PURGATORY GARDENS

A Novel
by
PETER LEFCOURT

Skyhorse Publishing

Skyhorse Publishing books may be purchased in bulk at special discounts for sales promotion, corporate gifts, fund-raising, or educational purposes. Special editions can also be created to specifications. For details, contact the Special Sales Department, Skyhorse Publishing, 307 West 36th Street, 11th Floor, New York, NY 10018 or info@skyhorsepublishing.com.

Skyhorse® and Skyhorse Publishing® is a registered trademark of Skyhorse Publishing, Inc.®, a Delaware corporation.

Visit our website at www.skyhorsepublishing.com.

10 9 8 7 6 5 4 3 2 1

Library of Congress Cataloging-in-Publication Data is available on file.

Print ISBN: 978-1-163220-640-4
Ebook ISBN: 978-1-63220-796-8

Printed in the United States of America

To Charlie Berns, who keeps refusing to die.

1
SAMMY

The thought of having the African whacked first occurred to Sammy Dee (née Salvatore Didziocomo) at a homeowners' meeting to discuss the mold problem in the laundry room at the Paradise Gardens condominium community in Palm Springs. The man was wearing a brightly colored native robe with a hat that made him look like a cross between a sushi chef and a kamikaze pilot, and he was hovering over the onion dip, putting the make on Marcy Gray, the former actress—territory that Sammy considered his own.

The African was at least six-three and dripping sweat into the dip. And, if that wasn't bad enough, he was speaking French. The onion dip was beyond help, but the affections of Marcy Gray were another matter. The woman had given Sammy reason to hope that he wouldn't have to pack it in for the duration.

She was an attractive (if slightly reconstructed) woman of an indeterminate age. Sammy put her in her sixties, but these days you could never be sure. They were getting better and better with the knife. Nine o'clock every morning she did a couple of miles on the treadmill in the exercise room and, though you could never tell with Spandex, it looked to him like she was holding up decently well.

They'd had mochaccinos at Starbucks, for openers; a few days later, lunch at Denny's; and the following week, dinner at the Olive Garden with a bottle of Valpolicella. She had been chatty and flirtatious and had led him to believe, over the spumoni, that had she not been suffering from some undisclosed female ailment at the moment, he might have gotten lucky that night. So, as far as Sammy Dee was concerned, Marcy Gray was low-hanging fruit. *His* low-hanging fruit. Not a French-speaking African's, in native robes with tribal scars on his cheek, and, Sammy suspected, a machete in his pants.

Sammy walked across the room to insert himself into the scene. He was wearing hand-tailored gabardine trousers, a cashmere sweater he'd paid two hundred bucks for at a Nordstrom outlet store in Palm Desert, and a pair of Italian loafers that were so soft he had bruised his toe on a table leg.

"Sammy Dee," Marcy Gray smiled, revealing some very expensive dental implants.

"How're you doing?"

"Do you know Didier Onyekachukwu?"

"Haven't had the pleasure," Sammy said, sticking out an indifferent hand to the big African, who crushed it in his meaty grip.

"Didier is from Ivory Coast. And he speaks French."

"No kidding?" Sammy said, trying to communicate just how fucking unimpressed he was by this fact.

"Didier is going to give me French lessons," Marcy went on.

"Dee Dee Yay," the African corrected the pronunciation of his name.

"My French could use some brushing up. Mind if I join you?" Sammy volunteered. He would do it in self-defense—to keep Marcy Gray from too much one-on-one time with Diddly Shit.

"It will be easy for you, Mr. Dee. French is very much like Italian."

As far as Sammy was concerned, he didn't look Italian. Well, not terribly Italian. Dee was supposed to be a swing name—some perversion of a Jewish or Russian name—suggested by the WITSEC people to widen the scope of the identity they were trying to conceal. You were encouraged to use the same initials, and possibly the same first name, but *Sal* was a little too Italian for a guy trying to hide from the mob.

"I don't speak Italian," he protested, as if maintaining that he wasn't a pedophile.

"Sammy's Jewish," Marcy said, repeating the fiction that he had told her over dinner the night he didn't get laid.

"Half. On my father's side. He got his name changed on Ellis Island."

"*Intéressant*," Didier Onyekachukwu said, dropping French into the onion dip along with his perspiration.

Sammy was thinking about cold-cocking the guy when Ethel Esmitz, the president of the PGHOA (Paradise Gardens Homeowners' Association), banged a spoon against a coffee mug and called the meeting to order.

Sammy and the African flanked Marcy Gray—each attempting a possessory posture—as the pros and cons of spending money to obliterate the laundry room mold were debated. It came down to those who were willing to increase their assessments to spiff up the place pitched against those who had better things to do with their money.

Sammy wasn't planning on spending the rest of his life, such that it was, in this middle-market condo community on the outskirts of Palm Springs, a home he was occupying very much as a matter of convenience. He had chosen it over similar arrangements in Ypsilanti, Jacksonville, and Tempe because he wanted to be in driving distance of a major city in the event that he felt like doing something besides play golf or get skin cancer growing tomatoes in his yard.

But he was there until the DOJ in Washington approved a new place for him to live—or washed their hands of him. Fuck mold in the laundry room. As it was, he never set foot in the place. His cleaning lady shoved his washables into a machine once a week and sat with the other wetbacks jabbering in Spanish while his jockeys shrunk from the hot water he kept telling her not to use.

The Finnish dykes across the hall—Tuuli and Majda, or vice versa—led the faction supporting bringing in the Mold Busters: "*Vee mussed kill de mold.*"

This from two women whose unit smelled of cat piss. When he'd told them that the odor drifted across the hall, they accused him of being a cat hater. He *was* a cat hater, and he wasn't particularly fond of Scandinavians or lesbians either, for that matter. Sammy wouldn't mind having them whacked along with the African. Maybe he'd get a package deal and do his WITSEC handler, Marshal Dillon, as well.

Ernest Dylan was a United States marshal and Sammy Dee's conduit to the outside world. He was the only person in the state of California who knew that Sammy Dee's real name was Salvatore Didziocomo, and that he had been—until eighteen months ago, when his testimony led to a sentence of twelve to fifteen for Phil "Three Balls" Finoccio on charges of extortion, tax evasion, and receiving stolen property—a member of the Finoccio crime family on Long Island.

He had been drifting for years as a semi-retired made guy, overseeing a bunch of younger button men carrying out the dwindling mob business in Nassau County. Just as he had been contemplating pulling out and moving to Tucson, using his asthma as a pretext and getting by on the stash of krugerrands he had been putting aside for this moment, they nailed him. The fucking IRS.

His longtime accountant and laundryman, Lennie "The Kike" Baumberg, gave him the bad news.

"They got you six ways to Shavuos, Sal. It's not just deductions. Deductions we could live with. It's failure to report. They audited that housing project in Wantagh where you been washing your laundry. You're looking at seven to ten, if you luck out with the prosecutor. They could go for ten to fifteen, and sell it to a jury."

Salvatore Didziocomo took a long, hard look at his options. Seven to ten would have taken him into his mid-seventies, probably in Otisville or Butner, where he could hang out with Bernie Madoff and get gang-raped by felons who had lost money in the market. Or he could commit the worst act that a made man could commit. He could sing.

That was, if he actually *could* sing. They were getting pickier in witness protection. You had to deliver the goods before they set you up with a new life. It wouldn't be enough to tell them that Phil Finoccio's nickname came from a third testicle that he had been born with, or so he claimed. Jimmy Bassio said he'd been in a steam room with Phil and that the guy had the smallest dick this side of Tokyo.

In his early days, Sal had seen his share of shit. He had been on the janitors' squad—guys whose job it was to clean up messes and dispose of bodies. There were things he had seen that he was still trying to forget—basements and garages with blood-splattered cement. They'd had to go in there with bleach, scrub out the DNA traces, and then drop the body from a boat twenty miles off of Freeport.

It had been some time since that stuff went down, but when it had gone down, it had gone down with canaries. Breaking *omertà*. There was no mercy for guys who blew the whistle. You were lucky if they just killed you.

Over the years, he had heard people talk about approaching the feds. There was an office in Washington you contacted to set up an interview. You met them in a restaurant, and you told them what you would be willing to testify about in court, and they told you whether or not what you had was worth their protecting you.

His meeting had been in a McDonald's in Silver Springs, Maryland. The guy was wearing a Washington Redskins windbreaker and sipping a milkshake through a straw. He told Sammy his name was Gary, no last name, suggested he order something, and said they would continue the conversation in his car.

For the next hour and a half, they sat in the guy's immaculate Chevy Malibu and negotiated. Gary told him that the bar was high, since the agency's budget was being slashed by Congress. They weren't going to spend the two hundred grand it took to set a guy and his family up for years unless he could deliver a really big fish.

Sal told him he had stuff on several high-ranking lieutenants in the Finoccio family. Gary shook his head. "It's going to have to be the man himself. And we're talking major felony. I'm not interested in tax evasion or securities fraud. I'm going to need murder one or two, conspiracy to commit, or extortion with bodily harm. And it's going to have to be firsthand testimony, no hearsay."

Sal chewed his Big Mac thoroughly, trying to remember exactly what he had seen with his own eyes and what he had heard about. He could give places and dates, and who was going to contradict him in court by saying that they were actually there and that it didn't happen the way Sal said it had?

"I can put Finoccio in a room where people were killed. I can give you dates and locations."

"Okay," Gary said, like a poker player calling the bet and then raising. "Did you participate in any of these acts?"

"What difference does that make?"

"I need to know if I'm going to have to get the Justice Department to sign off on not prosecuting you. That's a whole different deal. That deal is we put you in prison, in a protected situation, for two, three years, whatever we can get you reduced to, and then relocate you when you get out."

"Why the fuck would I agree to do that?"

"It's a way out."

"Once I testify, what's to keep you from reneging?"

"We'll sign a contract guaranteeing you a new identity, social security number, employment resume, a certain amount of cash, and suggestions for several locations to relocate. You'll have someone from the Marshals Service as your liaison in one of these locations. It will be well handled."

"How do I know that?"

"We've been doing this for a while."

"You never lost anybody?"

"Not if they followed the rules."

Then he explained the rules. No one, absolutely no one, from his old life could know where he was or his new name. They were prepared to relocate a wife and minor children with him, but no one else. He would have to break ties with everyone and everything from his past. Mail could be exchanged through a letter drop that the Marshals Service administered, but everything would be subject to inspection and redaction.

He was divorced, with a grown daughter and two grandsons living outside of Philadelphia. As far as his ex-wife, Joyce, was concerned, if he never saw her again, it would be too soon. The divorce had been ugly, to the point that Phil Finoccio had offered to have Joyce's lawyer's kneecaps adjusted. Sal had declined, not wanting to give her the satisfaction. He wrote a big check and walked away clean.

The WITSEC deal could be his best, if not only, shot to live the remaining ten to fifteen years of his life in relative comfort. He could circle the wagons and drift away without having to worry about what he was going to tell the IRS when they called him in for the audit. *I bought the house, put my daughter through Penn, and paid off my ex-wife on tips I got working in a bar on Northern Boulevard.* Even if they had him only one way to Sha-vuos, it was enough to put him behind bars for serious time.

It came down to only one real regret. His daughter, Sharon, and her sons, Mikey and Jeffy. His son-in-law, Howard, was an asshole. The guy taught junior high school gym, jogged four miles a day, ate like a fuck-ing rabbit, and told Sal, every time he saw him, that he was a heart attack waiting to happen. *You gotta lose the carbs, Sal. Or else they're going to lose you.* On Thanksgiving they would have vegetable stuffing and turkey with the skin peeled.

Was Thanksgiving dinner, a couple of Sundays in between, and the oc-casional phone conversation enough to make it a deal-breaker? He could write to her, find out how she was doing, get photos and news of Mikey and Jeffy. At this point, wasn't that really what this relationship amounted to? Nostalgia for a family life that, to tell the truth, was marked mostly by his absence?

He concluded that it was mostly the *idea* of not seeing them that was bothering him. So he made the deal. Six months later, after a series of clan-destine interviews with Justice Department lawyers, he was shuttled in a windowless van into federal court in Manhattan and, avoiding eye contact with Finoccio, recited a carefully rehearsed chapter and verse of the capo's sins. And when it was over Sal Didziocomo was relocated to the Paradise Gardens Condominium Community in Palm Springs, California, with a new name, new social security card, sixty grand a year living allowance, and a phone number he could call when he needed something.

So as far as Sammy Dee was concerned, he had bigger problems in his life than mold in the laundry room. He was about to express this opinion when Marcy Gray declared that she was joining the Mold Busters faction, along with the African. Sammy found his hand shooting up when Ethel Esmitz asked for a show of hands to support the dues assessment to deal with the mold.

There went a couple of hundred dollars he'd never see again. He'd try to think of it as a bad bet on a horse, and forget about it.

But Marcy Gray he couldn't forget about. She had gotten his dormant juices flowing. Even before he was relocated, when he was living alone in the house in Roslyn and had the money and the inclination, he hadn't bothered much with women. The business of taking them out to dinner, telling them their hair looked good or that they had a nice smile, just to get laid, didn't seem to be worth it.

He had just turned sixty when he and Joyce split up. It got easier to do without as he got older. By sixty-five, his testosterone was down a quart and his blood vessels were constricting. Performance had become an issue.

"Relax, Sal, it's normal," his doctor told him. "If God wanted guys your age to be having kids, he would have done something about the vascular system in the penis. You're lucky we got things to treat it now. Our fathers and grandfathers were shit out of luck."

He gave Sal a prescription for erectile dysfunction medication. He hated the term: it sounded like an abstract problem, like mold. Sal didn't like the flushed feeling and the sense that he was artificially dilating his blood vessels, and he used it grudgingly, hoping that someday, miraculously, it would all start working again without it.

There had been the occasional $500 hooker in Vegas, or the tipsy divorcée he'd pick up late at night at a bar out on Sunrise Highway. He could spot them as soon as he walked in, perched precariously on a bar stool, too much eye makeup, wearing a skirt a size too small, and smoking lipstick-stained cigarettes. All he had to do was buy them a drink and avoid taking them to his place, so he could leave afterward when they were out cold snoring.

And since he had been living the life of Sammy Dee, retired cement contractor, in Palm Springs, it had been cold turkey. Abstinence had proved to be a lot easier than he would have thought. In spite of the availability of well-heeled widows, he found it easier to spend his evenings watching ball games or old movies than dropping a pill and going at it with some predatory middle-aged woman with a tummy tuck.

And then, lo and behold, just when he had decided to pack it in, the unexpected occurred. The first time was in the exercise room, as he was pedaling his stationary bike and watching Marcy Gray's Spandex-encased rear bounce up and down on the treadmill. He wrote that one off as a freak short circuit. But then at the Olive Garden, when she bent over the table and he saw the swell of what looked to him like reasonably firm breasts and got a whiff of perfume, the blood vessels started dilating again, without the benefit of pharmaceuticals. His first unassisted hard-on in years.

He was eager to go for a test drive and had been counting on the night of the mold meeting to get behind the wheel, when the fucking African entered the picture. It was clear that he now had a rival for Marcy Gray's attention. Someone who was six inches taller than him and spoke French.

In his Salvatore Didziocomo days, he would have just had a couple of gorillas pay the guy a visit and make sure he knew that she was off-limits. Sammy Dee didn't have any goons he could call to pay the African a visit. He didn't even own a gun. It was against WITSEC rules. His new name was on a national no-sell database. If he got so much as a parking ticket, they could revoke his protected status and leave him out there exposed for Finoccio's people.

Sammy was thinking, more or less idly, about who he could safely contact for a referral to someone in LA—not taking the thought seriously or, at least, indulging in the notion that he wasn't taking the thought seriously, when his eye landed on a man leaning against the wall across the room.

The guy was wearing a cardigan and Hush Puppies and looked like he had better things to do. He was a former movie producer named Charlie Berns, who had actually won an Academy Award. Sammy found himself wondering why a guy who had won an Oscar would be living in a dump like this, but then what was a made man who'd had a split-level on the north shore of Long Island, a Cadillac Sierra, and ten grand worth of suits in his closet doing there?

In the spongy recesses of his memory, Sammy dredged up the title of a film that Charlie Berns had produced, something called *The Hit*, or *The Hit Man*, or *The Big Hit*. He had seen it on television late one night. It was about a mob contract man who falls in love with one of his targets.

He'd drop by for a cup of coffee. Find out if he had done any research to make the film. You never knew. What else did he have to do with his time?

"I'm sorry about this, Sammy. But my hands are tied."

"Your hands are always fucking tied."

"It's ten percent across the board. Everyone in the program."

They were sitting, Ernest Dylan and he, in a non-descript Mexican restaurant in a shopping mall in Cathedral City. The marshal was dipping nachos into the guacamole and dabbing at his trim mustache with a napkin.

"What about you? They cutting *you* ten percent?" Sammy glared.

"Different budget."

Now he was going to have to stretch things on fifty-four grand. The krugerrands had gone for his car and the $397,000 he paid for the condo. The government money was supposed to be subsistence. Food, gas, and lodging. Try living on five fucking grand a month. Taxable, no less.

"They just raised my monthly charges. We have a mold problem in the laundry room."

"Sorry about that."

"Do you really give a shit, Dylan?"

The marshal looked up from his refried beans, a hurt look in his eyes.

"Actually, I do, Sammy. I want you to be a happy camper."

"Or what? I break cover and get whacked by Finoccio's people?"

"We don't like to lose people."

"Not on your watch, right?"

"That's right."

"Sets a bad example. You'll have trouble recruiting more of us to spill our guts."

"You are free to drop out at any time. You know that."

"Oh yeah, I know that. You never fail to remind me."

"Look, Sammy, I understand. There's a lot of stress involved in living a new life. If you want, you can see a psychotherapist. We have several that work with us."

Sammy imagined himself on the couch. *I'm living in purgatory with a mold problem, doc. I can't get it up without pharmaceuticals, and I'm thinking of having a guy whacked because he's coming on to a woman I want to fuck. Apart from that, it's all good.*

He looked at the marshal in his Banlon T-shirt and wash 'n' wear slacks, thinking of James Arness in *Gunsmoke* with the big hat, and Dennis Weaver saying, "Yes, Mister Dillon. . ." as he shuffled out of the marshal's office.

"Get out of Dodge," Sammy muttered, laughing.

Ernest Dylan wasn't even born when the show went off the air.

"Listen, Marshal, you don't happen to know where I can hire a good hit man around here, do you?"

The guy didn't crack a smile.

"What about Craigslist?"

"I think we're done here."

"The least you can do is pick up the fucking check," Sammy said to Ernest Dylan's retreating back. He watched him grab a toothpick, walk outside, get into his car, and drive away, dissolving into the 102-degree heat.

That night, sitting in his unit listlessly watching a ball game, Sammy did something he wasn't supposed to do. He dialed his daughter's number in Philadelphia. Even though the government had given him an untraceable cell phone, it was against the WITSEC rules to use it except in the event of one of a small and carefully enumerated list of emergencies. Missing your daughter was not on the list.

"Dad?" She made his voice on the first bounce. Nearly two years in California hadn't bleached out the Long Island accent.

He looked at his watch, and realized it was after eleven on the East Coast. Howard had them all in bed by ten.

"Sorry. I forgot about the time change." They hadn't spoken since he'd called to tell her that he was going into witness protection and would be unable to visit or talk to her for the foreseeable future.

"You okay?" she whispered.

"Yeah."

There was a long silence. Neither knew what to say next. Finally, Sammy flipped into autopilot. "How're the kids?"

"Good."

"They . . . ask about me?"

"Sure."

He could hear the lie in her voice but was grateful for it.

"I . . . met a woman."

He didn't know why he said that. Maybe it was just something to say.

"Great. What's her name?"

"Marcy."

"Nice name."

"Yeah. She's nice."

"That's good. I'm glad you're with someone."

"We're not actually together yet," he said. "We've had a couple of dates."

Then he heard Howard's voice in the background, undoubtedly asking her who she was talking to, or maybe knowing it was him and telling her to hang up, and she asked if she could call him back.

"It's okay. I know it's late. I'll call you some other time," he said, and hung up quickly before she could protest.

As he lay on the couch, listening to the air conditioner wheeze, he wondered whether he'd hung up because he didn't want to cause problems between her and Howard, or because he'd had nothing more to say.

The thought upset him enough that he took an Ambien with his nightcap of nine-dollar cabernet. And, as he did more and more frequently of late, he fell asleep on the couch with the television on.

"Sammy, good morning." Her voice penetrated the sleeping pill fuzz. He could barely hear it over Katie Couric.

"Did I wake you?"

"No," Sammy lied. "Been up for hours."

"You said you wanted to have French lessons with Didier and me. . ."

Oh fuck.

"So I thought we could start today. We can have lunch. My place. Twelve-thirty?"

"Uh. . .sure."

"Terrific. Anything you don't eat?"

"Escargots," he said, and she laughed. If he could make her laugh and she could make him hard, they would have a good thing going. All he had to do was get the African out of the picture.

He showered for twenty minutes to wipe out the cobwebs, made himself some espresso (the last Italian thing he permitted himself), and took care in selecting an outfit, settling on a pair of cotton slacks and a Mexican peasant shirt that effectively camouflaged his expanding gut. He shaved, gargled with Listerine, slobbered his armpits with deodorant, and showed up a respectable seven minutes late to find his rival sitting on a kitchen stool with Klaus, Marcy's brown and black dachshund, in his lap.

The African was wearing a colorful native top over Bermudas with a pair of flip-flops. One of his wrists featured a Rolex, the other a gold bracelet. He reeked of Old Spice.

The French lesson, it turned out, amounted to learning the French word for everything they ate: a *crevette* salad with *endive* and *concombre*.

Marcy's place was modestly furnished. There were framed glossy photos showing her in her younger days with Hollywood people—her arm in "Sly's" and "Jimmy's," poured into a strapless gown, circa 1975, smiling at the camera.

With lunch she served a bottle of *vin blanc*. The African drank most of it, but it didn't seem to affect him. He maintained a serious demeanor except when he laughed, and then it was in a giggly, adolescent manner, and mostly at his own jokes.

He revealed nothing at all about himself, dodging Sammy's leading questions and keeping his attention fixed on the hostess, who seemed susceptible to his flattery.

It was clear that they were auditioning for the same job. It was like the finals of fucking *American Idol*. The prize was visible through the open bedroom door, where a Californian king bed was topped by a collection of fluffy pillows. One of them was going to have the pleasure of tossing those pillows to the floor.

Klaus glared when Sammy looked through the bedroom door. *Don't even* think *about it, you fuckin' wop*. The dog, she told him, was a trained attack dog that she had gotten from a former German intelligence agent who had a security business in Rancho Cucamonga. There were certain commands that only she knew which, when uttered, would instantly turn the dachshund into a killer. The dog was trained to go for the gonads or the jugular—two distinct commands. To avoid her inadvertently using one of the attack commands, the words were in German.

"I had him in the car once at the Volkswagen dealer, and one of the mechanics said something in German, and Klaus almost went through the windshield. So don't speak German in front of him. Just in case."

"No danger of that," Sammy said.

"So, Monsieur Dee, you are in the cement business?" Didier said, in a tone that implied that Sammy spent his life digging ditches.

"Retired," he responded, meeting the African's eyes.

"And what do you do now?"

"What I feel like."

"Of course." This with a Maurice Chevalier toss of his head.

"And you?"

"I am in the import/export business."

"Didier deals in African art," Marcy said.

"Benin bronzes, and the like," the African elaborated.

Sammy had no fucking clue what a Benin bronze was, but he wouldn't be surprised if there were AK47s in the crates with the bronzes. The guy looked like Idi Amin's kid brother.

"You would perhaps be interested, Monsieur Dee, in some Nigerian statuary? They are reputed to restore virility."

"No problem in that area. . ." Sammy lied with a big smile on his face.

The conversation lurched forward with this kind of limp repartee, each of the two suitors waiting for the other one to leave first. Finally, Marcy said that it was time for her and Klaus to take their afternoon nap and kicked them both out.

Back in his unit, Sammy lay down on the couch and turned on a ball game. Tomorrow, he resolved, he would pay the movie producer a visit. See if the guy could put him onto someone to do the African. The sooner, the better.

Charlie Berns's unit had no air conditioning.

"Can't stand it," he explained, as he led Sammy to an armchair near an open window. An overhead fan made little headway against the heat. He brought a pitcher of iced tea from an asthmatic refrigerator and poured a couple of glasses.

The producer was wearing a faded T-shirt, shorts, and sandals. He didn't seem to be sweating. Sammy was already dripping from his armpits.

"You from New York?" Sammy asked, picking up on the East Coast accent.

"New Jersey. But I've been out here since the seventies."

"Movie business, right?"

"If you can call it that. It's actually a crap shoot."

Sammy smiled. He might get to like this guy. Most of the people at Paradise Gardens had had their sense of humor bleached out by the sun. Charlie Berns looked like life still amused him.

"You made a picture called *The Big Hit* or *The Hit,* or something like that?"

The man thought for a moment, as if trying to remember the names of his children.

"I made a lot of pictures, most of them not very memorable."

"This movie, *The Big Hit* or whatever it was called, was about a hit man who falls in love with his target."

Charlie Berns's eyes screwed up, trying to focus, and then came out with, "Right. The guy decides not to kill her, and then they go after him, and the two of them run away, and then something else happens. The movie crashed and burned right out of the gate. Never made back its costs."

"I saw it on TV the other night."

"Shit. I probably owe somebody a residual. Goddamn Writers Guild is going to be on my ass."

"Did you have to do research on how contract guys work? You know, like to get the story right?"

"Yeah, yeah. . .The writer and I talked to an actual hit guy."

"How'd you pull that off?"

"If I remember correctly, it wasn't easy. It was like applying for a bank loan."

"Huh?"

"These guys had a routine, you know, to protect themselves. You called this number and there was a recorded message, asking you to leave a mailing address. A week later they sent you an application form. I'm telling you, it was like qualifying for a mortgage. You had to provide a social security number and bank references, and tell them the dimensions of your patio. These guys were very thorough. They had two covers apparently—patio decks and vermin. I didn't use that for the movie, though. Who would believe it?"

"Did you actually meet them?"

"We chickened out. I mean, we would have had to come up with a target, and though we both had a number of people on our shit lists, I wasn't sure I wanted them snuffed. So we decided to tell them the truth, that we were doing research for a movie. They told us to try the Internet."

"Do you know what they charged?"

"No idea. We made up a figure for the movie. Twenty-five grand. It sounded right."

"Well, at least you know where to go if you ever need someone rubbed out."

Charlie Berns uttered a short, dry chuckle, more a cough than a laugh.

"You know, I'm thinking about writing a book."

"Oh yeah, what kind of book?"

"A novel, maybe."

"About the cement business?"

"Who would buy that? No, some kind of crime thriller. I read a lot of them, and I'm figuring how hard could it be? Maybe I can come up with something good, and they'll make a movie out of it and I'll get rich."

"Why not?"

"I got a lot of time on my hands. What do I got to lose?"

"Sure. Will you give me first refusal on the film rights?"

There was just a trace of irony in the producer's eyes. He seemed like a man who spent his life throwing stuff against the wall to see what stuck.

"Just don't stiff me on the residuals."

"You kidding? You'd hire a hit man to do me?"

This time Sammy laughed. He let it settle for a while, then asked Charlie Berns if he still knew how to get in touch with the hit guys. For research for his book.

"1-800-XTERMIN."

"Come on. *Really*?"

"You don't forget that number."

For a number of reasons, Sammy Dee did not immediately call the number that Charlie Berns had given him. The chances were these guys were no longer in business. It wasn't a profession that people tended to stay in long. Maybe the cops had flipped them, and the number was used to entrap killers. Maybe they were in fucking WITSEC just like him, getting their maintenance cut ten percent.

He was looking at twenty-five, thirty grand, on the inside. And the only way he would be able to get his hands on that type of money would be to mortgage the condo. He could maybe get twenty-five at five percent, but if Dylan found out—and they seemed to have ways of finding these things out—he'd have to justify it or get his maintenance cut, if not eliminated.

Doing the hit himself was not an option. In his thirty years with Phil Finoccio, Sammy had never pulled the trigger on anyone. He had roughed people up, he'd even stuck a gun in a guy's mouth and threatened to pull the trigger if he didn't pay up, but he had never actually offed someone.

There was probably a millimeter of Catholicism still left in him— somewhere, he wasn't sure where—and he was concerned it might resurface, dormant from the days as a teenager when he would go to confession after jerking off.

As it was, he slept okay at night. It had taken him a while to get over flipping on Finoccio, but he had managed, through an elaborate set of rationalizations, to see it, ultimately, as self-defense. If he hadn't sung, he would have shriveled away in some small apartment in Garden City, living on handouts from Finoccio until the man himself pulled up stakes and moved to Tempe.

No, he had done what he had to do. And he wasn't going back there again. He was moving forward with his life, living, if not off the fat of the land, at least not off the gristle.

Two days after his lunch with Charlie Berns, however, Sammy Dee's resolution to leave well enough alone began to falter. He was sitting under an umbrella by the pool. Across from him were Chris and Edie, Paradise Gardens' resident swingers. They were a couple of leathery sun freaks pushing sixty. They hosted parties in their unit. Couples their age would get together, swill gin fizzes, and swap partners while the CD player belted out Johnny Mathis.

They had approached Sammy one day and asked if he had a girlfriend he wanted to bring by for drinks. Chris had actually tilted his head in Edie's direction, suggesting that all that could be his if he provided tit for tat.

"Thanks," he had said. "But I'm between girlfriends."

"Guy like you shouldn't be without one for long," Edie purred.

"With any luck, I will be," he replied. The sarcasm went right through them and out the other side.

Edie waved to him from the other side of the pool. She was wearing a bikini that accentuated her tit job. The effect, in the morning sun, was of a car with protruding headlights. Sammy waved back minimally, avoiding any expression that would encourage them to come over and talk to him, and closed his eyes to indicate that he was about to take a nap.

He drifted into a doze and was daydreaming about autumn on Long Island, the smell of leaves being burned in his neighbors' driveways, when he heard his name. He opened his eyes to see Marcy Gray standing over him.

She was wearing an age-appropriate bathing suit, a straw sunhat, and a pair of heels. "What you doing?"

"Not a whole lot," Sammy managed, telling the truth.

Taking the chaise longue beside him, she stretched out, kicking her heels off in a little coquettish move.

Even in the flat desert light, she looked appetizing. She was one of those women who knew how to present themselves. All those years facing cameras had taught her how to angle herself in the most attractive manner.

She opened a copy of *Entertainment Weekly*, absently leafed through it.

"Crazy world, the movie world, huh?" he said.

"Tell me about it."

"I bet you know a lot of people in Hollywood."

She nodded. Sammy wondered whether she still expected the phone to ring. The town was full of aging starlets living on the fumes of their careers.

"You know Charlie Berns?" he asked.

"The producer?"

"Yeah. He lives here."

"No kidding? I didn't know that."

"Had lunch with him the other day."

She perked up. "Didn't he win an Academy Award?"

"Twenty years ago."

"Oh, right. It was some kind of period piece, with Jeremy Ikon and Jacqueline Fortier, I think. . ."

Sammy shrugged. During that period of his life he hadn't gone to the movies much. All he could remember was seeing *The Godfather* with Joyce. It turned out to be the beginning of the end of their marriage. She started doing a Diane Keaton number, wanting to get out. It was downhill from there.

"I should get him a headshot," she said with sudden determination. "You never know, right?"

"Right."

As he was wondering whether she was delusional or merely hopeful, Diddly Shit showed up. With a thermos full of margaritas and two glasses.

"Cocktail hour," he said from behind his Porsche Aviator sunglasses, helping himself to the recliner on the other side of her.

"Would you care to join us, Sammy?" He pronounced the name *Sahmee,* with the accent on the last syllable. The insincerity of the invitation was evident.

Sammy passed, getting up and surrendering the field to his rival. He wasn't going to take sloppy thirds on the margaritas. He had better things to do.

Inside his unit, he went directly to the telephone and dialed 1-800-XTERMIN.

The voice mail picked up. "Hello, you've reached Acme Exterminating and Patio Decks. Please leave your name, a brief description of your vermin problem, the dimensions of your patio, and a mailing address. You will receive an estimate in the mail. Have a nice day."

Sammy did not leave his name and address. Not yet, at least. First he would find out how much cash he could pull out of the condo. And while he was doing that, he hoped that maybe the whole idiotic notion of having the African whacked would collapse under its own weight.

A loan officer from Wells Fargo came out to appraise the condo. Millie Peterman, a desiccated, fiftyish woman—a widow, he figured, whose husband had carried cut-rate life insurance—asked him questions. How long had he owned the unit? What was his equity? Any termites or mold?

"Lot of mold out here in the desert," she said.

"None in this place." Sammy held her look.

They'd let him know in a week. In the meantime, he had to say something to Marshal Dillon, who would no doubt find out about the loan app. WITSEC had wires into the banking system, to monitor money laundering operations, and they got notification of any kind of large money transaction.

"I'm thinking of starting a little business," he told the marshal, in the front seat of the county car parked in the Home Depot lot out on Indian Canyon Road, near the airport.

"That's good, Sammy. Being self-sufficient is the first step to getting your self-esteem back."

"Right, not to mention the fifty-four grand added to *your* self-esteem."

The marshal didn't dignify Sammy's crack with a response. Instead, he asked what kind of business.

"Import/export."

Dylan gave him a look that said, *it better not be drugs.*

"Strictly legit," Sammy added quickly. "African art. Fertility statues, that kind of stuff. Should sell good with the old ladies around here that want to start another family."

"Don't get cute with the IRS, Sammy. You know, your returns get audited automatically. Nothing personal. Everyone's in the program does."

"It's nice to know that you guys are looking after us."

Marshal Dillon took a toothpick out of his pocket and started working over his teeth. "One other thing, Sammy."

"What?"

"Your phone log registered a 610 area code on the 19th."

"You guys check my fucking phone?"

"You know we do."

"No, I didn't. I thought there were some things that were private."

"Afraid not. We know you called your daughter."

"It was her birthday."

"Her birthday's in February."

The marshal exhaled deeply, as if he were about to scold a six-year-old for not cleaning up his room. "Sammy, you know the drill. We were very clear about it. You don't call anybody from your old life."

"I just needed to say hello."

"You can send her a letter."

Sammy nodded slowly. He wasn't holding the cards, and he knew it. What he would do, he decided, was get another phone. One that wasn't tapped by the fucking Marshals Service. Either that, or a carrier pigeon.

Millie Petersen called to give him the good news—twenty-five grand at 5.02 percent with a balloon payment in seven years. With any luck, Sammy wouldn't be around to pay it. They could have his unit in Paradise Gardens. Mold and all.

To celebrate, he invited Marcy Gray to dine at Le Vallauris, an overpriced French place in town that dialed a 28 Zagat rating. She looked scrumptious in a black sheath that wrapped itself around her like a cigar leaf. She didn't have one of those reedy model's bodies that were fashionable these days. You got the feeling that she didn't starve herself on yogurt and cottage cheese. She was definitely a meat and potatoes woman.

Which didn't stop her from ordering the Russian River Petrossian caviar. At $85. She applied the bitter little black pellets liberally on her rosemary baguette, smiling beguilingly over a glass of Château something or other, recommended by the wine guy to "complement" the Beef Wellington.

It was going to be three hundred bucks with the tip, but it would be worth it if, afterward, he could sweep Klaus out of the bedroom and roll around on the big bed with her.

She asked him about the cement business. The WITSEC people had told him to research his cover in the event that someone wanted to know about it. Sammy had subscribed to *Cement Industry News*, but glazed over after a couple of pages. Nevertheless, he'd made himself memorize a couple of facts that he could toss out like confetti strands when needed.

"Did you know that the U.S. produces ninety-three million metric tons of cement every year?"

"Wow."

"Of course, with the mafia going out of business, we get fewer requests for cement boots."

She laughed, loud and full. He loved it. He imagined that she made love the way she laughed, holding nothing back.

"But, like I said, I'm retired," he protested. "I'm in the investment business these days."

"I bet you do very well," she said, with a touch of coquetry.

"I make a living. It's basically a crap shoot. Like your business, right?"

He wanted to get her talking about herself. With women, listening was an aphrodisiac. Though it hadn't worked very well with Joyce, who could go on for hours without his uttering a word and still wear cold cream to bed.

"You know what they say—you can't make a living in show business, but you can make a killing."

"So what was it like working with Sly and Jimmy?"

"They're actors. Like all of us. They slap some makeup on, say their lines, and hope they don't wind up on the cutting room floor. The way to survive is just to keep swimming. We're like sharks—we stop swimming, we die."

"What was your favorite film role?"

She told him. At length. And while she did, Sammy was deciding whether they ought to skip the after-dinner drink. They had polished off a couple of Mai Tais and a bottle of expensive red. It was clear that she was already lubricated, and any more might be counterproductive. Not to mention dampening.

The little blue pill was in his wallet, stashed there like the rubber he used to carry around as a teenager. He didn't want to drop it unless he knew he was going to use it, but by then it could be too late. Or unnecessary.

Wouldn't that be nice? Capillaries dilating like they used to. *Let's twist again like we did last summer*.

Worst-case scenario, it would be redundant. High-class problem.

When she went to the ladies room, he washed it down with a glass of the $9 San Pellegrino. They were twenty minutes from home, forty-five to lift off. The timing should be optimum.

He paid the check and was on his feet, her wrap in his hands, when she emerged. She had touched up her lipstick and looked even more appetizing. Her perfume mingled with the night-blooming jasmine as they stood outside waiting for the valet to bring the car.

When she leaned against him in the car, he could feel the heat emanating from her. He kept his attention on the road, convinced he would never pass a Breathalyzer. He didn't want to be sitting in the Palm Springs Police drunk tank, all alone with his hard-on.

He managed to get the car safely into the garage and parked in his space, more or less. Charlie Berns's old diesel Mercedes was, as usual, badly parked, and Sammy had to help Marcy wiggle out of the passenger seat. She pressed against him, and he could feel his blood already moving south.

As they went up the elevator and stepped out into the lobby, the your-place-or-mine moment arrived. Sammy had been debating the question all the way home. Her place had Klaus, but it also provided an escape hatch if things did not go well. He could beat a retreat back to the safety of his own place.

Their units were both on the ground-floor level, hers closest to the elevator. He would let her make the decision. It was always the woman who made the decision anyway, wasn't it? They knew, usually even before they agreed to go out with you, whether or not you were going to get lucky that night.

She had given him all the right signals. He decided that wherever it happened was okay. The way he was feeling, he could have done it standing up in the garage. It was all systems go.

And then disaster struck. As if he had been lying in wait, Diddly Shit opened the door of his unit.

"*Mais bonsoir, mes amis. . .*"

There was a bottle of cognac in his large hand. And a big smile on his face. "A *petit cap de nuit?*"

Sammy followed Marcy in the door, if only to keep her out of the African's clutches. It would be a fucking shame if he had gotten her prepped and then Diddly Shit swooped in for the kill. An hour or so later, drunk and pissed, he escorted her to her door and got nothing more than a sloppy kiss, somewhere near his mouth.

Back at his own place, he went directly to the phone, dialed the number. "Hello, this is Sammy Dee. Could you mail me a brochure?"

He gave his address, enunciating as best he could, then took off his shoes, plopped onto the couch, and fell into a remorseless stupor.

It took a week to get a response from Acme Exterminating and Patio Decks. During that time, he had to endure more French lessons and an untimely bout of prostatitis that ruled out any action with Marcy Gray.

Mel Cardazian, the Armenian urologist he went to see for his prostatitis, told him that he needed to "regularize" his sex life.

"It's a feast or famine kind of deal," he said, as Sammy bent over the examining table in serious discomfort. "Like any other muscle, the prostate needs to be exercised in some sort of systematic manner. You go out and run once a month, you're going to feel it the next day, right?"

Sammy pulled up his shorts, exhaled deeply, and collapsed into the chair in the examining room.

"I'm going to be seventy in December, doc. I'm not married. I don't think I'm a good candidate for the feast deal."

"Women are not your only option."

"I'm not going there."

"That's not what I'm talking about. Your prostate doesn't care if you ejaculate inside or outside a vagina. It just needs to be exercised."

"You want me to start jerking off?"

"Either that, or you could avoid sexual stimulation."

"How do I do that? Join a monastery?"

"Get a girlfriend," Mel Cardazian said.

Now, Sammy told himself, he was having the African whacked for medicinal reasons.

Returning from the urologist, Sammy found the application in his mailbox from Acme Exterminating and Patio Decks. They redid your patio while they took out your enemies. One-stop shopping. On the surface, it looked like an ordinary work contract, the estimate to be filled in after a visit to the site and an agreement on the size of the patio and the materials to be used. But, unlike most contractors, they required a great deal of personal information, things you wouldn't think necessary to resurface a deck. They wanted his social security number, bank references, last three addresses, employers' name(s) and address(es).

Sammy Dee had been provided with all the fictitious information he would need for his adopted life, including, as it turned out, for ordering a hit. He possessed a computer-generated social security number, tax returns, and names and addresses of former employers—actual WITSEC personnel possessing fabricated work records for him.

Acme Exterminating and Patio Decks clearly had some sort of method of determining from the required information if the applicant was working for the police or the Justice Department. Or did they just want you to run through hoops? Make sure it wasn't just an impulse buy?

When he dropped the application in the mailbox, he felt as if he were inching closer to a cliff. But the way down wasn't as long as it used to be. He found it strangely comforting to think that, one way or the other, he would be dead in less than twenty years.

This time, it took only three days to get a response. It was written on Acme Exterminating and Patio Decks letterhead, setting up a consultation to discuss the work the following Tuesday at the Tahquitz Creek Legend Golf Course. They would meet on the first tee at 6:45 a.m. He was instructed to reserve and pay for a tee time and carts for three people, himself and two guests.

The note was signed by hand. *See you there, Walt.*

Six forty-five in the morning was not Sammy Dee's best hour, but given that it was September in the low desert of Southern California, it wasn't the worst time to play golf. It would be ninety degrees by ten, a hundred by noon.

Up until the moment he was in his car driving to the golf course, and even then, he toyed with the idea of just turning around, driving home. For all he knew, the whole thing could be a con job. Or an Internet scam. The contents of his bank account could already be on the way to Nigeria.

But he had to admit that he was, at the very least, curious about these guys and their operation. It all seemed so painless. Arranging a hit over a round of golf. Maybe it was cheaper and easier than he thought. He was on his way to a public golf course. At six fifteen in the morning of a typical California day, the sun peeking over the rim of the San Bernardino Mountains.

At the pro shop, Sammy paid for the rounds, bought a range ball card and a couple of sleeves of Titleist Pro V1s, picked up a golf cart, and told the starter that he would meet his guests on the first tee.

Sammy sat down on the bench beside the tee box at the first hole and waited, staring off at the beautifully manicured fairway. At six forty-five on the nose, a cart with two men in it approached from the pro shop. They got out and walked over to Sammy.

"Walt and Biff Keller," they announced, with creased smiles on their faces and outstretched hands. One of them was in his fifties, the other in his thirties.

Father and son exterminators? A family business?

They were in immaculate Nike golf shirts, pressed Banlon slacks, and white Footjoy Icons. They each had a set of Prestigio Japanese clubs, probably three grand worth of irons alone.

"Go ahead. Give it a whack."

"Blues or Tips?"

"Let's go for it, what do you say?" Walt responded. There went at least ten strokes off his score. Sammy would be lucky if he broke a hundred.

He walked over to a spot between the championship tee markers, teed up, took a deep breath, and brought his hands back slowly, keeping his left forearm straight and his head still, and proceeded to slice the ball two hundred yards into a thick copse of Joshua Trees.

"Take a mulligan," Biff said.

The mulligan went half the distance, disappearing into the rough at the side of the fairway. "That'll work," Walt said.

The father teed up and hit the ball two-seventy, easy, right down the middle. The son beat him by thirty yards. By the third hole, the son was two under par and the father even. Sammy was five over, with a double bogey.

Conversation was confined to golf platitudes. They were jovial, relaxed, playfully taunting each other. "We got five bucks on this round," Walt said.

"Kiss it goodbye, Dad." Biff punched his father's shoulder with manly playfulness.

They had the preppy Southern California allure of Nixon's bagmen, smiling cheerfully while they squeezed your balls.

Sammy began to wonder if the whole thing was a wild misunderstanding. They were scratch golfers who looked like they'd never gone near a cockroach, let alone a hit. Maybe it was just a convoluted way of getting a free round of golf.

It wasn't. At the ninth hole, with Sammy fifteen over, Biff asked him if he would care to step into the restroom.

"No thanks, don't have to go," Sammy replied.

"Yes, you do," Walt said with his have-a-nice-day smile.

Sammy looked at the little shack with the doors marked Men and Women and wondered if he wasn't the target instead of the client.

Biff took an OUT OF ORDER sign from his golf bag and hung it on the door. The cloying odor of air freshener hung in the room. Biff locked the door behind them and told Sammy to take off his clothes.

"You're kidding."

"Nope. All of them." The preppy pleasantness was no longer in his voice.

"You think I'm wearing a wire?"

"You better not be."

"Is this really necessary?"

"You bet. And get a move on it. There's a foursome right behind us."

After his shorts were off, Biff made him turn around and spread his cheeks in case he had the wire up his ass.

"You ought to work out a little," the man said. "Get yourself a personal trainer. I know a chick in Rancho Mirage who'll harden you up a little. One way or the other." Biff smiled at his joke and told Sammy to get dressed and meet them out at the tee.

His clubs had been transferred to Walt's cart.

"Get in," the father ordered.

"I haven't teed off yet."

"Yes, you have."

Sammy climbed in. They took off down the cart path with Biff following.

"Let me ask you a question, Sammy. How come you didn't let your own people handle this?"

Sammy tried to conceal his astonishment. How did these guys make him?

"I don't know this for a fact, but I'm guessing you're mobbed up, or used to be until you dropped out or copped out."

"Does it make a difference?"

"We like to know as much as we can about our customers."

He stopped the cart a hundred yards from the hole and handed Sammy a golf ball. "Drop it in the middle of the fairway. I'd use a pitching wedge—well, the way you hit, maybe a nine."

His nine iron in hand, Sammy walked to the middle of the fairway. He dropped the ball and sliced the shot badly into the greenside bunker. He walked back to the cart, got in, and said, "I'm in the cement business."

"Okay. We'll go with that."

They rode up to the green, where Sammy hit out of the bunker fat and then three-putted for another double. On the way to the eleventh tee, Walt got down to business.

"Here's how this works. You give us five grand to study the problem. We check it out, see how difficult the job is, then quote you a price. If we proceed, the five grand goes against the price of the job."

"If you don't?"

"We keep the money. Think of it as research and development."

"Can you give me a number?"

"There's a big range, depending on who we're doing. You talking about Obama, we're into seven figures. You talking about a guy works nights at the 7-Eleven, we could do it for twelve. . .maybe fifteen. This is not a one-size-fits-all kind of business, you understand?"

Sammy nodded reflexively, understanding only that the negotiation had already begun. It was like buying a car. There was a price point that they each had in mind. Where they wound up would be determined by who needed the deal more. And at this point, he wasn't sure.

"My guy lives alone," he said as they drove up to the eleventh hole, a short par 3 over an artificial lake.

"Where?"

"Condo complex out on 111, toward the airport."

"He work?"

"At home. He's in import/export."

"Drug dealer?"

"Not that I know of."

"What do you mean, not that you know of?"

"I don't know the guy very well."

"Well enough to not want him around."

"Long story."

Actually, it wasn't a long story. It was short and sweet. Marcy Gray. A woman he barely knew. A woman he was spending twenty-five grand over. It didn't make any fucking sense. But nothing much in his life did any more.

"The guy is a foreigner, an African."

"Black?"

"Yes."

"That's gonna jack up the price."

"Huh?"

"They could consider it a hate crime. White on black. We get caught, they could go for life without parole."

Sammy watched Biff hit a beautifully lofted nine-iron shot that plunked on to the green and rolled to within three feet below the cup.

"I've got twenty grand. All in."

Walt nodded, then got out of the cart, grabbed an eight iron, and hit his ball between Biff's and the cup. Then he turned back to Sammy and said, "Tell you what—you get it on the green from here, we'll do it for twenty. You wind up wet, twenty-five."

"Come on. You see the way I play golf."

"That's why I'm offering the bet."

A hundred and sixty-five yards over water. Cross-wind, sun in his eyes. His knees were already shaky. He hadn't driven the green on the two previous par three's. It was dumb. Stupid dumb. But no dumber than anything else he had been doing lately.

He decided to let the golf shot determine whether or not he went through with putting a hit out on the African. Leave it in the lap of the gods. Why not? At this point, rational thought didn't seem to matter.

Reaching into his bag, he took a seven iron, then switched to a six. A little extra distance wouldn't hurt.

As he stood over the ball, he almost broke out laughing. This was fucking ridiculous. A five-thousand-dollar golf shot.

He concentrated so hard on getting lift on the ball that he jerked his head up just enough at the last moment to top it. It flew low over the grass and right into the water.

"Fuck!" As the word escaped his lips, he saw his ball skid over the surface like a skipped stone, hit the wooden piling on the far side, bounce back off it with enough spin to hop onto the green and come to rest between Walt's ball and the cup.

Holy shit. The gods were talking to him.

The five thousand dollars he'd saved on the eleventh hole was to be delivered to Acme Exterminating and Patio Decks—in non-sequential hundred-dollar bills, stacked in rubber bands and placed in a FedEx envelope—at a car wash on Gerald Ford Drive.

Between the eleventh and eighteenth holes, Sammy provided as much information as he possessed on Didier Onyekachukwu. Walt seemed not to know or care where Côte d'Ivoire was, but he asked very specific questions about the African's habits, acquaintances, business, vehicle, sexual proclivities, health—very few of which Sammy was able to answer.

"The guy a diabetic?"

"What difference does that make?"

"Overdose of insulin is much cleaner than a shot in the temple. Heart problem, we can O.D. him on digitalis."

On the eighteenth green, Sammy asked them for a time frame.

"We'll let you know. A lot of variables."

"A week? A month?"

"Let's say sometime between tomorrow and Christmas."

"That the best you can do?"

"You want it done well, or you want it done Thursday? One other thing—your patio?"

"My patio?"

"Right. The twelve by fifteen concrete slab you indicated in your application. We're going to redo it for you. It's part of the deal. You want to do business with us, you need to have your patio redecked."

"I don't get it."

"You don't have to get it. We're going to send you a construction contract. Twenty grand. Out the door. You'll need to get it co-signed."

Sammy three-putted to 109. They shook hands and Walt said they'd give him a better time frame as soon as they cased the job.

"Remember. We haven't committed to do this yet. If we don't like the way it smells, we walk away. By the way, if I were you, I'd fix that slice. You're coming over the top. Try keeping the right elbow in."

Sammy watched them walk to a van with ACME EXTERMINATING AND PATIO DECKS: WE GET THE JOB DONE lettered on the side. Biff got behind the wheel, and Walt waved goodbye as they pulled out of the lot and onto Route 111.

The license plate read: PATSNUFF.

ll
MARCY

Marcy Gray (née Madeleine Greenspan) had slept with a number of men for more or less professional reasons. From the perspective of time, however, she had to admit that she hadn't slept with the right ones. If she had been more judicious in her choice of sexual partners, she may not have found herself at a delicate age living on a SAG pension and social security in a one-bedroom condominium on Paradise Road in Palm Springs.

The problem began with her choice of husbands. There were two of them, one still alive. The dead one hardly counted. They had met just out of college, in an acting class on Hollywood Boulevard, in a storefront east of Highland, doing *Breakfast At Tiffany's* in front of a group of wannabes.

His name was Troy, and he was seriously gorgeous. Six-two, slim, pale blue eyes, with a dancer's grace and a soft Kentucky accent that rolled off his tongue like a shot of Jack Daniels. She had seen him do Nick in *Virginia Woolf* and had been smitten enough to approach him to do a scene from the Capote play with her.

When he suggested that they, in the interest of authenticity, rehearse the bathtub scene naked, she was there. Why not? Be in the moment. It was the sixties. Everyone took their clothes off. Everyone slept with everyone.

Five minutes into the scene, they were rolling around on the carpet of Troy's studio apartment on Wilcox. The scene killed, and a couple of weeks later, they took a trip to Vegas in Troy's '65 Mustang, top down all the way. They won twelve hundred dollars letting it ride on a two-dollar crap table, decided it was an omen, and went off, stoned out of their gourds, to a wedding chapel downtown to get married with an Elvis impersonator singing "Love Me Tender."

The hangover didn't kick in for a while. They were running to auditions, dreaming the dream, living off the State of California's liberal unemployment benefits. Life was good. Everything was possible. They were more like roommates than a married couple sharing a life plan. The sex was more often than not stoned and athletic, lacking, she began to realize, any sense of intimacy. Afterward, he was up, bouncing around the apartment, showering, and checking his messages, instead of lying with his arms around her.

Little by little, the picture began to get clearer. Troy spent a great deal of time grooming himself, joined a gym they couldn't afford, avoided kissing her on the mouth. He had more clothes than she did in their communal closet. And she caught him with tears in his eyes while watching *Shane* on TV.

"I bet he likes to do it doggie style," her girlfriend Kay said when Marcy had confided her feelings. *Duh. . . .*

But it wasn't until she came home and found him in the shower with a waiter from their favorite Mexican restaurant that she had to admit that she'd married a gay man. They hung on for six more months, distracted by the erratic adrenaline hits of auditions, scenes, workshops. This producer might be coming to class, that agent was looking for new clients, this casting director was a cousin of someone that someone used to know. . .

The gossamer labyrinth of Hollywood dreams.

But it was a losing battle, and they both knew it. They stopped having sex, stopped talking about anything important, started stashing money away separately and fighting over who was paying for what. Marcy saw the fear metastasize inside him as he realized that his desire for men could sabotage his career as an actor, that he was destined to live his life in the big closet that Hollywood provided for gay actors.

She found a place to live in Laurel Canyon, and he became just another girlfriend. They stayed in touch—long phone conversations, dishing late at night when both of them were blue and drunk—until years later, when they bothered to get divorced so that she could marry her second husband. They drifted apart. One phone call a week, then one a month, twice a year, and finally a Christmas card. She had been married to Neil for five years when she went to Troy's memorial service—dead from AIDS at 44.

Neil was at least straight, though she wouldn't have minded if he was just a little bit gay. With some of the wit that her gay friends possessed. He was a writer she'd met when she'd landed a job on *Owen Marshall: Counselor At Law*. Or was it *Petrocelli*? During the seventies, she was booking jobs as damaged women—junkies, abused wives, schizophrenics—and they all blurred together in her memory.

In theory, Neil Breslau was the nice Jewish boy her parents had always wanted her to marry. He was Jewish, all right, but he wasn't all that nice. Deep inside him was a vein of passive aggressive anger that bubbled up to the surface and expressed itself in a wounding sarcasm that she grew to hate. Over the six years of their marriage, his frustration with a writing career that remained below the radar expressed itself by his inability to find any pleasure in anyone else's success. Including hers.

Not that Marcy Gray had ever become a marquee name. But she managed to cobble together a decent living from guest actress jobs on television and the occasional damaged woman role in low-budget features. She got so good at it that she could virtually phone in the performance: vacant eyes, aspirated, brittle voice. In the early eighties, Marcy Gray was the go-to actress if you needed a hooker, a junkie, or a divorcée, with or without a heart of gold.

She didn't get rich, but she wound up taking home more money than Neil, and that turned out to be the deal-breaker with a man whose self-esteem was as flimsy as Neil Breslau's. He spent his days writing depressing, bitter scripts about depressing, bitter men that no one wanted to make. He refused to get a day job or consider Plan B. When she came home at night, it was like coming home to a beaten dog who didn't even want to go out for a walk.

She began staying later at classes, auditions, eating out with her actor friends, avoiding going home. From some primal sense of morality, she avoided having the affairs that she easily could have had. They were out there—smart, good-looking, funny men who came on to her. But she remained faithful to the sullen depressive she had married. For five years, at least.

Then she met Yves, a French director fifteen years older than her, who had a brief flash of cachet in the movie world. Marcy met him on a movie he directed about a drug dealer. Who else but Marcy Gray to play the damaged junkie who falls in love with the lead? She nailed both the audition and the director. And after the first day of shooting, she broke her wedding vows and slept with him in his hotel room in Fresno, where they were filming. And the second and third night as well.

It was clear to both of them that the duration of the affair would be the length of the shoot. Six weeks. And it was. It barely outlasted the wrap party. He flew to Vancouver to cut the movie, and she never saw him again. Or the movie, which, thankfully, was never released.

But he left with her the desire to rediscover men—and the conviction to dump Neil. When she told him she wanted out, he became nasty. If she wanted a divorce, she could pay for it. They had been married for six years with no children, and the only asset of any value was the small two-bedroom house they had bought, with her money, in Silver Lake. It had gone up in value during their marriage, and he wanted not only half of it, but a piece of her SAG pension, and an alimony payment until he "got back on his feet."

He had hired a lawyer and was threatening to take her to court. She couldn't fucking believe it. During their six-year marriage, he had earned next to nothing, and now he was claiming that he "took care of her needs, sacrificing his own career for hers."

The divorce dragged on for almost a year, with the lawyers milking it for all it was worth—which wasn't a whole lot, but more than what they had been fighting over in the first place. Marcy got to keep the house and the Fiat Spider with the bad rings, but she had to give him half the SAG pension accumulated during their marriage, and fifty thousand dollars "to get him back on his feet."

So Marcy found herself skidding into her forties unattached, undiscovered, and unloved by anyone but a series of rescue dogs she adopted and showered inordinate amounts of love on. She had good friends, mostly fellow struggling actors, with whom she shared the ups and downs of the bumpy road of a film career. She continued to take classes, perfecting her technique, rejoicing in brief interludes of glory when she got to do some marvelous scene in class, and became, for those fifteen minutes, Anne Bancroft, Shirley MacLaine, Meryl Streep, or the occasional Equity Waiver play in a ninety-nine-seat theater in East Hollywood, where she got to play damaged women of a somewhat higher pedigree—Lady Macbeth or Blanche DuBois.

And she continued to hope that there would be a man with her name on him, someone she could love the way a woman was supposed to love a man—fully, madly, deeply. But as she climbed into her late forties, the opportunities began to narrow. Men her age were able to trade down, scooping up women in their thirties and younger. What was left were divorced guys—bitter neurotics like Neil—or men in their fifties or sixties, who were ignoring women their own age to trawl among the recently dumped women in their forties.

As far as she was concerned, it was bottom-feeding, and she wasn't interested. Instead, she indulged in flings with below-the-line crew guys and struggling young directors, boozy weekends in Baja or Vegas, where she would wake up on Sunday mornings and long to be lying next to some warm and witty man who cherished her, instead of some semi-literate grip who just wanted to fuck her.

Through it all, she continued to work, playing older damaged women, auditioning for medication commercials—middle-aged women with dry skin, arthritis, insomnia. She drew the line at laxatives. And now and then, there was a role with a little meat on it, and for a week or two she felt like an artist and not merely a caricature of a type that she could barely relate to.

At heart, she was Madeleine Greenspan, a nice Jewish girl from the Valley, and not Marcy Gray, the damaged soul she had made a living playing. She could have been very happy, she sometimes thought, with a lawyer or orthodontist, children, a nice house, and maybe a job teaching acting or decorating houses, or whatever.

But, for one reason or another, it hadn't worked out that way. Instead she had spent the last twenty years watching the ship drift out of the harbor without her. And now she was, as the French say, "a woman of a certain age," living in narrowed circumstances in Palm Springs with a spoiled dachshund.

The truth was that she wasn't entirely sure just how old she really was. She had lied so often about her birth date, had written various numbers on various work forms, that the only way to find out the truth would be to send for a copy of her birth certificate. This she assiduously avoided doing. She couldn't face seeing the actual number in the glaring California sunlight.

At sixty, or some approximation of that age, she had gone under the knife. Twenty-five grand to a top-of-the-line Bedford Drive plastic surgeon, who had done such a good job that you couldn't really tell. Or so she allowed herself to think. There wasn't a working actress in her age range who hadn't gotten work done. It was self-defense, she told herself. Eat or be eaten.

The surgery didn't do much for her career, which continued to dissolve by imperceptible degrees. Every six months, when she got her SAG dues form, the numbers stared her in the face. She had moved from damaged girls, to damaged mothers, to damaged mothers with teenage children. There weren't a lot of roles for damaged grandmothers. Casting directors continued to call her in for oddball roles, but she booked maybe one in ten, and that one was rarely more than a day's work.

It was time to move on to Plan B. Which involved selling the house in Silver Lake and getting a condo somewhere she could afford. The options were narrow. She couldn't face living in the Valley, north of the Boulevard, in some six-unit, one-bedroom place with a postage-stamp pool and cottage-cheese ceilings, surrounded by out-of-work actors and laid-off aerospace engineers.

An actor-realtor friend told her she could get a decent place for her money in Palm Springs. It was only a ninety-minute drive from LA, had a great climate (in the winter at least), and was full of aging gay couples who would be more convivial neighbors than those she'd find in Canoga Park.

It took her a while to give up the ghost and admit to herself that it was time to leave Hollywood. Her therapist told her that she was in an abusive relationship with the business. It didn't value her, or nourish her. It just beat her up.

"Would you put up with this shit from a man?" Janet Costanza, a no-nonsense, transactional type, asked her, before SAG cut down on the mental health benefits and she couldn't afford to see her regularly.

Marcy sat in Janet's big overstuffed armchair next to the tissue box, tears in her eyes, makeup running.

"What else am I going to do?"

"Live your life. Face it: you're a woman in a bad marriage. So do you hang around and put up with the abuse, or do you get out and make a fresh start?"

"I've never done anything else but act."

"Yes, you have. You've lived your life. Acting is just a way of making a living."

So she sold the house in Silver Lake and moved to Palm Springs. She enrolled in yoga classes, painting classes, cooking classes, and real estate classes, and she tried not to look at the phone. Unable to make a complete break, she didn't tell her agent that she was out of the business—just that she was in Palm Springs and would only come up to audition for real jobs.

"What's a real job?" Artie Reman, her agent of twenty years, asked her over lunch at a sushi place on Santa Monica Boulevard.

"One that has a little meat on it."

"You mean, the stuff that Meryl turns down?"

Artie Reman cut to the chase with a ruthless economy of words. He would call her and say, "You're not getting the job." Or, "They think you're too old." Or, "They wrote the role out."

And this time he was no gentler. "Look, I got women fifteen years younger than you who can't get arrested. Actresses have a shelf life, and yours is past due."

"Jesus, Artie, do you have to compare me to a container of milk?"

"Delicacy is not my strong suit."

She sat there eating her raw vegetables, hoping for at least a lifeline to be tossed her way. And though he was indelicate, Artie Reman was not without feeling. Or at least nostalgia.

"I'll keep my ear to the ground for something right for you. If I can get you in, you'll drive up from the desert and read. Okay?"

So off she went, her belongings in a small truck driven by moonlighting, out-of-work actors who moved things by night so as not to be unavailable for auditions. Marcy took with her cartons of headshots, old scripts, videos of her performances, photos of her at the craft-services table with actors people might recognize. She'd had one line in *Cat Ballou*—"You look like a man who could use some company"—in which she played a damaged saloon hussy putting the moves on Lee Marvin, and the actor had graciously signed the on-set photographer's still of them. *Love ya, Lee.*

She had chosen Paradise Gardens from all the other condominium complexes in Palm Springs because the ground-floor units each had a little patio. Her resolution to take up gardening, however, didn't last longer than one summer, during which everything she had planted died an agonizing death. If there was an Association for the Prevention of Cruelty to Plants, she would have been outed, her very funny, very gay neighbor, Stanley, told her.

Stanley Hochberg was a retired choreographer who had worked on several of the big production musicals of the fifties and sixties. Stanley being both gay and Jewish, they bonded. They drank wine, cooked for each other, watched old movies on television. He told her she was gorgeous, and that if he'd had an ounce of hetero blood in him, he'd be all over her.

He constantly cracked her up. Waiting for the light to change, some delicious young man would walk in front of them in tight jeans, and Stanley would say, "Be still, my beating dick." Or his description of Chris and Edie, the middle-aged swingers of Paradise Gardens, as "Sonny and Cher on Quaaludes." It was Stanley who coined the phrase "Purgatory Gardens" to describe the thirty-unit complex on Paradise Road they lived in. *It's not quite up to the standards of hell.*

And it was to Stanley that she had confided that she felt her life, at that point, was mostly about damage control. She needed to circle the wagons and figure out a way to get through the years in front of her.

"I'm a single, childless woman, living in genteel poverty. A couple of bad breaks, and I could be a bag lady," she told him.

"Don't be a drama queen, sweetheart."

"Seriously. Who's going to take care of me in my old age?"

"I will," he'd said, and meant it. And she was convinced he *had* meant it, until he got ill and died of stomach cancer. She had nursed him as much as he would let her, fighting back tears as he went not so gently into the night. *Why the fuck couldn't it have been AIDS? I would at least have had some decent memories. . .*

Without Stanley, she felt that there was no human presence to keep her from winding up with a cardboard sign at a freeway on ramp. WILL ACT FOR MONEY. Or give head, for that matter, but that would be a hard sell in this market. In her day, she had been proficient at that particular craft. *If only she had sucked the right cocks.* The thought made her laugh until she cried, and she missed Stanley even more.

The strategy was clear: find someone to take care of her. He didn't have to be Mr. Right, just not Mr. Wrong. Surely there was someone around, some decent-looking man her age, or maybe just a little older, who didn't have pee stains on his underwear and drove at night. And she wouldn't mind a little sex now and then, just enough to remind her that she was still a woman.

She had narrowed it down to two candidates—both, conveniently, residents of Paradise Gardens. For once, they would be auditioning for her, though they didn't know it. It wasn't a cattle call. She was already at callbacks, having scouted the available talent and come up with the only two men who were presentable and straight.

The safer choice was a retired cement company owner named Sammy Dee, who had hit on her while she was on the StairMaster in the exercise room. He was on the short side—five-nine, maybe five-ten in shoes with heels—and could lose a few pounds, but he had a rich head of undyed hair and nice skin.

Sammy Dee was from somewhere on Long Island, and had just enough of the East Coast accent to attract her. His nails were impeccably manicured—the sign of a man who took care of himself—and he was rarely more than a few hours away from his last shave. In the right light, he reminded her of Lino Ventura (in Lelouch's *Happy New Year*).

Sammy was soft-spoken and polite. She liked the way he listened with full attention, never interrupting, keeping his eyes focused. And he had old-world manners. He opened car doors, pulled chairs out, got up when she entered a room.

There was something about him, however, that didn't quite add up. Apparently he had no family, or at least none that he was close to. He told her he'd never married, was an only child, and his parents were long dead. He'd left home at seventeen to work in construction, and owned his own business by the time he was thirty. For the last ten years, he'd been an independent investor.

What to make of a straight guy pushing seventy who had never married? There had to be some skeletons in his closet. Long-term relationships, girlfriends, women who left him or were left by him? Judging by the lump in his gym shorts, she was convinced he was playing for the right team.

More importantly, if he had owned his own business for all those years, why wasn't he living in Boca Raton or Beverly Hills?

Google was no help. *Did you mean Sandra Dee?*

On the surface, at least, he seemed to be comfortable. His wardrobe was expensive, he drove a new Lexus, and he had some serious jewelry—a gold ring, a neck chain, and a Philippe Patek.

But she had no idea what he had in the bank. If anything. The last thing she needed in her life, at this point, was another dependent. Klaus was bad enough. The dachshund had a series of chronic ailments that caused her to drop serious change at the vet's.

She knew even less about the second candidate, the African who lived in a two-bedroom unit, the second bedroom used as an office for his import/ export business. Didier Onyekachukwu was from Ivory Coast—a place that, to her, was just a colorful name somewhere on the map of Africa.

He was tall, heavy-set, and wore mother-of-pearl reading glasses on a chain around his neck. On one of his cheeks was a scar that he told her was a tribal marking, which she found, for some reason, sexy. He spoke English erratically, but with a perfectly charming French accent. English was his third language—before French, there had been a tribal language that he had spoken until he was ten, when he'd been shipped off to a missionary school.

There was a sing-song quality to his speech, an exotic cadence. He called her Mar-*cee* and smiled through a set of incredibly white teeth. He moved gracefully for his size and liked to dance. A major plus, in her book—and an area in which Sammy Dee couldn't compete. *I don't dance—don't ask me.* Marcy had yet to find a straight man who could dance.

Didier called her *ma petite* and *ma belle* and had a lovely, rich, full-bodied laugh that filled the space around him. It was hard to dislike him. Even Tuuli and Majda, the Finnish lesbians who didn't like anybody, would allow smiles to leak from their icy Scandinavian features when he joked with them. He called them Inga and Binga, to their faces, and managed to sell them a mahogany statue of a tribal princess with a large pointed head-dress that, he assured them, was used as a sex toy by Sapphic Fulani women.

Now that she had narrowed her suitors down to the final two, she missed Stanley's perspective. He would have guided her, helped her formulate a strategy, spotted things about the two men that she could be missing. He would have been her consultant, her coach, her confidant.

Chris and Edie had no doubt cruised them, interviewing them as possible additions to their swinging parties. Edie had approached Marcy one day at the pool and suggested that she show up with *one of the new guys for a couple of Mai Tais and a little you-know-what.* Marcy passed, explaining that she didn't indulge publicly in *you-know-what.*

"You don't what you're missing."

"I'm afraid I do."

The night of the mold meeting, the contestants came face to face. It was obvious to her, and probably to them, that they were in competition. Didier was cordial, jovial, diplomatic, but Sammy looked like he wanted to put his rival through a wall. Frankly, she wasn't sure which of the two attitudes was more attractive. Stanley Kowalski, even with Brando playing him, didn't race her motor. But, then, a touch of the Neanderthal wasn't entirely unappealing either. Though Marcy considered herself a feminist—what woman who supports herself isn't?—she wasn't above being titillated by the thought of a man throwing her over his shoulder and dragging her off into a cave.

When Didier had proposed French lessons, Sammy had invited himself along. It was clear that Sammy was more interested in preventing her from spending quality time with the African than in learning French. It was almost like high school—boys competing to drive her home. She loved it.

The French lesson didn't turn out well. The lunch she prepared for the three of them had been an awkward affair, the two of them going out of their way to belittle the other as if they were peeing on trees to claim their territory. She threw both of them out after an hour and took her nap with Klaus.

There was a third man who interested her (professionally, not romantically) at Paradise Gardens, a movie producer named Charlie Berns. The man had flown in under her radar. She knew of him vaguely, the way everyone in show business knows everyone else, and had been surprised to learn that he was a neighbor.

She knocked on his door one evening, and he invited her in for a cup of coffee. His unit looked like it was occupied by transients. The decor consisted of cheaply framed one-sheets of movies he had done, low-budget genre films without notable actors or directors. And it was dreadfully hot, even at night. He told her that he was allergic to air conditioning.

The man had a scattered, vacant manner to him, an expression on his face that seemed to indicate that nothing you could tell him would in any way disconcert him. Producing movies taught one to roll with the punches, and Charlie Berns looked as if he had been down for the count a number of times and yet still managed to get up off the canvas.

He pretended to know who she was, or, more accurately, who she had been, nodding as she recited her more noteworthy roles. Between them, they had a long list of mutual friends—acquaintances actually, since friendship in the film business rarely survived the duration of a shoot. The alcoholic wrap party embrace. *We must get together.*

As she sat drinking coffee with him, she experienced a confusion of motives. Was she adding him to the short list, or was she interested in a job working for him? Over the years, she had developed the habit of auditioning for anyone who was in the position of hiring her. It was an unconscious instinct, even with people as low down on the food chain as Charlie Berns appeared to be.

Unlike Sammy Dee or Didier Onyekachukwu, however, Charlie Berns didn't move the needle on her chemistry test. Though he was not unattractive, there was something detached, almost asexual, about him, which seemed to indicate that he had other things on his mind than women.

Still, he had won an actual Academy Award. Years ago. She vaguely remembered seeing him on TV in an ill-fitting tux, mumbling his acceptance speech. The movie, *Dizzy and Will,* was a ponderous period piece starring Jeremy Ikon and Jacqueline Fortier that had snuck in when the two leading candidates canceled each other out.

"Where's your Oscar?" she asked him.

"I got $375 for it on eBay."

Unbelievable. If she had one, she'd have put it in the middle of the living room with a spotlight on it.

"So what's your next project?"

He smiled dimly and shook his head. "I'm retired."

"Oh, come on. Really?" Unconsciously, she switched into coquette mode.

"Let me put it this way—as far as the people who finance movies are concerned, I'm retired."

"Even if the right script came along?"

He looked around him, as if to say, "*Here?*" How was the right script going to make its way into Paradise Gardens?

"You never know," she said with a smile.

That phrase had been her mantra for all the years she was in the business. Everything she did, every attempt to land some improbable role, was motivated by her telling herself that *you never know.*

Unfortunately, now she *did* know. Or at least she should have. She had known when she sold the house in Silver Lake and moved to Palm Springs, when she had applied for her real estate license, and when she walked into Charlie Berns's condo with a retouched headshot.

And yet here she was, batting her eyelashes like a starlet, violating another of the fundamental principles for surviving in Hollywood: don't shit where you eat. The man was a neighbor, someone she would likely see again, and you didn't want to have to run into anyone if the project you had worked on together was a train wreck.

"You never know," he repeated.

She found herself liking the man. He had an impish, ironic smile that flickered at odd moments. He had walked the same highway she had, dealt with the same bullshit, and was suffering from the same sort of dim nostalgia that flared up into an occasional rebirth of interest.

Charlie Berns accepted her headshot and promised to keep her in mind for his next picture, whenever or whatever that might be. Why not? At that very moment, someone could be busily writing a brilliant script about a damaged woman in her sixties, her *early* sixties. *You never knew.*

The first date she had with Sammy Dee was at the Olive Garden. The two-hour dinner revealed very little about him, except that he had good table manners and liked his wine. He skillfully evaded her questions about his past, as well as about his present and future.

"What do you do when you're not investing?" she'd asked.

"Play golf."

"Is that all?"

"I go see movies."

"You don't travel?"

"Not if I can help it."

On their second date, he took her to a high-end French restaurant in town, where he ordered off the top of the wine list. He dropped a couple hundred on the dinner. That went into the credit column. She drank too much and got cuddly in the car on the way home. There was no telling what would have happened if they hadn't run into Didier in the hallway as they were heading for her condo. He was standing there, a bottle of cognac in his hand, like a parent waiting up for kids who had broken curfew.

She wasn't ready to go to bed with either of them. Not yet. It wasn't that she was an old-fashioned girl in this respect. But she was a smart girl. She knew that one way to keep a man interested was to keep him horny. And she needed them interested while she did her due diligence.

Didier Onyekachukwu's courting consisted, for the time being, of showing up with margaritas at the pool, or knocking on her door at odd hours with a bottle. His past was a great deal more exotic than Sammy Dee's. He grew up in a bush village in Africa, with no electricity or running water, where people sacrificed goats. He was educated by French priests, had studied and lived in Paris. The timing of all this was left vague. She had no idea how old he was.

He had been married years ago in Côte d'Ivoire to three different wives. At the same time. Polygamy was the African way of dealing with the demographic problem of too many women, he explained. He had at least a dozen children whose names he wasn't entirely sure of. There were three Kodjo's (the Duala name for children born on Monday), a couple of Kumlas (girls born on Thursday), a Thomas, a Victoire, and maybe a Marie Genevieve. Occasionally someone sent him a photo of a grandchild.

He told her that he had been involved in politics, first in the liberation movement against the French, and then in the young republic's government, and had risen to some sort of powerful position before things got nasty and he fled to France. "I am fortunate I am not dead," he said with perfect equanimity. "Terrible things have happened to my country." He didn't elaborate.

Marcy Googled Côte d'Ivoire and learned that the country used to be called the Ivory Coast. Its capital was Yamoussoukro, the life expectancy was forty-one years, the per capita annual income was $1,062, and its history was marked by a series of bloody coups and ruling family infighting that was too complicated to keep track of.

Unlike Sammy Dee, Didier Onyekachukwu didn't mind talking about his past, but much of it was so foreign to Marcy that it didn't shed a lot of light on who he was now. He was cheerful, forthcoming, and fun to be around. But was he the man to take care of her? Would he take her to Paris and the south of France, to the châteaus of the Loire, and to all the other places she longed to visit? Would he allow her to shred her real estate license and pass on driving up to LA for an audition for some role she didn't even want?

And was he a better bet than the retired cement company owner with the good manners and the pinkie ring? It was a tough call. What she really wanted was to see their tax returns. And their medical records. Preferably both.

Marcy found JB INVESTIGATIONS: DISCREET, RELIABLE, REASONABLE on Angie's List. They had seven reviews, six As and one B. The website listed "asset search" among the services provided and offered a free consultation. They did not include the evaluation of potential romantic prospects, but she assumed it went with the territory.

The office was located in a strip mall in Cathedral City, above a Chinese take-out place. Marcy had, naturally, dressed for the interview as if it were for a role. She was playing the damaged wife of a scoundrel in some 1940s film noir, and wore a black dress, heels, and some costume jewelry. The only thing missing was the Barbara Stanwyck hat and veil.

She had expected Robert Mitchum, or at least Elliott Gould doing Robert Mitchum, and was surprised to discover a hefty middle-aged Jewish woman named Evelyn Duboff behind the desk. The woman was dressed in a Loehmann's pantsuit and a pair of Adidas tennis shoes.

"Sit. Take a load off. You want a cup of coffee?"

"No, thank you," Marcy said, sitting down.

"So how'd you find me?"

"Angie's List."

"You ever wonder who this Angie is?" Marcy could hear Brooklyn in her voice. "Must be a very rich woman by now."

Marcy nodded, unconsciously looking around for a cue card. As if she were doing a take of a scene and had gone up on her lines.

Though the air conditioning was on, it wasn't making a lot of headway against the midday desert heat. The odor of soy oil wafting up from the Chinese place below made her feel queasy.

"So what can I do for you, Miss. . .?"

"Gray. Marcy Gray."

Evelyn Duboff looked at her a little closer and smiled. "Wait a second, you were in pictures, right?"

"Still am. Well, sort of. . ."

"I've seen you on television. In a movie or two."

"They show them late at night."

"Facacta business, the movie business. You make a million, or you starve."

"I did all right, for a while. Now. . .well, anyway, that's not why I'm here. Your website says you do asset searches."

"Bread and butter business these days. Used to be women wanted to know whether their husband was screwing around on them. Now they want to know where he's stashed the 401K."

"This isn't that. . .exactly." It was at times like this that she wished she had her own private screenwriter writing her dialogue. She sat there for a moment, not sure how to present the problem.

"Darling," Evelyn Duboff said, "don't be shy. This is a privileged conversation. We do everything within the law, more or less. And, between you and me, we can stretch that a little bit, too."

"Well, it's sensitive."

"What isn't? If I could tell you the things people want to know, you'd plotz. So what's going on? Married?"

Marcy shook her head.

"Ex-husband hid his assets during the divorce, and now he's taking bimbos to the Caribbean?"

"Actually, it's two men."

"Two? Nice, very nice."

"And I've never been married to either of them. But I'm thinking about it."

Evelyn Duboff digested this for a moment, nodding slowly. "Uh-huh. And you want to see what you'd be marrying into. Am I right?"

"Sort of. I mean, I just want to know a little more about them."

"Don't blame you. Far as I'm concerned, anybody gets married at our age deserves complete disclosure. You wouldn't buy a used car without getting it checked out by a mechanic. Right?"

"Right. So is it. . .legal to do that?"

"Legal enough."

The woman shifted her bulk in the chair and emitted a sound that was somewhere between a belch and a yawn.

"Banks are forbidden by law to disclose information on depositors except to law enforcement, and even that has to have a court order. But there are ways of getting the information without dealing with the bank."

"I just kind of want a rough idea of. . .their. . .assets."

"I'll give it to you down to the penny. Including real estate, stock positions, annuities, commodity futures, puts and calls, partnerships, precious metals, you name it. Anything else?"

"Well, you know, past marriages, ever been arrested type thing."

"No problem. Tell you the truth, most of that is public record. You could get it yourself. But I'll throw it in."

She wished she had a prop cigarette. This would be the moment that the director would have her lift the veil, and Robert Mitchum would take the gold-plated lighter out of his double-breasted suit and light her cigarette. *I'm not sure I can afford your services, mister.* He would crease his cheeks a millimeter and say, *Don't worry about it, ma'am.*

"This sounds kind of expensive," Marcy said.

"Depends. Anything I can do without moving my ass out of this chair you can probably afford. Surveillance is the expensive item. Sitting in a car waiting for a man to walk out of his girlfriend's apartment type thing. That can add up."

"I don't have a lot of money."

"Neither do I. But I'll tell you what—my usual price is five hundred an hour, but for you, I'll do it for three-fifty. With any luck, you're in for a thousand, maybe twelve hundred. Out the door."

Marcy screwed up her features. She could afford a thousand dollars. She had spent that much money on shoes.

"Look, the more information you give me—past addresses, social security numbers, date of birth, mother's maiden name—the cheaper this is going to be."

"All I know is their names and where they live."

"Can you get me license plate numbers of their cars?"

"I think so."

"Okay, that's a start."

Evelyn swiveled in her chair and turned on her computer. She hit a few keys, brought up a screen, hit a few more keys, and pages came out of her printer.

"This is a contract. It's the usual mishegoss about no liability on my part and what happens if you don't pay me. It's standard. Relax. It's not going to be worth my while to hire a lawyer if you stiff me for a thousand dollars."

"I'll pay you, don't worry."

"Of course you will. And you're going to write me a retainer for three hundred and fifty dollars right now. A bargain. You couldn't even get your carpet cleaned for that money."

Marcy gave the contract five seconds of her attention, signed it, and took her checkbook out. She started to write the check, then stopped.

"There's no way they're going to find out, right?"

"They'll never know, darling."

She wrote ACTING LESSONS on the memo line.

Evelyn Duboff glanced at the check. "You're going to write it off. Why not? It should be tax deductible anyway. Information on a potential investment."

The tax deduction hadn't even occurred to her. She was more concerned with covering her tracks. Three-quarters profile to camera right, her good side, she rose and headed for the door. She got it in one take.

It wasn't until she was driving home that Marcy realized that she didn't know if Didier Onyekachukwu even had a car. She had never seen him outside of Paradise Gardens. How did he live in Palm Springs without a car?

Pulling into the parking garage, she drove past Sammy Dee's space and saw the Lexus, glowing from the car wash. She memorized the license plate. In her condo, she picked up the phone and dialed Didier's number.

"Good morning," he answered in his endearing, sing-song voice.

"*Bonjour*, Didier." He liked it when she tried her French out on him. "*Come unt tally too?*"

"*Comment vas-tu?*" He corrected her.

"Of course. Listen, *mon ami*, my *voiture* is *malade*. I wonder if you can give me a lift to Ralphs. I need to pick up a few groceries."

"*Désolé, ma petite. Je n'ai pas de voiture.*"

"*Pardon?*"

"I do not have a *voiture*. I take the taxi when necessary."

"Oh. . .I see. Well, I'll give a Sammy a call."

"No, no, no!"

"I'm sure he won't mind."

"No, no, no!" he repeated. "I, too, have a need of the groceries. I shall call the taxi, and we shall procure our groceries together. *N'est-ce pas?*"

"It's really not necessary."

"I insist."

A half hour later Marcy found herself in the back seat of a taxi with Didier Onyekachukwu and a shopping list of items she didn't need. There was an intimacy to the excursion that she found a bit uncomfortable. Even though she was auditioning life partners, she would have preferred working up to shopping together more gradually. At this stage, it seemed to fall into the too-much-information area.

She avoided cosmetics and stayed away from cleaning supplies. She walked right by the bathroom deodorizer, even though she actually needed a replacement for the jasmine-lavender mélange atomizer she kept on the toilet lid in her powder room.

Instead she bought canned goods, soups and vegetables, coffee and sugar, and then bought some yogurt and cut fruit when she realized that she had presented this excursion as something more pressing than stocking up on soup for September in the desert.

His shopping cart contained exotic fruits and vegetables—kiwi, papaya, figs, mangos, artichokes, plantains, yams, garlic—as well as sesame oil, noodles, spices, nuts. And, incongruously, a large box of Fruit Loops.

"I like to eat them as I watch the television," he explained.

As they stood in line waiting to be checked out, she restrained herself from leafing through the latest issue of *People*, even though she was dying to know who Jennifer Aniston was dating. She had subscribed to the tabloid until she realized that she was going through it unconsciously searching for evidence of the declining careers, or incurable illnesses, of people she didn't like. Or worse, the obituaries of women she had been in direct competition with. *One less rival.*

As soon as she got home, she called Evelyn Duboff and gave her Sammy Dee's license number. She told her that Didier Onyekachukwu didn't have a car.

"Red flag," the detective said.

"What do you mean?"

"He could have lost his drivers license. DUI, reckless driving, whatever. . ."

"Wouldn't that be on his record?"

"Not if he knows how to keep it off. There are people who can get it done for you. And clean up your credit rating at the same time."

"So...when do you think you might have some answers for me?"

"Depends."

"On what?"

"On whether either of these guys has gone to the trouble of purposefully clouding the trail. There are people you can get to do that for you, too."

"So you'll let me know?"

"You'll be the second to know, darling."

Ten minutes later, the doorbell rang. Sammy Dee was standing there in a pair of neatly pressed trousers and a Lacoste T-shirt.

"Something wrong with your car?"

It took her a second to connect the dots.

He answered her unuttered question. "I saw you pull out in a cab."

Now what? A little improv routine. It was something she did well in acting class. You just went with whatever your scene partner gave you—like hitting a tennis ball back over the net.

"I didn't want to drive my car."

"How come?"

"It's kind of acting up."

"What's wrong with it?"

"The. . .motor sounds funny."

"Let me take a look at it."

"I'll take it in tomorrow. No big deal."

"Hey, you never know. Maybe it's something simple. I'll take it for a spin."

She had painted herself into a corner. If the intention of the scene was to avoid his finding out that there was nothing wrong with her car and that she took a taxi with Didier Onyekachukwu for some other, compromising reason, she wasn't accomplishing it. She dredged down into the improv well and came up dry.

Marcy got her car keys, handed them to Sammy, and watched him head off toward the parking garage. "Thanks," she called after him.

Then, as he disappeared into the elevator, she remembered that she had left Evelyn Duboff's name and address on a Post-It note on her glove compartment. JB Investigations: Discreet, Reliable, Reasonable.

Okay. There were a number of reasons one could consult a private detective besides investigating other people's assets. Right? She poured herself a glass of cranberry juice and sat down to come up with a plausible reason for why she had seen the detective.

She worked up a scenario. Research for a movie role she had been offered. A female private detective movie she was up for—a kind of modern film noir. Opposite Russell Crowe—no, Jimmy Caan, more age-appropriate. Warner Brothers. Shooting in Rancho Cucamonga, maybe Fullerton, in December or November, depending on locations. Soderbergh was supposed to direct, but they were talking to Ang Lee. . . .

All this because Didier Onyekachukwu didn't own a car.

Sammy didn't ask when he returned with her keys. Instead he told her that she needed a tune-up.

"Your plugs are dirty."

Tomorrow she would take her car in for a fucking tune-up, she promised. She would sneak out early before the African was up so that she wouldn't have to explain why her car was no longer *malade*.

Four hundred and fifty-nine dollars later, her car was running beautifully. They found a couple of other "little problems" in addition to her dirty spark plugs that needed to be taken care of. Shopping for a man was getting more expensive. Marcy was up to fifteen hundred dollars and counting.

A week later, the detective called and suggested she come into the office.

This time Marcy skipped makeup and wardrobe. She wore a lightweight tracksuit and had her hair tied up in a ponytail. More Diane Keaton incognito at the dry cleaner's than Barbara Stanwyck with a private eye.

Evelyn Duboff was eating a tuna sandwich at her desk, which was littered with file folders. "Sorry," she apologized. "I missed lunch today. What's with the schleppy wardrobe?"

"I just didn't feel like dressing."

She leaned back in her swivel chair and said, "You got some taste in men, darling."

What the hell did that mean?

"I don't know quite how to put this but, well, neither of these guys are who they're supposed to be. Let me rephrase that. They have both gone out of their way to disguise their true identities. I can't prove this, but I'd bet my bippy that Sammy Dee and Didier Whatchamacallit are not the names they were born with."

"How do you know that?"

"I've been doing this long enough to develop a seat-of-the-pants feeling about this kind of thing, and let me tell you, my backside is ringing off the hook. You're dealing with a couple of real shifty characters here."

Marcy slumped into her seat. This was not what she wanted to hear. She had come to this woman for reassurance, and it looked as if she were getting anything but. Was she going to have to start auditioning all over again?

"Let me give you an example. Sammy, the Jewish one? First of all, if he's Jewish, I'm Mormon. Some people have, what do you call it, gay-dar, you know, they can tell if a man is gay. Well, I got Jew-dar. And, you ask me, this guy is about as Jewish as the Pope."

"He said his father changed their family name on Ellis Island."

"Maybe on Staten Island. Dee is a Polish Ellis Island name. Sandra Dee? Her real name was Sandra Cymboliak. There's no will. No divorce records, no next of kin anywhere. What kind of Jew has no family anywhere? Jews have families, even if they don't like them. No ex-wife? Really? Guy's not a faygeleh and he's pushing seventy, there's got to be at least one, if not a couple of women, in his past. *Zero* women? Please. Cement business? Pretty squishy, if you'll pardon the expression. Most of the cement in this country comes from Mexico. Wait, it gets better. Did you know he was getting into the art business?"

"Sammy? No, that's Didier."

"That's what I thought, too, but guess who just borrowed twenty-five grand from Wells Fargo to open an art gallery. And this is just the obvious stuff. It's the numbers that give him away."

"Huh?"

"Social security number and driver's license number. A person's social can tell you something about their age, where they were born, how long they've been in this country. There are sequences that have meaning, and, with the right databases, you can make certain assumptions about someone. And then there are the funny numbers. Funny numbers are computer-generated numbers that the government comes up with when they're trying to conceal someone's identity."

"Why would the government want to do that?"

"I thought you were in the movie business. You never heard of witness protection?"

"You mean, like, for the mafia?"

"It's not just for the mob. The SEC's doing it, too. When the government wants someone to blow the whistle on some big fish, they make a deal. They set you up with a whole new life—new name, new location, new social security number, new everything."

"You think Sammy is in witness protection?"

"Maybe, maybe not. Maybe he did it all himself. Look, there are a number of reasons someone does an identity scrub that have nothing to do with crime. Could be romantic disappointment, business disaster. It's the modern version of the French Foreign Legion. You become Monsieur X."

Evelyn Duboff polished off the last of her tuna sandwich, chugged some orange juice straight from the container.

"I don't know any of this for a fact, but I'll bet you his name isn't Sammy Dee, he's not Jewish, and he's never been in the cement business. The rest, I don't know."

"Does he have any money?"

"Not in the bank, at least. Apart from the twenty-five grand he borrowed from Wells Fargo, which is down to nineteen as we speak. The car is a three-year lease, five-ninety-nine a month. He's into MasterCard for over eleven grand."

"Jesus. . ." Marcy sat there, exhaling, shaking her head slowly, as if a doctor had just given her bad news.

"You want to hear about the African?"

"I don't know—do I?"

"Well, the good news is that I know a lot less about him. Most of the schmutz on him is in France. And it's in French. I could get a translator involved, but we're talking serious money. You're already over a thousand."

"Just tell me, is he really from Côte d'Ivoire?"

"I couldn't find any birth records for him. But then, African birth records are a little approximate. Sometimes they forget to write things down. Ivory Coast is a former French colony, and a lot of them go to France, so I tried running the name there and came up with a match. Of course, it could be a different Didier Onyekachukwu, but with a name like that, I doubt it. He pops up in Nice in 1984, working in the—you'll love this—fashion business. Right? This guy is giving Yves Saint Laurent a run for his money. You ask me, the fashion stuff was a front for something else. I smell drugs. Or maybe guns. But not high-class rags, that I can tell you. A straight African in the shmata business? I don't think so."

"He says he's importing African art. Sculpture, fertility statues. . ."

"Probably is. The thing is, do you know what's in the statues?"

"C'mon, *really*?"

"Darling, I'm just doing my job here. Guy with his background in the art business? Living—no offense—in a down-market Palm Springs condo development? If he's in the drug business, he's not very good at it."

Marcy sat there inhaling the soy oil fumes drifting up from below. She felt exhausted. Depressed. Defeated. And she must have looked it.

"Look, tell you what. I'll keep looking, see if I can turn some more stuff up. Maybe I'll find something good."

"I can't afford any more."

"I'll do it off the clock." She shrugged and said, by way of explanation, "We girls got to stick together."

Marcy drove home through the frying-pan heat, feeling worse than she had in a very long time. How could she have been so stupid?

What was it with her taste in men? Two dreadful husbands, a profusion of sub-standard lovers, and now, when she should have known better, was this the best she could come up with? An ex-mafioso and an African gunrunner?

As she drove in to Purgatory Gardens, she saw Didier at the pool playing Scrabble with Tuuli. Or was it Majda?

He waved. She didn't wave back. She went inside, curled up with Klaus, and had herself a good cry.

III
DIDIER

When he was Minister of Economics and Finance for one of Burkina Faso's unelected presidents, Didier Onyekachukwu (née Koffi Gbadabo, a.k.a. Blaise Gbadabo) had managed to make a number of people rich, including himself. Not bad for a young man from the bush of Upper Volta, the seventeenth child of a yam farmer with three wives, an earthen-walled house with an ostrich egg on the roof, a scrawny goat, and a patch of reluctant soil.

In spite of the poverty, it wasn't an unhappy childhood in Gouya. Koffi and his brothers and sisters had the run of the village. There was no electricity or running water, and no school to speak of—except the Muslim religious school, which his father, because of his fondness for palm wine, spared his children from attending. Before he was old enough to help in the fields, Koffi was allowed to run free, swim in the stream, torment the dogs, and climb the baobab trees.

All this bliss came to an end when his father decided to send him to a missionary school in a neighboring town. Koffi had to leave his happy home to learn about the Stations of the Cross. The adjustment wasn't easy for an eight-year-old who had never worn shoes or eaten with a fork. The monks were intolerant of any divergence from *"le chemin au ciel."* As far as Koffi was concerned, he had already been on the path to heaven, splashing in the stream, dropping baobab nuts on old men passing under-neath, happily playing with his budding penis. Now he wasn't allowed to touch it except to pee, which he had to do in a ceramic bowl instead of in the fresh air, competing with his friends to see who could arc the stream farther.

Koffi did well in school. He grasped the cold beauty of the Pythago-rean theorem, as well as the imperfect subjunctive of irregular verbs. The monks gave him a new name—Blaise, after the seventeenth-century French philosopher.

By the time he was thirteen, he barely resembled the little savage who had arrived at the school five years before in a pair of torn shorts. He could solve quadratic equations, list the kings of France from Charlemagne all the way to Louis-Philippe, and quote large portions of the gospel accord-ing to Luke.

At the same time he began sneaking out the window to visit the village girls at night after the friars had locked the dormitory door. After he im-pregnated a fourteen-year-old girl, the friars hustled him off to complete his education in their school in Ouagadougou.

The capital resembled a dusty French provincial town, with open sewers and enough eclectic European architecture to give it delusions of gran-deur. Blaise Gbadabo, as he was now known, became a student at the Lycée Voltaire, earning his room and board by washing dishes in the refec-tory kitchen.

Blaise finished fourth in his class at the Lycée Voltaire, and he was of-fered a scholarship to attend the Sorbonne. He didn't hesitate. Two months before his eighteenth birthday, he was on an Air France flight to Le Bour-get Airport in Paris, carrying nothing but a cardboard suitcase with two pairs of trousers, a half-dozen shirts, and the bible that the friars had given him as a graduation present.

As soon as he got off the bus at the Gare de Lyon, young Blaise was overcome by the energy, the color, the smells of food, perfume, and wine. And women. All those women in their cotton dresses, legs exposed, eyes and mouths made up alluringly.

What he loved most about Paris was the feeling that, at any given mo-ment, anything could happen. Life swirled around him on the streets, in the cafés, on the métro. He was convinced that on every street there was an adventure awaiting him. All he had to do was turn the corner.

Blaise walked the streets of the city, soaking it all in—the architecture, the history in every stone, the blur of color. He loved sitting in a café for hours with nothing but a three-franc cup of coffee, watching the movie of life around him. He loved the rich subtlety of the language, the ability to find meanings within meanings, to discover what he thought in words. He loved the food—the complexity of its textures and sauces—and the variety of wines, each one a little different from the other.

But mostly, he loved the women. Unlike in Ouagadougou, where if you looked at a French woman too pointedly you risked getting rebuked (or worse), here the women returned your look.

Blaise was tall and slender and moved with natural grace. He got invitations to dances, to picnics in the Bois de Boulogne, to swim at the Piscine Deligny—the public pool beside the Seine where women sunbathed topless—and often to girls' rooms late at night. He would arrive at these small *chambres de bonne*, walking up the six flights of stairs, to be greeted at the door by Brigitte, by Marie-Louise, by Agnès, in a pair of American blue jeans and a tight sweater, which he would soon have the pleasure of removing.

When Upper Volta became the autonomous *République de Haute-Volta* in 1960, Blaise decided it was time to go home. There were too many opportunities for a young man with a degree in economics from the Sorbonne. Four years after he had left, he returned, this time with a Louis Vuitton suitcase containing silk underwear, cashmere sweaters, and a bottle of Yves St. Laurent cologne.

Back in his village, there was a feast in his honor, with roasted goat meat, manioc, cassava, and palm wine. The drums beat under a harvest moon, and Blaise danced until he collapsed. In the middle of the night, he was visited by his father's youngest wife, a comely girl named Afia from a neighboring village, and nine months later his stepmother made him a father for the first time.

By that time, his own father could no longer keep track of whom among his wives he was sleeping with and when, so the child was assumed to be his. The result was that Blaise's son was also his stepbrother, but in rural Africa these distinctions didn't count for much.

In Ouagadougou, he found work as an uncertified accountant for a cotton dealer. Moussa Doukabe, a former schoolmate at the Lycée Voltaire, offered Blaise a job helping him run the business. Moussa knew cotton, but he didn't know numbers, and he needed the Sorbonne graduate and his knowledge of economics.

It was both an exhilarating and dangerous time to be in West Africa. Africans were running their country for the first time, learning on the job how to do the things that the French had always done for them. There was a great deal of both idealism and corruption. The fault lines of tribal differences, smoothed over by the colonial powers, reemerged and replaced meritocracy with favoritism.

It didn't take long for the young Sorbonne graduate to get noticed. By his second year in Ouagadougou, he was a man about town, spending his days making money and his evenings in the city's nightclubs, dancing the High Life and going home with his pick of pretty young women.

A year and a half into his work with Moussa Doukabe, Blaise was offered a government job. He would be making less money than he had been exporting cotton, but he realized he could acquire two things that, at his stage in life, were worth even more than money—contacts and influence. So he left Moussa and went to work in the Ministry of Economics and Finance.

At the Ministry he saw firsthand how influence was peddled, how money was channeled to friends and family, siphoned off by those who knew how to disguise what they were doing. While the vast majority of the people of Upper Volta remained mired in poverty, a small cadre of them became rich. They lived like feudal lords, driving Mercedes, keeping mistresses, and treating their servants worse than the French had.

Ouagadougou in 1960 was like Dodge City a century earlier. You needed a big gun and a bigger set of balls. Blaise Gbadabo had the latter, and he compensated for his lack of family connections with audacity and brains. The Sorbonne had taught him how to read the market fluctuations, and his vantage point in the Ministry of Economics and Finance enabled him to exploit this knowledge. He knew who to pay off, how much to give them, and how to tap dance around the repressive tax laws enacted by the legislature.

It was soon clear to his superiors at the ministry that this young man was worth knowing. Undersecretaries came to him for advice, gave him money to invest, and rewarded him with promotions. Two years in, he was working directly under the deputy minister, Etienne Tsadeko, a fun-loving man with a similar taste for good living. At night, the two young bachelors prowled the *bas fonds* of Ouagadougou, returning to Etienne's house in the wee hours with a bottle of Remi Martin and a couple of young women to help them drink it.

Etienne told Blaise that the military was planning a coup, that the young, French-trained colonels could be running the country within a year. Accordingly, Blaise began to cultivate the men in the stylish, Paris-tailored uniforms and sunglasses. They, too, had a taste for women and money, and Blaise knew how to provide them with both. It wasn't long before the young man with the Sorbonne degree was speculating successfully on the cotton market for his new friends.

By the time that Colonel Jean-Baptiste Zenbo occupied the presidential palace, after a bloodless coup, Blaise Gbadabo was a frequent visitor. A few months later, the colonel made him the new Minister of Economics and Finance in the not-so-provisional government of Haute-Volta. Promised elections were continually put off due to "threats of tribal violence and election irregularities."

Now Blaise had his hands not only on the cotton market, but also on the tax revenue of the republic. And plenty of influence to peddle. His office featured a Directoire desk and a Louis XV armoire filled with Napoleon brandy and Davidoff cigars. He had a deputy minister, with an office right beside his, and three personal secretaries.

Supplicants were in and out of his office—regional governors asking him for more development funds for their districts, foreigners wanting contracts to do business in Upper Volta, and, of course, anybody and everybody who had known him before his success.

Blaise Gbadabo skillfully made himself invaluable to the country's rulers with his talent for manipulating money. He knew enough about finance to make them rich without looking like they were plundering their own country. He set them up with Swiss bank accounts and foreign residences.

Inevitably, the educated underclass began to understand that Upper Volta under the army was no better than Upper Volta under the French. Now they were merely being exploited by their own people. Anti-government sentiment began to sprout.

At first, Colonel Zenbo blithely ignored the protesters, claiming that they were "neo-colonialist elements" or communists, depending on whom he was talking to. Then he expropriated their property and tossed a few in jail on trumped-up charges—income tax evasion, illegal foreign speculation, or the convenient catch-all "activities detrimental to the democratic republic of Upper Volta." Finally, he just shot people.

Though Blaise Gbadabo was never called upon to shoot anyone, he was instrumental in keeping money flowing to the colonels, permitting them to retain power by an artful mixture of bribery and intimidation. And with his impeccable French and undeniable charm, he became a diplomat.

Zenbo dispatched him to Paris to reassure the French that their former colony was still a democracy, albeit in transition. It would require time for democratic institutions to become fully rooted in a country still torn apart by tribal rivalries, he told them. Rivalries that were made worse by their fifty years of colonial exploitation. Very effectively, Blaise mined the residual guilt that the liberal elements in Europe still felt about their former possessions.

Blaise spent a week at the Georges V, had dinner at Le Tour d'Argent, and went to the Folies Bergère, enjoying all the luxuries he couldn't afford when he was a student there. He was invited to give a talk at Sciences-Po on economic development in West Africa and was the guest of honor at a cocktail reception at the Élysée Palace, where he assured Charles de Gaulle that he was beloved throughout West Africa and told Andre Malraux that French culture was thriving in the République de Haute-Volta. Neither of which was true, but it went down easily with the Dom Perignon.

On his way back to Ouagadougou, Blaise stopped off in Zurich to deposit the letters of credit he was carrying from the French government into the people of Upper Volta's account, with some spillage into the colonels' accounts and his own.

To consolidate his position in Ouagadougou society, Blaise married one of Colonel Zenbo's nieces—a plump nineteen-year-old named Marie-Laure, who besides being cheerful and compliant, was a member of the ruling Mossi tribe. It was a dynastic marriage that would keep him insulated from any sort of tribal purge within this or future governments.

Marie-Laure bore him two children in quick succession and was content to stay at home in their spacious colonial house, paddling around the swimming pool and ordering the servants around—and not interfering with either her husband's political life or his dalliances.

Blaise got richer, put on weight. He had three more children, out of wedlock, with three different women, and provided generously for all of them.

Nevertheless, he made an effort to keep his profile low enough to stay below the radar of the growing underground opposition. Blaise was enough of a student of politics to know that if the government fell, he would be out the door with them—or worse, lined up against a wall. There were only so many people that Colonel Zenbo could throw in prison before the Bastille would be stormed.

The country was a mess, and Blaise Gbadabo knew it. By 1980, he had made sure that he had enough money stashed abroad so that when the time came, he would be able to get out quickly. He avoided going to public places without a security detail, convinced that his name was on someone's hit list.

By that time, he had already divorced Marie-Laure in an amicable settlement, offering a generous sum of money and the use of his name—the latter of which she politely declined as the political situation darkened.

"I don't want to have to collect your body from the firing squad," she told him in her usual affable manner. "And I don't want my children to have to live with your legacy."

"That's very considerate of you," he said.

When the inevitable coup came, Blaise was fortunate enough to be in Lomé attending a conference on economic development, the pretext for a trip to visit a phosphate mine he had invested in. When he heard the news that Colonel Zenbo had been arrested, Blaise didn't bother returning to his suite at the Hotel Benin. He went directly to the Air Afrique office and bought a one-way ticket to Paris.

He arrived at Orly Airport at 2:00 a.m. with nothing but a toothbrush, purchased at the airport, and ten thousand Central African francs—just enough to get him on a train to Zurich, where he withdrew a comfortable sum of money and checked into the Baur Au Lac under an assumed name. He lay in the marble bathtub, sipping Courvoisier, watching television reports on the chaos in Ouagadougou, and contemplated his next move.

Switzerland, fortuitously, had no extradition treaty with Upper Volta and, even better, was the home of some of the world's most adroit international lawyers and plastic surgeons. It was a country where you could get almost anything done discreetly if you had enough money—in short, the perfect place for a man with several million dollars and a desire to bury any trace of his former life.

It cost him $48,000 to have a new identity created and $73,000 to have his face redone. He was now Didier Onyekachukwu from Abidjan, Cote d'Ivoire. He barely resembled Blaise Gbadabo, from Ouagadougou. The surgeon added tribal scars that identified him as a member of the Ashanti tribe in Ivory Coast, and while he was at it, he altered the nose just enough to give him a more European look.

As soon as the bandages were off, he shaved his head, started a beard, and considered where he wanted to live. Wherever it was, it shouldn't be on the continent of Africa, where there were traces of the former Blaise Gbadabo. He had no doubt that the new rulers of Burkina Faso, as Upper Volta was now called, had put his name on a list for prosecution. He could be facing twenty years in a prison in the north, on the fringe of the Sahara, where the temperature hit 120 degrees.

In the end, he decided to go to Nice—because it was warmer, because they spoke French, and because he had liked what he had seen when he'd visited the place en route to Colonel Zenbo's villa in Juan les Pins. Compared to Zurich, the place was Sodom and Gomorrah. It was full of restaurants, discos, color. And, of course, women. Lots of them, walking the streets in heels and designer dresses, an aroma of $200-an-ounce perfume trailing after them, or lying topless along the gravelly beaches, breasts saluting the Mediterranean sky.

He found an apartment on a street off the Promenade des Anglais, with a balcony from where he could gaze out across the Mediterranean and imagine Africa burning.

For several months, Didier enjoyed getting up late, brewing coffee in his De Longhi coffeemaker, reading through *Le Figaro*, taking walks on the beach, having dinner at one of the excellent seafood restaurants along the Promenade, watching *Starsky and Hutch* dubbed in French, and going to sleep to the sound of the surf lapping the shore.

But he began to realize that this wasn't a life. It was an existence. Outgoing and charming by nature, he missed people. He had avoided making friends because of his residual paranoia that someone would recognize him and he would be dragged back to Africa in chains.

And, more serious, if he continued to live as well as he had been accustomed, he would eventually burn through his money. The cost of living on the Cote d'Azur was not cheap, and neither were his tastes.

It took him a while to find something that could occupy him and, at the same time, serve as a front for laundering his Swiss francs. The idea occurred to him while observing women—an activity he indulged in often, sitting in cafes sipping pastis and watching the parade go by him. He noticed that the French women and the African women were borrowing fashion ideas from one another, creating an unconscious fusion of chic, an amalgamation of styles that reflected both cultures.

It came to him all at once: a Franco-African fashion line. The idea seemed so self-evident to him that he was surprised no one had thought of it already. The fact that he knew absolutely nothing about *haute couture* did not deter him. What had he known about cotton before he made a fortune speculating in it?

He would need a partner—someone who could execute his idea creatively by designing the clothes that he would sell, both to French and African women. He found Jean-Marc Métanu, a young, high-strung gay man who had worked for Givenchy in Paris and spent some time in a boutique in Dakar.

"We can call it VPD—Via Paris Dakar."

"How about just PD—Paris/Dakar?"

"There is the unfortunate pun PD. . .Pédé."

And Didier laughed, the first good belly laugh he'd had in a while. Jean-Marc joined him. They drank a little more pastis and talked some more.

And decided that PD, the word play on *pédérast*, might just be the kind of inside joke that would give the enterprise both pizzazz and notoriety.

"It is better to be shocking than to be ignored, *n'est-ce pas?*"

In September they had a gala opening at their boutique on the Avenue Felix Faure. Members of the fashion press, glasses of Veuve Clicquot in their hands, watched the French and African models, at 2,000 francs an hour, display the line. Didier stayed in the background as Jean-Marc was interviewed and photographed by *Paris Match* and *Elle*. In spite of the plastic surgery, Didier did not want any traces of Blaise Gbadabo's face in magazines.

For the first year or so, the line sold well. Didier expanded PD with a store in Paris and explored starting another one in Abidjan. He took his first trip back to Africa with his Ivorien passport and discovered that he was now on the other side of the table. This was Africa, after all, and there were a number of people he had to bribe. In effect, he was dealing with himself just a few years ago, when he was extorting businessmen for pay-offs in Ouagadougou.

The good times didn't last. Within a year, he was starting to lose money. The fashion business, he was learning, didn't follow the same economic principles as the cotton business. Cotton was cotton, but fashion was whatever was fashionable at any given moment. The initial success of PD created a number of imitators—rip-offs, knockoffs, hybrids—all taking a bite out of his sales.

It took some time to find a buyer, and when he did, he dumped the business fast, getting out with his shirt and little more. He was back walking on the beach and reading the paper, licking his wounds, trying to understand what had gone wrong. Nothing, he concluded. He had just chosen the wrong product. What he needed was a product like cotton, with a steady demand that was not subject to the quirks of malleable taste. Something like drugs. Why not? Limited supply, high demand.

So Didier Onyekachukwu became a drug dealer. As usual, he did his homework, learning what he could about sources and markets. Most of the narcotics business in France came through Marseille, where the French mob had a stranglehold on import and distribution throughout Europe. He knew enough to understand that he didn't want to mess with these people—Corsicans with nasty manners who had little compunction about slicing you up into small pieces and scattering you in the Mediterranean.

The heroin came from Central Asia, transshipped through Tbilisi, Baku, and Istanbul. Didier decided to take a trip to Uzbekistan to see if he could find a supplier. Tashkent, recently liberated from the Soviets, was a frontier town that reminded him of Ouagadougou after the French had left. The Uzbeks were figuring out how to get along without the Russians and weren't doing much better than the Africans thirty years previously.

He sat in nightclubs with fat strippers and blaring music, drinking vodka and writing numbers on a napkin, just as he'd done with Jean-Marc in Nice. He learned that he could get as much as he wanted at a very decent price. The distribution end of the business was trickier. He needed people in France to peddle the product for him—a squad of street-level salesmen who would deal directly with the users, a population he had no desire to have personal contact with. In short, a subcontractor.

Finding the right man took some time. Didier hung around the bars near the old port in Nice among the unsavory population of the drug business, keeping his eyes and ears open.

The right man turned out to be a woman, and an African to boot. Fidèle Kpajagba was from Chad, another former French colony on the edges of the Sahara that was even more god-forsaken than Upper Volta. A large, garrulous woman, she had made money in N'Djamena cornering the melon market, branching out into palm oil and manioc and eventually opium.

She took her cash to France, where there were more addicts with more money than in Chad, and started selling heroin, hashish, and anything else she could get hold of. She operated out of a tiny couscous restaurant on the Quai Lunet with a largely North African clientele. Close to three hundred pounds, she sat at a table in the corner of the restaurant drinking rosé and dispensing envelopes to customers. She was not reluctant to confide her difficulties to Didier.

"I tell you, *cheri*, if I didn't have to pay off half the cops in Nice. . ."

"The cost of doing business, *n'est-ce pas?*"

"In Africa, where you and I come from, perhaps, but here I thought it would be better. And my suppliers, they're just as bad. They don't deliver, they raise their prices, they give me bad stuff. If I could get a consistent supply at a decent price, I would do very well."

"What if I handled that end for you?"

"You?" She looked at him and laughed, her whole body shaking like a bowl of couscous. "You are an Ashanti from Cote d'Ivoire. What do you know about the heroin market?"

He told her. She became interested. After a few glasses of rosé, she said she would buy a shipment from him if it was good quality and the right price. And if that worked out, they'd be in business.

He named a price. She looked at him skeptically. "How will you make *your* money?"

"Quantity," he explained. "I sell enough, I do very well."

What he didn't mention was another of the principles of business he had learned while buying and selling cotton: develop a market first, then make money. Build demand, then manipulate supply.

The drug business was both exhilarating and lucrative—beyond his expectations. Eventually, he needed a front to launder his profits, and he started a high-end gallery near the Hotel Negresco, where well-heeled customers could wander in and spend three thousand dollars on a watercolor of the old port. Prices could be moved up and down to satisfy his tax sheltering needs. To facilitate his dealings with the rich tourists who stayed at the high-end hotels along the Promenade des Anglais, he took English lessons. He had long, lovely lunches, cultivated artists, went to openings, parties, movies, concerts.

It was around this time that he took up with an American woman. Nancy Nemeroff, an heiress and patroness of the arts, wintered every year in Nice, where she indulged her exotic sexual tastes. They met at a disco very late at night, both drunk, and wound up in her suite at the Negresco on a canopied Louis XV bed.

In the morning, room service was brought by a waiter in eighteenth-century costume, replete with wig, gold-plated shoes, and knickers. They sat on the balcony in fluffy robes eating eggs Benedict and drinking coffee from Sèvres china, looking out over the beach.

They spent most of that day, and the days that followed, in bed, with nourishment breaks from room service. He learned that she was the granddaughter of the man who invented Velcro and lived, when she wasn't in the south of France, in Palm Springs, a hundred miles east of Los Angeles.

Every year when Nancy Nemeroff relocated to Nice for a month, they got together. And it was because of the Velcro heiress that Didier sought refuge in Palm Springs when his drug business went south.

Unlike the fashion business, where he was simply outmaneuvered by time and changing tastes, he was squeezed out of the drug business by the Corsicans and the cops. The Corsicans arrived first, offering to become his partner, taking 20 percent of his net in exchange for not tossing him to the seagulls. They were extremely cordial, smiling through capped teeth while assuring him that he would very much want to consider their proposition.

The cops didn't threaten him. He was tipped off by one of his paid informants, a lieutenant in the *Gendarmerie Nationale*, that his name was on a list of narcotics dealers that they were going to indict in the next few months.

So Didier Onyekachukwu moved to his third continent in thirty years. This time, his exit was not quite as precipitous as the one that Blaise Gbadabo made from Africa years ago, but he was gone within a month, taking with him very little outside of the cash from the fire sale of his apartment and gallery.

There were three places outside Europe where he knew people: Ouagadougou, Tashkent, and Palm Springs. The decision was a no-brainer.

Nancy Nemeroff granted him asylum in her twenty-acre compound outside Palm Springs, consisting of a twelve-thousand-square-foot main house, and a couple of five-thousand-square-foot guest houses that she filled with an eclectic group of artists, writers, and hangers-on. Didier had the run of the place—the enormous swimming pool, the north/south tennis court, the wine cellar, and her—until he was replaced by a younger model. The heiress took up with an ex–Los Angeles Laker basketball player, half a foot taller than Didier and thirty years younger.

Jamal Jefferson moved into the main house, and Didier was moved to one of the guest houses, becoming a sort of major domo, looking after the wine cellar, advising the chatelaine on art purchases, trotted out for dinner parties to regale her entourage with his invented stories of growing up in the bush of Ivory Coast.

The Velcro heiress never knew that he had been a drug dealer, let alone the Minister of Economics and Finance for the Republic of Upper Volta. As far as she was concerned, he was an affable African art dealer who liked to have a good time, knew about food and wine, spoke impeccable French and colorful English, and kept her happy in bed. At least until the basketball player showed up and he was moved to the bench.

Didier knew that his days as a hanger-on in Nancy Nemeroff's compound and life were numbered. He was a court jester whose job it was to entertain her and her guests. Worse, she had taken to lending him out to her friends. He didn't mind being a drug dealer, but he drew the line at being a whore.

He considered his next move. This time, money was a major factor, since he had fled France with enough cash for only a year, maybe two if he stretched things. All he had was a couple hundred thousand in the bank— no pensions, no social security, no medical insurance. Now, he didn't need a front business to shelter income; he needed income to survive the twenty—if he was lucky—years in front of him.

Didier decided to stay in Palm Springs. The clean desert air and hot, dry climate agreed with him. The city was full of older wealthy people, refugees from Los Angeles, and New York, in search of a sybaritic lifestyle. They had money and leisure, two attributes that made them a promising market.

The art business once again was an obvious choice. This time, however, he would actually have to make money at it and not merely launder illegally earned cash. The city was full of galleries, most of them pedestrian— the kind of paintings you hung in your desert pastel den, sculptures you planted outside in your succulent garden. He needed an angle, a specialty, something that would distinguish him from all the other art dealers in town.

It was Jamal Jefferson who gave him the idea. The ex-Laker was going through an African roots phase. He had started to wear a dashiki and play drums.

"What tribe you from, man?" he asked Didier one day.

It took Didier a moment to remember. "Ashanti."

"You like speak Ashanti and shit?"

"Well, not really anymore. I used to."

"You ought to go back there and rediscover your roots, man. My people are from Kenya. I got like Maasai ancestors. That's why I'm so tall, see. The Maasai were warriors. They kicked ass. Big time."

Of course. Why hadn't he seen the next opportunity? It was right in front of him. He would import African art. It would sell, and not just to blacks rediscovering their roots, but to all those people looking for things to put in their sunken living rooms to show how interesting they were.

When Didier looked into it, however, he discovered that the authentic stuff was no longer being exported. African governments, in their desire to rediscover their "Africanness," had decided not to let their heritage migrate out of the country and had put limitations on what you could take out. Customs officials at airports from Lagos to Lomé had been trained to recognize authentic Benin bronzes, Yoruba masks, and ebony fertility sculptures.

But then he had a better idea. Why smuggle the real stuff? It would be the usual daisy chain of payoffs, all those unwanted partners who could blow the whistle on him at any moment. Besides, how many people in Palm Springs, California, could tell the difference between an authentic pre-Colonial fetish sculpture and something manufactured and aged to look like one?

He would make imitations of authentic pieces and sell them as the real thing. He would stay below the radar by keeping his prices low enough that his clients wouldn't bother with appraisals. He had the market; now all he needed was the supply. And cheap labor.

The cheapest labor this side of Bangladesh was actually not far from Palm Springs. They weren't all working in the casinos. The Cahuilla Indian tribe had a reservation nearby and their own native craft racket going. They were undoubtedly skilled at creating authentic works of Native American art, so why not African?

Didier had to do a number of things in preparation for launching his new business. He needed to find the right Indians. He needed to learn everything he could about African art, so he could talk a good game. And he needed to locate affordable gallery space, not to mention a place to live.

The gallery turned out to be a converted shoe store on the northern end of Palm Canyon Drive, and the condo in a complex less than a mile away. He wanted to be within walking distance or a short cab ride to the gallery. He had never bothered to get a driver's license—a superfluous document in 1960s Upper Volta and a luxury in France that he had decided he could live without.

Paradise Gardens, thirty-five units, each with its own patio, was afford-able and well located for him. He put a 10 percent down payment on a $350,000 unit and moved in. Two months later, he was selling African art made by Cahuilla Indians in a converted garage in Cathedral City and attending meetings of his condominium complex's homeowners' society. And he had his eye on a woman.

The first time Didier Onyekachukwu saw Marcy Gray had been late at night, watching a very bad movie on his television. He was jolted out of his stupor by a pair of eyes staring out at him from the fifty-two-inch flat screen on his wall.

She was in bed with an actor whose name he couldn't recall, staring across the man's bare chest, through the cigarette smoke, right out at Didier in his condo in Palm Springs, as if to warn him to stay away. She was damaged.

Two days later, unloading groceries from his taxi, he saw her again—at least twenty years older, but still striking—getting out of her car with a small dog in her arms. The dog growled at him.

"*Seien Sie ruhig*, Klaus," she said, quieting the dog.

"He is just being gallant," Didier said. "When a man has the attentions of a beautiful woman, he doesn't like to share them."

He walked over, subdued the dog with a commanding scratching of the ears, and introduced himself.

"Didier Onyekachukwu, at your service, *madame*."

Thirty minutes later, they were sitting on her patio, surrounded by suf-fering plants and sharing a bottle of Bourgueil that he had brought over from his modest wine cooler—a luxury from Costco that he had permit-ted himself.

It didn't take him long to appraise her surroundings and realize that she was not going to be a customer for his African art business. There was nothing displayed of any value or taste. But there were a number of framed photographs of Marcy Gray with actors he recognized. And a modest statuette.

"That was a SAG award for Best Guest Actress on a Drama Series," she explained. "*Quincy, M.E.*"

"And you are still acting, I hope."

She smiled, lapping up the flattery like a starving kitten. "That's very kind of you to say, but the phone isn't ringing much these days."

"Nooooo." He painted incredulity on his face.

"I'm afraid so. There's very little work for. . .mature actresses."

"You see, that's the problem with this country. Americans do not appreciate women in the full ripeness of their beauty. In France, they have an expression, *une femme d'un certain âge*. It's meant as a compliment—a little vague, suggestive, exotic. . ."

"I wish I spoke French. It's such a beautiful language."

"Would you like lessons?"

"Really?"

"It would be my pleasure."

The next time he saw her was at one of those ridiculous homeowners' association meetings to discuss maintenance problems. This time it was mold. He had no idea what mold actually was, besides the topping on aged cheese. In this country, they hired exterminators to destroy snails instead of cooking them in butter and garlic.

She looked particularly alluring that night, wearing a pair of reasonably snug-fitting leopard skin slacks and two-inch heels that added to her natural grace. She knew how to make an entrance, coming into the multipurpose room as if she anticipated that all eyes would be on her.

In addition to Didier's eyes, she attracted the attention of a man whom he had noticed before sitting at the pool reading magazines and looking as if he was just about to drop off to sleep. The night of the mold meeting, the man interjected himself into a tête-à-tête he was having with Marcy Gray. She introduced him as Sammy Dee, from New York. Though he claimed to be half-Jewish, Sammy Dee reminded Didier of the Corsicans he had dealt with in Nice, with rough-hewn features set off by delicately groomed hair and nails.

It was clear that Sammy Dee entertained an interest in Marcy Gray as well. Without the slightest bit of encouragement, he invited himself to join the French lessons Didier had proposed for her. Two days later, he showed up for lunch at Marcy's place, dressed like a *Boulevard des Italiens* pimp.

They ate crab salad and drank white wine as Didier sprinkled French words on the table and did his best not to cringe when they mangled the pronunciation. The two men lobbed little conversational hand grenades at each other.

The Italian claimed to be retired from the cement business. That Didier could believe. He had about as much charm as a slab of concrete. Conversation was more of a trial than an art with him. But he hung around long enough that Marcy finally excused herself to take a nap, effectively throwing them both out.

After that lunch, it seemed that every time he was making a move with Marcy, Sammy Dee showed up. Worse, he took her out to dinner, and Didier had to ambush them as they staggered home from the parking garage, tipsy with wine, and thwarted what was clearly going to be some sort of consummation.

In his days as Minister of Economics and Finance of the République de Haute-Volta, he could have dealt with a rival by having the colonels stick him in prison for twenty years. When he was in the drug business, he could have, for a price, had the Corsicans dispose of him. But now, he didn't know who to contact to get the job done.

Didier had no doubt that there were people in Southern California, if not in Palm Springs, that you could hire to deal with this kind of problem. If there were people who removed mold and snails, there must be people who removed people.

The solution to his problem came through an open window. Didier was out on his patio one afternoon, snoozing in his hammock. It was a Monday, a day off from his gallery, which he had named "Afrique Ouest." He had hired someone to run it for him, a post–middle-aged *pédé* named

Clive who, Didier hoped, would bring his friends in to buy art. Clive's friends came in, hung around, gossiped and talked about how "arresting," how "primitive" the art was, but they didn't buy any.

The immediate neighbor to his right was a former movie producer named Charlie Berns. He was not particularly interested in African art, but he was friendly enough and apparently the only other straight male in the complex under eighty, besides Didier and the Italian.

Lying in his hammock, hovering on the edge of sleep, Didier heard the gravelly voice of Sammy Dee coming through the window of Charlie Berns's condo. Who keeps a window open in 104-degree heat? He was asking the producer about the movie business, specifically about a film he had made about a mafia contract killer. He wanted to write a novel, he explained.

A book? The man could barely talk. How was he going to write a book? A thriller about the cement business? But what Didier heard next changed everything. Charlie Berns gave Sammy Dee a telephone number, supposedly of an actual hit man he had contacted for research on a movie. The number implanted itself in his mind, lodged there like an errant strand of mango between his teeth.

He woke up with the telephone number in his teeth every morning and went to bed with it at night. More often than not, he would wake up at 4:00 a.m. with it, and during those sleepless hours before dawn, he would permit himself to consider how far he might go to get rid of his rival.

Besides being an impediment to Didier's romantic plans, the man was of no use to anyone. The Italian had no friends, no family, no job. He did nothing but take up space. The Finnish lesbians accused him of being cruel to their cats. Klaus barely tolerated him. What kind of person was disliked by dogs and cats?

The art gallery wasn't thriving. He had managed to sell a few pieces of his locally manufactured "authentic" African art to his neighbors at Paradise Gardens, but not enough to make up for his costs.

The boat was taking on water, and he couldn't bail fast enough to stay afloat. His best—maybe his only—shot at this point was the actress. She could be his life raft. Perhaps she wasn't a Velcro heiress, but she had to have social security, some sort of pension, friends with money, maybe even a little property somewhere. They could move in together; she could help him sell his art. It would all work out splendidly. If only he could get rid of the strand of mango stuck in his teeth.

Who would miss Sammy Dee? Not Marcy Gray, he hoped. *À la limite*—she might mourn for a couple of days, at most a week or two, and then welcome Didier with open arms. He would emerge the victor and claim his spoils.

Didier wrote 1-800-XTERMIN, the number he had heard through Charlie Berns's open window, on a piece of paper and put it in the hollow penis of a Yoruba fertility fetish on his mantelpiece. The disturbing strand was no longer stuck between his teeth. It was out, loaded and ready to fire. The next time the Italian got in his way, he was a dead man.

IV
SAMMY

Acme Exterminating and Patio Decks sent Sammy Dee an envelope in the mail. Inside he found a construction contract for a rebuilt deck, a demand for an initial payment of $10,000 for "equipment and materials," and a line asking for a co-signer. All of this was to be signed, notarized, and delivered in person to the same car wash on Bob Hope Drive where he had handed over the $5,000 for the initial "appraisal."

Attached to the contract was a page of legal boilerplate. There was a paragraph that stated that "in the event that the signer is unable, for any reason, to fulfill the contractual obligations stipulated above, the co-signer assumes full responsibility thereof."

Sammy had never seen anything like that in a construction contract. Unable *for any reason*? Like if he died? Between now and Christmas? Was this a threat? Or a promise?

On the golf course, they had made it clear that the patio deck bullshit both created a front and established grounds for them to pursue you legally if you backed out on the deal. They could go to court with evidence of services rendered. And your only defense would be telling the judge that you wanted a hit, not a new deck.

Sammy knocked on Marcy Gray's door in the late afternoon, the construction contract in his hand. Klaus uttered his usual low growl, sniffing him through the door, and Sammy kept himself from growling back. He would have to find a way to win the dog over, but first things first.

The actress came to the door, in sweatpants, no makeup—clearly not expecting anyone.

"Sammy?" Klaus amped up the growl a few decibels. "Klaus, *hör auf damit*. It's just Sammy."

The dog slunk off to the corner of the living room, as if to say, *Just give me the command, and I'll tear this wop to pieces.*

"Sorry to barge in on you, but I have a small favor to ask."

"Sure. Come on in. I'll make some coffee."

"No thanks." Her coffee was awful, watery and bitter. Judging by the way her garden looked, she must have fed it to her plants.

They sat in her conversation nook, furnished with two rattan chairs and an ugly horsehair sofa and looking out on the pool, where Chris and Edie were plying a couple of middle-aged swingers with sangria.

"So how you doing, Sammy?"

"Good. Good. How about you?"

"I had to take Klaus to the vet this morning. He's got some intestinal thing."

"Sorry to hear that." *With any luck, it's pancreatic cancer.* Sammy put on his best sympathetic look. "So, anyway, here's the deal. I decided to get my patio deck redone."

"Great. I should do it, too. Mine is in terrible condition."

"So the thing is, they want me not only to sign a construction contract, but get a co-signer. I mean, it's ridiculous. For a patio deck? It's not like I'm taking out a mortgage. But nowadays, everyone's got lawyers telling them what to do."

"You want me to co-sign the contract?"

"I'd really appreciate it. They want someone local, and I haven't been in Palm Springs long enough to know anyone that well. I mean, it's nothing that you'd have to worry about. The work is only a couple of grand. There's no way I'm not going to pay them."

"Of course. I would be happy to do it, Sammy."

"I really appreciate it. And just to thank you, let me take you out to dinner Saturday night."

"I'd love to, but I promised Didier I'd go to that karaoke bar near the Marriott with him. He's going to sing French songs. You want to join us?"

"Thanks, but I don't sing."

He managed to walk out without coffee and with Marcy Gray's signature on the contract. As he passed the African's condo, Sammy wondered if there was a way to get the deck built before Saturday night. A rush job.

When he met with Biff at the car wash to give him the signed contract and the up-front payment, he learned that his patio deck resurfacing job would start that week.

"Is it really necessary?"

"You bet."

"I'm going to pay you the money."

"That's why they invented contracts, Sammy. Listen, your guy, the African? He doesn't own a car."

"So?"

"It makes it harder to hit him. We don't want to do him in his home, if we can help it, and we don't want some taxi driver as a witness."

"What are you going to do?"

"We're going to need to get creative."

"Like what?"

"The less you know, the better."

They were sitting in the front seat of the van, eating tacos.

"Look, promise me you won't do anything to the woman who co-signed."

"Why would we?"

"You know, if something happened to me."

"We'll just sue her."

"That's comforting."

"It's not personal."

"She doesn't know anything about this."

"I should hope not. By the way, we've got a Facebook page. It would help if you liked us."

"You're on fucking Facebook?"

"Cost of doing business."

"Jesus. . ."

"Rebuilding patios is a loss leader. The snuff business is the cash cow."

"Any better idea of a time frame?"

"Nope. This one is problematic. If we had known he doesn't drive, we would have charged you more money."

Biff finished his taco, folded the perfectly clean napkin up and put it in a plastic trash bag hanging from the dashboard. The van reeked of air freshener.

"What do you do with the body?"

"Not our problem. We're in the exterminating business, not the disposal business."

"Yeah, but with all this DNA shit you see on TV, don't you take risks leaving a body behind?"

"Nothing for you to worry about. You're just a guy getting his patio deck redone. You got the cash?"

Sammy handed him the FedEx envelope with the hundred-dollar bills inside, and Biff stuck it in the glove compartment.

"You're not going to count it?"

"Why? If it's not right, we just don't do the job."

"What happens if I change my mind?"

"You don't. This is an irrevocable contract. Once we're in business, we don't want to see you or talk to you again. When the job's done, you'll be given instructions on how and where to deliver the final payment."

"That's crazy. . ."

"You don't like it, you can try Craigslist."

Sammy studied the man's features. There wasn't an ounce of irony in them.

"One other thing, Sammy. Don't even think about stiffing us for the rest of the money. If you do, we're going to terminate you. With extreme prejudice."

"What does that mean?"

"You don't want to know, believe me. We're done here."

Biff started up the van's engine. Sammy digested a sense of finality along with his taco. This was it. As soon as he got out and Biff drove away, the plan would be in motion.

"So. . .this is it, huh?"

"You bet. The deck guys will be there on Monday morning. Early."

By *early*, Sammy thought he was talking about nine. But at thirty seconds past 7:00 a.m. the following Monday, two Mexicans in Acme Exterminating and Patio Deck jumpsuits started chewing up his old deck with a pneumatic drill. At seven fifteen, he was visited by Ethel Esmitz, who informed him, in her capacity as the homeowners' association president, that any kind of major construction work had to be approved by the PGHOA.

"It's in the CC&Rs."

"The what?"

"The CC&Rs. Covenants, Conditions, and Restrictions. You signed it when you bought your unit."

This conversation, carried on by shouting over the sound of the jackhammer, was followed by Tuuli—or perhaps it was Majda—arriving to tell him that the noise had traumatized their cats. Even Chris and Edie, hung over from whatever overindulgence they'd engaged in the previous night, complained.

Sammy went outside to ask the workmen how long the job was going to take, but they apparently spoke no English because they ignored him. His deck had been reduced to a rubble of slate fragments and a ground fog of dust. The Mexicans were wearing surgical masks and do-rags and looked like members of a heavy metal band.

They finally stopped for lunch at around eleven, and Sammy used the reprieve to pick up the phone and call Marcy. He wanted to see if Diddly Shit was still alive.

"Hey, Marcy, it's Sammy. Sorry about the noise. The deck guys are here."

"No problem. I slept right through it."

Sammy didn't like the idea of *that*. Was she so knocked out by postcoital bliss that she couldn't hear the jackhammer? Was the African lying in bed beside her, smoking a cigarette?

"So. . .how was karaoke?"

"Great. You should have come. Didier sang *La Vie En Rose*."

He would have paid a lot not to witness that.

"I didn't hear from him about the noise. Everyone else complained. Is he okay?"

"Yeah. He's out taking Klaus for a walk."

"That's nice."

"Klaus *loves* Didier."

Fuck him, and the dog he rode in on.

Sammy was in the CVS drugstore downtown, buying Prilosec for his acid reflux, when he walked past the condom display and had a thought. Maybe he should stock up. It had been years since he bought a condom. During his teen years on Long Island, buying a scumbag, as they were called by the Italian teenagers he hung out with, was a rite of passage. They were kept behind the counter, and you mumbled that you wanted some Trojans and cringed when the pharmacist repeated, loud enough for the whole store to hear, "What's that? Prophylactics? You want *prophylactics*?"

Then you would carry one in your wallet for months, if not years, until the outline of the condom could be seen through the leather, which you would proudly display to your pals every time you took your wallet out. *See? I'm prepared. For the innumerable opportunities presenting themselves every day.*

Now, fifty-plus years later, he felt a similar mixture of embarrassment and pride as he placed the condoms alongside his Prilosec on the checkout counter. The smart-ass clerk with the shaved head and the pierced eyebrow looked at the condoms, then at Sammy, and said, "Big weekend, huh?"

If it wasn't broad daylight, with a line of people in back of him, he would have cold-cocked the kid. Instead he smirked back and said, "You bet."

"Way to go, dude," the kid said, and offered him a high five, which Sammy declined.

He was walking out to his car when he heard something he hadn't heard in almost two years. It froze him in his tracks.

"Sal?"

All those years of conditioning made him turn toward the voice, instead of continuing toward his car, as he should have. Standing ten feet away from him, with a shopping cart full of stuff, was Nick Tuccieri. And a look on his face, caught between surprise and amusement.

"Jesus! Sal Didziocomo. . ."

Tuccieri was a made guy in the Finoccio family whom Sammy had known since their days together with the janitors. He was called Nick the Tip, because he chain-smoked tiparillos. Sammy had sat in cars with him, windows cracked only a fraction of an inch because of the Long Island winter, choking on his cigar smoke and waiting for some guy they were about to shake down.

A few difficult seconds elapsed, during which Sammy considered saying he wasn't Sal Didziocomo and getting into his car, but he knew Tuccieri had made him. The mobster was staring right at the plate of the Lexus.

"How you doing, Nick?" he said, finally, his mind shifting into overdrive. Phil Finoccio may have been in the joint, but he was still running things from the inside. Sammy had no doubt there was a price on his head—a big one.

"You live out here?"

"Just vacationing," Sammy said.

Tuccieri read Sammy's discomfort and tried to reassure him. "Hey, Sal, listen. You don't have anything to worry about. I'm retired. I'm not going to drop a dime on you."

Sammy nodded, bouncing up and down on his feet, as if he had to pee.

"Phil's not getting out for a while. The guy's pushing eighty. He probably doesn't even remember."

Right. Like he doesn't remember his own name.

"Vicky and I moved out here last summer," Nick the Tip went on. "We're living over in Palm Desert. Why don't you come by for dinner?"

"Thanks, Nick, but I'm leaving tomorrow. Early. Got to pack."

"Where you living these days?"

"Jacksonville. Florida."

"No shit? Good fishing down there, huh?"

"Marlin." The word slid out of Sammy's mouth. He hadn't the slightest fucking idea if there was marlin fishing in Jacksonville.

"Hey, listen, why don't you give me your number? We're thinking of going to Florida in February. We'll do a little fishing, catch up."

"Uh. . .sure. Listen, give me your email and I'll send it to you, okay?"

Tuccieri fished a card out of his wallet and handed it to him. It said just VICKY AND NICKY, and it had a phone number and email address.

"Thanks, I'll get in touch. Good seeing you, Nick."

Sammy was so eager to get away that he turned too quickly and the CVS bag slipped out of his hand. The condom package spilled out onto the ground.

As he stooped to pick it up, he heard Tuccieri say, "Way to go, Sal. Glad to see you're still in the ball game."

Sammy nodded stupidly and went to his car, opening it and getting behind the wheel. He started the engine and looked back through the rearview. There was Nick the Tip, staring right at his license plate.

As soon as he got home, Sammy dropped two Prilosecs. It had happened, the one thing that wasn't supposed to happen. His cover was blown—and to a guy who used to work for Phil Finoccio, if he didn't still. The witness protection people had stressed that one small breach was all it took. It was like a gas leak, they said. *The tiniest opening, and you're dead.*

He had been told to report any incident that could possibly reveal his former identity to the Marshals Service. Immediately. And as soon as he did it, he knew they would whisk him off to some safe house while they reconstructed a new identity and location for him. They were set up for it. It was like a fire drill. Just ring the alarm, and they would be ready to roll.

The thought of starting this whole game over made him ill. Another name, another home, another social security number, another marshal. . . and even worse, he would have to disappear from Marcy Gray's life. He wouldn't be able to say goodbye, or even send her a note explaining what had happened.

He poured himself a large glass of cabernet, which he knew from experience would neutralize the Prilosec, but fuck it. He needed to calm down, figure out what to do, and then do it. Fast.

The question was—was Nick Tuccieri to be trusted? Everything he had learned from his forty years in a crime family told him *no*. Loyalty to the family came first, and in spite of the guy's protestations to the contrary, Sammy knew that you never really retired. You just went out to pasture.

If Nick reported the meeting to Finoccio but bought the Jacksonville story, they would send people down there to look for him. But if they were still playing with a full deck, they would run Sammy's plate and learn that the car wasn't a rental, but was instead registered to Sammy Dee, of Paradise Gardens, Palm Springs, California. Then it would be only a matter of time before he started his car and was sent through the roof of the garage.

Well, maybe it was better to get sent through the garage roof than to have to go through this charade one more time. In the end, it was the thought of Marcy Gray and a possible future with her, not to mention the unthinkable thought that with Sammy gone Diddly Shit would have an unimpeded path to her bed, that made him decide to roll the dice and pray that Nick the Tip didn't drop a dime on him—or, if he did, that it was the wrong dime. She was the first woman in a long time who had gotten him interested in something other than golf and baseball. And if it was just his dick talking, so what? *Something* was talking to him.

The one good thing about his age and prospects was the fact that he didn't have that much to lose. Whatever happened, he had ten, fifteen more years on the outside. Might as well live them the way he wanted to. And if he was checking out, he would check out with a bang.

Sitting on the counter was a three-pack of lubricated Durex Extra Strength. He took one out and put it in his wallet. Then he thought better of it and put all three in there. Why the fuck not? Go for the trifecta.

Two days after his run-in with Nick the Tip, he was woken early in the morning by one of his neighbors from across the hall. Tuuli (or Majda) knocked loudly on the door, and when Sammy staggered to open it in his pajamas, he was greeted by a torrent of Finnish invective. When she switched into English, the only word he understood was *murderer*.

She turned on her heels and stalked across the hallway, entering her condo and slamming the door. Sammy stood there, feeling a sudden chill pass through him. Was it done? Was the African dead?

It was nine o'clock in the morning. He had heard no police sirens or ambulances. Cracking his blinds, he peered out the window. All was quiet at Paradise Gardens. There was no crime scene tape around Diddly Shit's condo, no cop cars or medical examiners in sight. The only activity was Bert Velum, the eighty-seven-year-old health freak, swimming laps in the pool.

As the morning dragged on, Sammy sat on a kitchen stool, drinking coffee and trying to figure out what had motivated the woman's outburst.

If Diddly Shit was, in fact, dead, how did she know that Sammy had ordered the hit? He couldn't call Biff to inquire. Was there something on their Facebook page? *Another first-rate snuff job done. Bravo!*

He was still in his pajamas, seriously over-caffeinated, when his doorbell rang. Standing there were two badly dressed plainclothes detectives from the Palm Springs Police Department.

Detective Melendez flashed an ID.

"Sammy Dee?"

Sammy nodded. He asked if he and his partner, Detective Guthrie, could have a word with him. Sammy took a deep breath, trying to keep his heart rate down, and nodded. He was frozen in place, and after an awkward pause, Melendez asked, "Mind if we come in?"

Sammy nodded again and led them to his kitchen table.

"Coffee?" Sammy offered, his throat thick.

"No thanks," Melendez replied. Then, matter-of-factly, "Can you tell us, Mr. Dee, where you were last night?"

"Something happen?"

The cop held his look for a long moment, as if trying to read guilt into his features. "There was a murder committed."

"What!?" Sammy tried to communicate both shock and outrage.

"About nine o'clock last night. Were you here?"

"Uh, I think so. . ."

"You think so?"

"I went out for dinner at one point. . ." Sammy lied and immediately regretted it. What was the point of lying about his whereabouts? He hadn't killed the African—not directly, at least. "But I was back by nine. I'm pretty sure. Who was killed?"

"You don't know?"

"If I did, I wouldn't be asking you."

"Do you know your neighbors across the hall?"

So that's why Tuuli (or Majda) was screaming at him. The other one was dead. They hit the wrong person. They must have got the condos mixed up. . .

"Something happened to them?"

The cops exchanged a look, and for the first time the other detective, Guthrie, spoke. "One of their Siamese cats was found dead this morning."

It took everything that Sammy had to keep from bursting out laughing. And it wasn't just the mix-up, but the fact that there'd be less cat-piss smell wafting across the hall. Bad news, good news.

"You mean, someone killed the cat?"

"The cat was poisoned."

"Poisoned? Who would do that?"

"That's what we're trying to find out."

"Why are you talking to me?"

Melendez took over again. The man was wearing the ugliest sports jacket that Sammy had seen since his days in the mob. "Mr. Dee, according to the cat's owner"—he checked his notebook—"Tuuli Rennholm, you had made threats against their cats in the past."

"She thinks I killed her cat?"

The cop rechecked his notebook. "Both women, Tuuli Rennholm and Majda Juntunun, as well as the homeowners' association president, Ethel Esmitz, have indicated that you have complained about the cats."

"Yeah. They smell the hall up. But that doesn't mean I killed one of them."

"Do you have any witnesses to your whereabouts at nine o'clock last night?"

"No. What kind of bullshit is this? You're spending taxpayers' money investigating a dead *cat*?"

This remark pissed Melendez off, as if Sammy was questioning his professionalism. "Murdering an animal is a felony in California."

"Look, it's true I don't like the cats, but I didn't kill one of them."

Melendez opened his notebook again. Then: "Have you ever ordered pizza from Pizza Hut on Arroyo Seco Drive?"

"Probably. I don't remember. The cat ate poisoned pizza?"

"Infused with strychnine."

"Cats don't like pizza."

"It had anchovies on it."

Melendez opened his notebook again, as if consulting a script. "Do you know anybody in the complex who orders take-out pizza from Pizza Hut?"

"Jesus, I don't know. I mean, it's the closest one, I think. And they deliver. Between you and me, I prefer the Domino's on Eucalyptus."

"So you didn't order the pizza or know anybody who may have?"

"Right."

"One more question. Is there anyone you think might be trying to kill you?"

"Me? You think the pizza was meant for me?"

"We don't know who it was meant for. The poisoned slice was in the communal garbage bin."

"No shit?"

"You have no known enemies?"

"No. I'm retired. I play a little golf, keep to myself. Who'd want to kill me?"

Melendez slapped his notebook shut with emphasis and said, "Thank you. Call me if you think of anything you forgot to mention." He handed Sammy a card: DETECTIVE SERGEANT JORGE MELENDEZ, PSPD, with a phone number and a website.

Jesus! Even the cops have fucking websites now.

After they were gone, Sammy poured himself his seventh cup of coffee and considered what the hell had gone down. It couldn't have been Finoccio's people. They didn't work that fast. Besides, poisoned pizza was not at all their style. They would have had a guy in a Pizza Hut uniform come to the door with an AK.

It had to be Acme. How did they know that Diddly Shit ordered a pizza? And if he did order it, how did they intercept it and get the strychnine in it? Did they have to whack the pizza delivery guy, or was he tied up in the crapper at the ninth hole at Tahquitz Creek? And how come the African didn't eat the pizza, but the cat did?

The only explanation was that they had bugged Diddly Shit's phone, found out about the order, then called back Pizza Hut, canceled it, and delivered their own poisoned pizza. And for some reason, the man had thrown it out without eating it, leaving it in the garbage bin for the cat.

Sammy wasn't the only one at Paradise Gardens who wanted to know how strychnine had gotten into an anchovy pizza from Pizza Hut. A wave of anxiety swept through the place, to the extent that Ethel Esmitz called an emergency meeting of the PGHOA for seven that night.

Everyone showed up, except the Finns, who were in mourning. There was a lot of chatter as Sammy, wearing a pair of pressed jeans that he was probably ten years too old to be wearing, entered the room. Why not? He was feeling good. One fewer cat in his life.

Various sets of eyes met his, radiating suspicion. It was no secret that Sammy Dee didn't like the Finnish lesbians' cats. Fuck 'em. He had an air-tight alibi—a signed contract to kill the African. There was no deal on the cat.

Across the room, Diddly Shit—alive and well and wearing one of his African dashikis—was standing with Marcy and Charlie Berns. Sammy sauntered over and said good evening.

"Isn't it awful?" Marcy said.

Sammy nodded, trying to infuse some conviction into the nod.

"Did the police speak with you, Sam*ee*?"

"Yeah. Couple of mugs from the Palm Springs PD showed up. They looked like they were auditioning for *CSI: Cucamonga*."

Nobody laughed. The mood was not jocular. The residents looked as if there had been a terrorist attack on the complex. Except for Charlie Berns, who had his usual air of detached bemusement.

"What do you think, Charlie, there a movie in this?"

"Afraid not. You can kill people, as many as you want, but you can't kill pets. No studio will touch it."

"Who do you think it was?" Marcy asked.

"You mean, who put the strychnine in the pizza?"

Marcy nodded, then shivered.

"Maybe it was the Helsinki mob."

Again, nobody laughed, or even smiled. Sammy was on shaky ground here and needed to lose the sarcasm. He changed tactics, coming about quickly into the wind. "Don't worry, Marcy, the cops'll deal with this."

"Well, I hope so. Klaus goes through the garbage sometimes."

"We must install sealed trash bins, that's it. No?" Diddly Shit suggested.

"That's a very good idea, Didier," Marcy said.

Fuck. Sammy was losing points by the minute. The African was not only not dead, but he was solidifying his position in the Marcy Gray sweepstakes.

Ethel Esmitz ordered them to grab one of the folding chairs against the wall and take a seat. As usual, Marcy sat between Sammy and his rival. Everyone started talking at once until the homeowners' association president gaveled them into submission.

"Please, we need to be calm," she said.

"Calm? There's a murderer on the loose!" Beverly Lipner, a desiccated matron from Canoga Park, exclaimed.

"We don't know that for sure," Ethel Esmitz insisted.

"There was poison in the pizza. Poison!"

"Yes, but it could have been from some household product. Or from the mold people. The police are looking into it."

The meeting lurched forward, accusations of malfeasance and negligence thrown around haphazardly.

When it was finally over, Sammy retreated to his condo, turned on a ballgame, and tried to unwind. Between the cat hit and all the coffee he had drunk, he was unable to relax. What the fuck had happened? Hours later, he drifted into a fitful sleep, the TV on, his head aching.

The phone woke him at nine. It wasn't his regular phone, but the cell that the Marshals Service had provided him with. What did *they* want? Sammy dragged himself into the bedroom, unearthed the iPhone 3 (the cheap bastards didn't even spring for the latest model), and growled into the phone:

"What?"

"Sammy, we need to talk."

"Talk."

"Kramer's on Main, next to the Movie Colony Hotel. Noon."

"I can't make it."

"Yes, you can." Marshal Dillon hung up. He took a twenty-minute shower, put on his orange Dockers, and, looking like some retired Borscht Belt comedian, headed off to meet his contact.

The restaurant, a Jewish deli, had large booths and gravel-throated waitresses who called you *sweetie* and gave as good as they got.

"Best pastrami in the Coachella Valley," the marshal said, biting into a mammoth sandwich.

"Is that like the best manicotti in Lapland?"

The air conditioning was on arctic, but you still didn't want to order the matzo ball soup. Not in this climate. Sammy had ordered lox, eggs, and onions, and would soon regret it.

"So to what do I owe the honor of buying you lunch, Marshal?"

As usual, the marshal didn't cut to the chase. There was always a fucking preamble. He put his pastrami sandwich down squarely in the center of the plate, as if it were a flower design.

"Sammy, you are aware that relocated witnesses have to be scrupulous in avoiding brushes with the law, aren't you?"

"You bet."

"It causes problems for the Marshals Service with respect to our relationship with other law enforcement agencies."

"Okay. I'm sorry. I made a right turn on a red the other day onto 111. There was a sign, but the fucker didn't have to write me up. I slowed down. There was no one in sight. It was eleven at night . . ."

"That's not what I'm talking about."

"All right, I give up. What'd I do?"

The marshal picked up his sandwich again and chewed meticulously, as if enjoying making him wait for the punch line. Sammy had never met anyone in his entire life who ate more slowly than this guy. If there was an Olympic event for this skill, he'd win the gold medal hands down.

"It has come to our attention, Sammy, that the Palm Spring Police Department has interviewed you in their investigation of a felony."

"You mean the dead cat?"

"The PSPD is treating it as attempted homicide."

"What?"

"They are surmising that the perpetrator was targeting a person and that the cat ate the poison inadvertently."

"I'm a fucking murder suspect?"

"No. You are merely a person of interest."

"Well, that's comforting. . . ." Sammy said. But sarcasm was out of the marshal's radio frequency range.

What the fuck. Had the clowns in the bad sports jackets put two and two together? Were they watching Walt and Biff? Sammy clenched his stomach muscles and convinced himself that he had nothing to worry about. All they had on him was his signature on a patio deck contract.

"Anything I need to know?" Dylan asked after a moment.

"You mean, like am I trying to kill someone?"

"I should hope you're not, because if you are, I am obliged to turn you in. Attempted murder is a federal crime, and I am a federal law enforcement officer sworn to uphold the law."

Sammy took a deep breath and exhaled, already feeling the lox and onions doing their number.

"Look, the only reason they talked to me was because I didn't like the cats. They smelled up the fucking hall. I had complained about it, and they thought maybe I was trying to get rid of them."

"Were you?" A completely straight face. The guy could have been holding the nut flush or a pair of deuces. You couldn't read him.

"C'mon, you think I did the cat?"

"If you did, I would prefer you didn't tell me."

Sammy had half a mind to confess to the cat hit, just to make Dylan squirm. One of the few pleasures he had these days was tormenting his handler.

"Let me ask you a question, Marshal. How would I have gotten strychnine into a Pizza Hut anchovy pizza and made sure the cat ate it?"

"I don't know. But I would like to be reassured that you had nothing to do with it, nevertheless."

"I had nothing to do with it, nevertheless."

"Thank you."

"You're welcome. How about you pick up the check, for a change, as a token of your gratitude?"

By way of response, the marshal pushed his plate away, wiped his mouth, got up, and walked out of the restaurant.

The cat business went down three days before Thanksgiving. The paranoia level at Paradise Gardens abated slightly, though no one ordered anything delivered from Pizza Hut. There was a story done by the local Palm Springs ABC affiliate *Eyewitness News* reporter, Tracy Tohito, about the poisoned cat. She stood in front of the complex, microphone in hand, and breathlessly reported.

"The suspicious death of a beloved Siamese cat has put the occupants of this Palm Springs condominium development on edge. The unfortunate cat, a six-year-old male named Lurjus, meaning 'rascal' in Finnish, ate a piece of anchovy pizza that pathologists later determined was laced with strychnine. The police are investigating the possibility that the lethal poison was meant for one of the occupants of the complex and not the cat. . ."

Sergeant Melendez had little to add when interviewed by the diminutive Japanese-American reporter. "Our investigation is ongoing." Period.

Tracy Tohito did get an earful from Chris and Edie, who said that no one was sleeping well these days with a murderer on the loose.

Sammy Dee wasn't sleeping well, but it had nothing to do with the dead cat. He was wondering when the next attempt to whack the African would go down, and whether it would be successful this time. Waiting for something to happen that you had no control over was like waiting for an earthquake.

Marcy Gray invited him, Diddly Shit, and Charlie Berns to Thanksgiving dinner. He and Charlie Berns brought wine, but the African brought a mahogany sculpture from Benin, which he claimed dated from precolonial times and promoted good health. To Sammy, it looked like a doorstop.

They sat around Marcy's kitchen table, a family of convenience, eating overdone turkey and pre-fabricated stuffing. Diddly Shit consolidated his position with Klaus by slipping pieces of turkey to the dog under the table.

Charlie Berns told war stories about their days in the trenches of Hollywood.

"It's a crapshoot masquerading as a business masquerading as an art form," he said. "Nobody really knows what they're doing. You roll the dice, and now and then you land on Go. Mostly then."

"How did you survive for so long?" Sammy asked him.

"Stupidity. I was too dumb to get out."

"Yeah, but you made a living, didn't you?"

"Occasionally. More often than not, I was scrambling. It was always trying to find the money, and then when I had it, trying to make it through production, post-production, publicity, the whole deal, without running dry."

"Even after you won your Oscar?" Marcy asked.

"After that I was able to skate for a year, year and a half, but then I caught a couple of bad breaks—script problems, lawsuits, stars sticking powder in their noses, deals falling apart—and pretty soon I was back in the pack of howling dogs, looking for funding with everyone else. The thing about the business now is that it's run by MBAs. For them, it's about stock price and exposure. Market share and risk management. There isn't an ounce of passion anywhere. You go to a meeting and they talk about four-quadrant demographics and multiple-platform releases. They could just as easily be making lawn mowers. . ."

"You mean you really wouldn't do another picture if you had everything tied up?" Marcy asked him.

"Of course I would. I'm still stupid."

She laughed, and Sammy found himself laughing with her. It was a lovely laugh, a laugh that he wanted to hear more of in his life. He was falling more in love with her every day.

A few days after Thanksgiving, Sammy received a note in the mail from Acme. It was brief: TUESDAY, DECEMBER 1, 6:45 A.M., TAHQUITZ CREEK, GREENS FEES FOR THREE.

Biff had said at the car wash that they didn't want to see him or talk to him again. Now they wanted to play golf? Maybe they were going to renegotiate. Up the price. And what was he going to say? Sorry, not interested? They had stressed that the contract was irrevocable. That if he backed out, they would do something terrible to him. *With extreme prejudice.*

There went another $375 into the project. Tahquitz Creek had just raised their greens fees to $125. Did they have to play at the crack of fucking dawn? And, of course, there was no way of communicating that you were not able to make it. With these guys, you showed up.

Sammy showed up. Armed with his clubs and a fleece vest for the chilly morning air. When Walt arrived on the first tee at 6:44, he was accompanied by a man Sammy had never met.

"Sammy, I want you to meet my periodontist, Ken Immelman."

Sammy shook hands with a puffy, sixtyish man with a Tommy Hilfiger windbreaker, yellow slacks, and a grip like a wet flounder.

"You got gum problems, Ken's your guy. An hour in his chair, and you could handle Dr. Mengele. You got the honors, Sammy. We're playing tips."

And that was that. They teed off on the 467-yard first hole, with Walt sharing a cart with his periodontist and Sammy riding alone. This arrangement precluded any conversation beyond the usual golf bullshit at the tee box and on the green. The guy was a seven handicap, and he and Walt were playing Skins at a dollar a hole.

When they got to the tenth hole, with Sammy seventeen over and getting more annoyed by the moment, he announced that he was taking a pee, hoping that Walt would follow him into the men's room so that they could talk. But the exterminator merely took his driver out of the bag and said, "Make it quick, Sammy. We got a tail wind going for us."

What the fuck was Sammy doing there, besides filling out a threesome? And where was Biff? The whole thing didn't make any sense. Meanwhile, Walt and the periodontist were enjoying themselves over what could, at most, be a twenty-dollar payoff. Sammy was hitting the ball all over the place, as usual, and putting like a weightlifter.

On the eighteenth green, the two of them putted out, and Sammy finally shoveled his ball out of a steep, green-side bunker and three-putted for a double. As they took off their hats and shook hands, he said to Walt, "Can I buy you a beer, Walt?"

"Gee, I'd love to, Sammy, but I got to run. Business lunch in town. How's the patio deck working out?"

"Fine."

"Glad to hear it."

Then he turned to Ken Immelman and put his hand out. "Three bucks."

"If I hadn't got that side-hill lie on the seventeenth. . ."

"If the queen had balls, she'd be king."

The periodontist handed Walt three dollars. Sammy stood and watched the two of them walk toward the parking lot until he heard someone yell "Fore!" and he looked back to see a foursome waiting to hit their approach shots.

He trudged to his car, put his clubs in the trunk, and slammed the lid. You could tell the kind of day a man had on the golf course by the way he slammed the trunk of his car. Sammy banged the shit out of the Lexus's trunk hood. He had stopped scoring at the turn, with fifty-three on his card.

It wasn't even eleven yet, and already it was hot in his fleece vest. He was tired. Worse, he was confused. Not to mention pissed. He had no idea why Walt had summoned him to play golf with his periodontist. It made no sense. Was the guy fucking with his head? Did he want a free round of golf? Or was there some other weird reason that he wanted Sammy to be at Tahquitz Creek between seven and eleven that morning?

Then he suddenly realized what was going down. While they were playing golf, Biff was doing the African. Yes, of course. That was it. This would give Sammy an alibi, should it ever come to that. No trail led to Acme. No breadcrumbs of any sort. Very neat work. These guys were good.

Nonetheless, as he drove down 111 into town, he felt queasy. He wasn't sure if he was ready to face the crime scene, police cars, reporters, crazed neighbors, a distraught Marcy Gray.

Well, the good news was that he had an air-tight alibi. He had the starter at the golf course who could put him there at 6:35 in the morning. Just to be on the safe side, he decided to stop at Vons and pick up a few things, so that he would get back even later and be seen by more potential witnesses. He needed a few things, anyway. He was out of frozen pizza and his shower drain was running sluggishly.

Sammy parked the Lexus at the Vons on Sierra Madre, got out, picked up a shopping cart. He grabbed a quart of Drano and was staring into the frozen foods freezer, trying to decide between pepperoni and mushroom, when he heard the explosion. Screams were heard. People dove for cover.

Pieces of the Lexus were found a quarter of a mile away.

After getting the report from Evelyn Duboff that both of her suitors had skeletons in their closets—or worse, recently decomposed corpses—Marcy Gray lapsed into a depression. She had a history of these bouts—nothing major, no suicidal thoughts or heavy-duty pharmaceuticals involved, just your run-of-the-mill depression, treatable with therapy and whatever SSRI the SAG health insurance was currently paying for.

She drove up to LA for an appointment with Janet Costanza, sat on the sun porch of her therapist's house in Nichols Canyon—a house that Marcy liked to think she had helped pay for—and unloaded.

"I mean, here I am, sixty. . . and I'm still making bad choices with men. You'd think I would have learned to recognize the danger signs by now."

"You're sixty-seven."

"How do *you* know?"

"It's in your SAG paperwork. We've got to start off with the truth. Here in this room, at least."

"Thanks a lot."

"Age is just a number, Marcy."

"Maybe for shrinks it is, but not for actresses."

"When's the last time you acted?"

"You mean, like a job?"

"Yes."

"I don't know. . .a year, maybe a year and a half ago. . ."

"Then why isn't your insurance current?"

"Okay, two years, maybe three. . ."

"So if that's the case, can we really say that you are still an actress?"

"Why not? How does it hurt?"

Janet Costanza gave her the look that Marcy hated. The therapist held her eyes and said, without words: *Let's cut the shit, shall we?*

"Okay, fine. So I'm not sixty, and I'm not an actress. What am I then?"

"You're a sixty-seven-year-old woman, living in Palm Springs and doing something positive with your life, I hope."

"Jesus. You make me sound like a statistic."

"I just want us to work within the real world, Marcy."

Marcy nodded her compliant nod—a nod that meant *you're right, and fuck you for being right.*

"Okay, so tell me about these men that you're involved with."

"I'm not really involved with them. I mean, not yet."

"Okay, so what are you with them?"

"I'm considering them."

"For what?"

"For involvement."

"Uh-huh. . ."

Marcy leaned back into the spongy cushions of the wicker couch that faced Janet's rocking chair. She didn't want to talk; she wanted to be comforted. She wanted a cup of chamomile tea, a good cry, and a prescription for Zoloft. But she knew that there was no way of getting out of this house that lightly. So she let go.

"I need a man in my life. Someone to take care of me. I'm sorry if that's anti-feminist or something, but it's what I need. I'm not sure I can make it alone. I don't have enough money. Or enough strength. I'm frightened at night that someone is going to break into my condo. I'm starting to have trouble driving at night. I'm constipated. I haven't had sex in so long I can't even remember what it feels like. I'm scared shitless of getting old and sick and having no one to take care of me, and winding up on the street like a bag lady. . ."

It had come pouring out of her like some underground lava stream that had been bottled up for a long time. And with it came the tears. Sobs, not tears. Her body shook with the convulsions. Janet let her go on for five minutes before saying (softly, for a change), "Didn't that feel good?"

Marcy sniffled and nodded simultaneously.

"The psyche cries for the same reason that the stomach vomits. It's a protective mechanism. It helps you get rid of the poison. And that's the first step to healing. So. . .now tell me about these men."

Marcy grabbed handfuls of tissues from the box sitting purposefully beside the couch, crumpled them in her hand.

"They're both my neighbors at Paradise Gardens. I almost said Purgatory Gardens. That's what Stanley used to call it. Remember Stanley, my gay neighbor?" She smiled dimly at the memory.

Janet nodded. She had the ability, like most good therapists, to remember the supporting characters in a patient's life.

"They're both, I don't know, about my age—maybe a little older. It's hard to tell with men. They age better than we do. Fuck them, right?"

The therapist actually smiled—a rare occurrence. Janet was maybe a few years younger than her and, as far as Marcy knew, not with a man. There were no family pictures in the office, except for her dog. Marcy had gotten a gay vibe from Janet, but she couldn't be sure. Maybe she was asexual. Maybe she was a nun or a cross-dresser. . .but what the fuck difference did it make?

"Anyway, so both of them are interested in me. I mean, I'm pretty sure they are. And what's really kind of cute is that they're competing. It's actually funny—they're like two dogs trying to hump my leg."

"Have you had sex with either of them?"

"No!"

"How come?"

"What do you mean, *how come*? You think I sleep with every man I meet?"

"You have a pretty good batting average, Marcy."

"Thank you," Marcy frowned.

"Just calling 'em as I see 'em."

Janet and her goddamn baseball analogies. It was hard enough for Marcy to get her insides vacuumed without having her problems translated into situations in a sport she barely understood.

"So I hired a private detective to look into these guys."

"Really? Isn't that a bit extreme?"

"There's a lot at stake."

"I don't understand. You hired a detective to check a man before you sleep with him?"

"For chrissakes, no!"

The process was clearly working. The therapist was getting her prepped for the transference process, in which she became her mother and Marcy became the spiteful fifteen-year-old daughter she was feeling like at the moment.

"Then what's the big deal?"

"The big deal is. . .the rest of my life. . ." And she started to cry again. By the time she was calm again, she had depleted the Kleenex box.

"Okay," Janet said in her most soothing voice, which wasn't all that soothing. "Let's take it from the top. It's the seventh inning—all right, we'll say the bottom of the sixth—and you're already worrying about the ninth. The ninth inning is three innings away. A lot can happen in that time."

"Can we lose the baseball metaphors, please?"

"You're creating anxiety about issues that may not even exist."

"How do *you* know?"

"I don't. But you haven't told me anything yet that I see is a problem. Once there is a problem, we can address it. Look, I can't do anything about the fact that you're sixty-seven and alone. Now, tell me, what are you really anxious about? Beside the fact that you're going to die someday. Because, let me let you in on a secret, we all are."

Marcy glanced at the clock. There were eleven minutes left. Time to cut to the chase. "Okay, according to the detective, both of these men have some sort of shady past. One of them may even be in witness protection. Sammy, the Jew—he claims to be a retired cement company owner, but I don't buy it. And he may not even be Jewish. I mean, what kind of Jew is in witness protection? The other guy is an art dealer. He's African. Black. My parents would turn over in their graves. Apparently he was involved in some weird stuff in France in the 1980s. There's no way of knowing. And here's the thing—both these guys have no ex-wives, or families, or anything. I think they're both bullshit artists."

Janet sat in her rocking chair digesting this information. To her credit, she didn't rock. But she did nod her head slowly, as if she were sifting the information through her various filters.

"Okay. Worst-case scenario, the Jew's an ex-mobster and the African was some sort of warlord, or gunrunner, or whatever. And here they both are, living in Palm Springs, your neighbors. They're interested in you. Romantically, we hope. Or at least sexually. So you succumb to their charms, go to bed with one, maybe both, and it's nice. You have a good time. You haven't forgotten how to make love. You like both of them. It's an embarrassment of riches. What's so bad about that? I've got women in here younger than you who would give anything to have one man, not to mention two, interested in them. See it as win/win. Pick the guy who takes the best care of you. See where it goes. Who knows? Maybe you'll keep both of them on the hook. Sounds pretty good to me. You ask me, you're at the plate with a 3-0 count. You're in the catbird seat."

Marcy plowed her way home through heavy traffic on the San Bernardino Freeway, without a prescription for Zoloft. *You don't need medication; you need new lingerie.* As usual, she left Janet's feeling worse than she'd felt before the appointment. *This isn't a massage, this is work. If your muscles don't hurt after a workout, you're not doing it right.*

She decided that she would try to enjoy her life in the catbird seat, wherever the fuck *that* was. There was a Victoria's Secret outlet store in Palm Desert. She'd stop off on the way home and see what she could find. Though it didn't look like either of these guys needed much enticement.

The question was—which one of them should she try out first? Though they were entirely different types, they both dialed about the same number on her chemistry gauge. Neither one was Brad Pitt, but she had to be realistic. Brad wasn't on her dance card. In her late sixties—God, she hated that number—she was looking at guys her own age, and likely older, who might be interested in a woman of mature charms.

Marcy walked out of the Victoria's Secret outlet with a push-up bra and a lacy peignoir with a pair of sheer panties. She passed on a thong. Not even on a good day. At the Fragrance outlet, she sprayed her wrist with a dozen scents before settling on a two-ounce bottle of Lady Gaga's "Fame."

Then she stopped off in town for a bottle of Piper-Heidsieck and some chocolates stuffed with truffles. All in, she had almost two hundred dollars invested in this seduction, and she still hadn't decided which of the two and when. She would let circumstances determine the outcome. The first one who got in touch with her, she would invite over for dinner.

As it turned out, neither of them called that day or the next. They weren't at the pool or in the exercise room. It was raining on and off, one of those November rains that hits the desert just as people were starting to forget that it ever rained at all. She began to wonder if they were out of town. There she was, all dressed up and no place to go.

And then, of course, when they finally got in touch, it was within fifteen minutes of each other. Didier invited her for a Scrabble game, and Sammy invited her to go shopping with him. The times conflicted, as if they had done it on purpose, as if they had each other's brain tapped and knew when they were going to make a move.

The next day, Sammy knocked on her door around four in the afternoon. She had just gotten back from taking Klaus for a walk and was in sweatpants and no makeup. It was not the right moment for the champagne or the chocolates, and, as it turned out, he had come on business. He had some sort of construction contract for a new patio deck that he wanted her to co-sign.

She signed it. Why not? She didn't have any money anyway, so what difference did it make if someone went after her? But it made her even more aware that he seemed to have buried his past. You would think he could get someone to co-sign the contract for him without his having to hit up a retired actress—or, as Janet would say, a sixty-seven-year-old woman living in Palm Springs, trying to do something constructive with her life.

That night she went to a karaoke bar with Didier and did a Peggy Lee version of "Fever" that killed. But when she got home, she was tired and didn't feel up to sex. She pleaded a headache and didn't invite him in. And then, ten minutes later, she regretted it.

She went to bed, resolved that she would wake up the next morning, flip a coin, and invite the winner for Piper-Heidsieck, chocolates, and a private showing of her Victoria's Secret collection. She was tired of all this equivocation. One of them, at least, would be road-tested.

But the next morning, before she could even flip a coin, let alone put her makeup on, she was woken by a loud knock on her door. Two Palm Springs police detectives were standing there.

"Miss Gray?" said the thin one, who resembled Jack Webb in a herring-bone sports jacket that she wouldn't have let Klaus sleep on.

For a moment she thought of denying it, looking the way she did, but they obviously knew who she was.

"Something the matter?"

They told her. Ten minutes later she was back in bed, hugging Klaus, sick with worry. There was a killer on the loose, murdering animals. If she had to use the *Töten!* command, she was ready.

Both of her suitors showed up at the emergency meeting that evening to discuss the security problem at Paradise Gardens. Sammy was flip about the dead cat, which she found totally inappropriate, and Didier moved up a notch. Not that she was in any frame of mind to break out the Piper-Heidsieck, in any event.

The police had suggested that the target might not have been the cat, but rather an occupant of the condominium complex. How creepy was that? As if she didn't have enough on her mind these days without having to worry about poisoned take-out food. A community watch deal was proposed, with the tenants taking turns patrolling the grounds, looking for suspicious activity.

"What kind of suspicious activity?" someone asked.

"Anything out of the ordinary," Ethel Esmitz replied.

"You mean, like take-out pizza?" Sammy asked.

Again with the sarcasm. She was starting to favor Didier, until he moved into the doghouse, along with Sammy, by speaking out against the tenant patrol.

"We are not trained law-enforcement people, n'est-ce pas?"

This was no time for French skepticism.

The motion passed on a voluntary basis, and Marcy was assigned the 4 to 6 p.m. shift, along with Chris and Edie.

She took Klaus with her for protection—more from the swingers than from the murderer. As they patrolled the grounds looking for suspicious activity, Edie asked if she wanted to join them in the sauna. These people never gave up.

"Chris and I smoke a joint, go in there and unwind. By the time we're done, we're seriously mellow."

"Sounds like fun."

"Come join us some time. And bring Sammy, or Didier. We'll have a little party."

Marcy nodded rhetorically, hoping they would drop the subject.

"So which one of them are you doing?" Chris asked her. "Edie thinks it's the Jew, but my money's on both."

"Neither of them, thank you very much, Chris."

"Right. . . ." The two of them shared a look.

"It's none of your business, anyway," Marcy said, petulance in her voice.

"Hey, sorry. No offense meant, babe. It's just, you know, a looker like you. . .I mean, it's a shame not to share the wealth."

"We believe in corporal communism. You know, from each according to his means to. . .whatever," Edie said, and the two of them laughed loudly. They were clearly stoned.

Over the next two hours, most of which was spent sitting by the pool listening to Chris and Edie talk about their sybaritic lifestyle, the only suspicious activity they observed turned out to be someone's new cleaning lady leaving the laundry room. When they asked her for i.d., she dropped the basket of clothes she was carrying and ran. It turned out that the woman was an illegal Honduran who thought they were the immigration police.

The next day, Sammy called to find out if she were all right. She was touched by his concern and moved him out of the doghouse.

"You looked kind of upset last night."

"I was. You know, it's upsetting, this thing with the cat."

"Yeah. Anything I can do?"

For a moment, she thought about inviting him for champagne and chocolates, but decided against it. She had gained three pounds since she had bought the peignoir, compulsively eating junk food to deal with her anxiety, and she could use a mani-pedi, not to mention a bikini wax.

"Thanks, Sammy. That's sweet of you, but I'm a little under the weather. Tell you what, though, why don't you come over for Thanksgiving dinner on Thursday? I'll invite Didier. And Charlie Berns, too."

He said he would, but there was a lack of enthusiasm in his voice, as if he'd had something else in mind. So had she. But if she really was going to plunge back in after all this time, she wanted it to be under optimal conditions. She wanted to be thin, or at least thinner, and well-coiffed. Maybe she'd go for a landing strip. The thought of getting her pubic area trimmed into a narrow rectangle made her laugh so heartily that she actually felt better. Why not get a full Brazilian, while she was at it? She was in the fucking catbird seat, right?

Marcy decided to cook up a storm for Thanksgiving. It had been a while since she had been motivated to bother making something special. Too lazy to cook for one person, her evening meals consisted largely of take-out or deli counter dishes in front of *Jeopardy*. Not since Stanley was alive had she spent any appreciable amount of time in her kitchen.

She had learned a lot from her former neighbor, who would teach her tricks he had learned during his student year in France. *It's not the meat; it's the sauce. Just like French women. No tits, no ass, but they know how to garnish themselves.* God, she missed him.

The boys showed up within two minutes of one another, bearing gifts. Sammy and Charlie brought wine, and Didier presented her with one of the sculptures from his gallery.

"An authentic Yoruba talisman," he told her. "It will bring you good luck."

"I could use it," she said.

"Now, now, we have much to be thankful for," Didier tried to reassure her.

"Right," Sammy quipped. "We could be starving in Africa."

"Not everyone is starving in Africa, S*amee*."

"Oh yeah? What's the per capita income of Darfur?"

"Hey, guys, this is a day to give thanks, not to bicker."

Marcy suggested that they join hands around the table and give thanks before they started eating. The three men reluctantly agreed, and they spent a moment pretending to be thankful for something—that is, everyone but Marcy, who decided that she really *was* thankful to have three men around her table for Thanksgiving dinner.

Sammy carved. Beautifully. His manicured hands sliced through the turkey with dexterity. On his right index finger, a large ruby reflected the light from the candles that Marcy had put in the sterling silver candlesticks that she hadn't used since the days of her marriage to Neil.

Sammy looked handsome in a light blue cashmere sweater and dark gray slacks. Beside him, Didier was wearing one of his native African numbers over pajama-like trousers and suede sandals. Charlie looked, as usual, like he had slept in his clothes—a creased linen jacket, a long-sleeve polo, and a pair of unpressed jeans over cut-rate Italian loafers.

She felt a sudden surge of unexpected pleasure. She felt good, better than she had for a while. Okay, maybe she was just a sixty-seven-year-old woman living in Palm Springs, but at her table sat three men, two of whom wanted to sleep with her.

Charlie Berns told stories about his days producing movies in Hollywood. It brought back memories of her long, intermittently rewarding career on the periphery of the movie business. Thirty years of incarnating various damaged women.

Now, she thought, she was no longer playing a damaged woman; she *was* one. As soon as the thought occurred to her, she banished it. No matter what happened, she wouldn't allow herself to sink into self-pity. She was healthy—more or less—and had a dachshund who loved her and two men who wanted her. She closed her eyes and silently gave thanks.

And prayed that somebody, somewhere, would keep her from being a bag lady. If she had to be bag lady, she would at least be an attractive one. She pictured herself standing at a Freeway onramp with Klaus, a Brazilian, and a cardboard sign reading: WILL ACT FOR MONEY.

A couple of days after Thanksgiving, Marcy found herself across the street from Didier's art gallery—a storefront, painted bright green and orange.

Colors, she assumed, that were quintessentially African. She had been shopping for shoes, saw the AFRIQUE OUEST sign, and decided to pop in and say hello.

The place was deserted, except for a bored-looking, middle-aged gay man sitting at a desk, talking on his cell. He didn't bother getting off the phone—barely even looked at her, for that matter—as she walked around examining the pieces of art displayed haphazardly around the place.

The man was speaking loudly enough for her not to be able to avoid overhearing.

". . .Bruno, it's not like he even looked at me. He was spending the whole evening talking to Malcolm. What he sees in him is beyond me, frankly. The man hasn't been near a gym in years. Besides, I think he's sleeping with Arthur. . ."

Gay dishing. She had heard enough of it in all the makeup trailers she had spent time in during her acting years, when her makeup artist and hair dresser would wittily assassinate their friends' characters while making her into whatever version of a damaged woman she was playing that day.

Eventually, the man got off the phone and, without getting up, called across to her, "Help you?" There was no sincerity in his invitation.

"No, thanks," she said. "Just browsing."

He nodded and was about to dial another number when she asked if Didier happened to be around. He put his phone down and looked more closely at her. "You a friend?"

"A neighbor."

"He's in a meeting. I can tell him you're here."

"That's okay," she said, and meant it. But just as she was turning to leave, the door to an inner office opened and Didier emerged, accompanied by a man in a braided ponytail and moccasins. The man was wearing sunglasses and had a manila envelope in his hand.

"Mar*cee*?" Didier seemed surprised to see her.

"Hi. I just happened to be across the street, looking at shoes, and figured I'd say hi. But if you're busy. . ."

"No, no. George was just leaving. George Kajika, meet Marcy Gray. *The* Marcy Gray."

The Native American showed no recognition of her name, or her face, for that matter. He merely nodded, minimally, and walked out of the gallery.

"I didn't know that Indians went in for African art."

"*Au contraire, cherie.* They are good customers. They appreciate the primitive in art. Do you know what Kajika means in Choctaw? Walks Without Sound. *Formidable, n'est-ce pas?* His family must have been stalkers."

And he let go with one of his high-pitched volleys of laughter that Marcy, quite frankly, was getting a little tired of.

There was a Starbucks on the corner, and she accepted his invitation for a latte. It was three in the afternoon; too late for lunch, too early for dinner. They sat outside, under an awning in the spraying mist, watching air-conditioned cars drive by, occupied by refrigerated senior citizens on anti-depressants.

"It's not quite Paris, is it?" she remarked ruefully.

"Alas, no. Perhaps you would allow me to take you there one day. For a holiday?"

"That would be lovely."

"We should go in spring. April in Paris. Chestnuts in blossom. . ."

That was still four months away. Anything could happen before then. Still, she liked the idea of it, the promise. She would put it in Didier's plus column, even if he didn't really mean it. He seemed as if he meant to mean it. Which, these days, might have to be enough.

Things became murkier when Evelyn Duboff called with an update. Marcy, who felt guilty that the woman was now working pro bono for her, offered to take her to lunch, but the detective said that they could talk on the phone.

"Your phone's not bugged, is it?"

"Not that I know of. But some weird stuff's happening around here. Someone's cat was poisoned, and the cops think it could have been that they were actually trying to kill someone in the complex."

"No kidding? Who?"

"Nobody knows. It's scary. We organized a community watch."

"Well, hmmn. . .I wonder if there's some connection. . ."

"Some connection with what?"

"How was the cat poisoned?"

"Take-out pizza."

"Hmmn. . . ."

Evelyn Duboff took a moment, as if she were putting something to-gether in her mind. Marcy could hear her heavy breathing over the line.

"I have some more information. And I'm wondering how this fits in."

"How *what* fits in?"

"I called in a favor with an old friend who lives in France. Asked him to do a little snooping around on your African. And he came up with some stuff. After he was in the shmata business, he went into the art business. He had a gallery in Nice, in the high-rent district near the big hotels, and was selling to rich tourists. Anyway, my guy is plugged into the gendar-merie, and he made a few phone calls. Apparently there was a warrant for his arrest in process when he left the country."

"Arrest warrant? For what?"

"Drug dealing. Heroin."

"Oh, my God. Really?"

"No one ever presented any evidence, and apparently there wasn't enough to start extradition proceedings, but the police believed that the art gallery could have been a money laundering operation. The *dossier*, as they call it over there, is closed."

"You think it's true?"

"I don't know, but when you told me about the poisoned cat, I thought about the connection. You see, if he had crossed someone, they could have put a hit out on him. Poison is a favorite contract killing method. Leaves no fingerprints or powder stains. The Russians put it in borscht. It dis-guises the taste."

"So maybe he's still dealing drugs, and this African art business he's do-ing now is just a front?"

"I don't know. But it's a hypothesis."

"Oh, wow. . ."

"Hey, I could be entirely wrong here. And the Frogs could've been wrong too. That happens a lot—they set up some guy to roll over on some-one else, and he implicates an innocent guy to get himself off the hook."

Marcy had trouble visualizing the jovial African dealing drugs. On TV, the drug lords were Colombian. Then she started thinking about the African art and wondering if the narcotics were smuggled inside the statues. And then about the Indian, George Walks Without Sound, and his manila envelope. Had the man just dropped off a shipment of cocaine?

"Here's what I don't get," Evelyn Duboff said, interrupting Marcy's paranoid scenario. "If he was in the drug business, why would he be living in a middle-market condo in Palm Springs? You want to make a living with drugs in this community, you deal Lipitor or Viagra. There aren't a whole lot of people shooting heroin around here."

"I think you're right." Marcy decided to indulge in wishful thinking, not ready to eliminate Didier from her short list.

"Yeah, probably. It's a long shot. Just doing my due diligence."

"Anything new on Sammy?"

"Nope. I can't even get a flicker. He's really covered his tracks."

"You know, maybe he really is who he says he is—just a retired cement guy with no family," Marcy said, deciding to extend her wishful thinking to the other name on the short list.

"Hey, why not? Give him the benefit of the doubt."

Then, a few days after that conversation, Sammy's car got blown up in the Vons supermarket lot. And things really got weird.

VI
DIDIER

When Didier Onyekachukwu called the telephone number he had heard through Charlie Berns's open window, he wasn't expecting to hear a message requesting that he leave his name and mailing address. Rattled, he hung up. Did he really want to leave evidence of his desire to kill Sammy Dee on an answering machine? The whole thing could be a sting operation. Or a joke.

But when the Italian started consolidating his position with Marcy Gray, inviting her to dinner, taking her to the movies, Didier realized that he would have to do something if he didn't want to watch the man walk off with the actress, right under his nose. It was, quite simply, unacceptable.

He had been through it in his mind and decided that he really didn't have a choice. With Afrique Ouest sinking slowly and the Indians putting a tomahawk to his head for more money, he'd be broke before spring. And then what? Find some rich old woman who was looking for something a little *défendu* in her declining years? Go back to Burkina Faso and live off the charity of his children, if he could find them? Go back into the drug business and spend the duration of his life in a federal prison, with the worst type of Africans—African Americans?

No. One way or the other, Marcy Gray was his lifeboat. If it sunk, he would go down with the ship. And there wasn't room in the boat for Sammy Dee. He would have to be disposed of.

So he called back the number and left the information. A week later, he got in the mail a questionnaire about his vermin problem, along with an application for a rebuilt patio deck, with a lot of questions—social security number, place of birth, previous residences. Didier had been very careful about disclosing details of the identity he had assumed in Geneva years ago, fearful that the *gendarmerie nationale* would learn of his whereabouts and try to extradite him.

A patio deck? His own patio deck was a naked slab of concrete. Since he bought the unit, he hadn't done a thing to it. Other tenants had put in gardens, barbecue pits, flower boxes, but Didier's patio had remained forlorn and neglected. Sammy Dee had recently had his patio deck redone. Maybe Marcy paid attention to these types of things.

Well, he rationalized, it wouldn't be a bad thing to improve his position with Marcy, as well as his property, while he was getting Sammy Dee disposed of. Two stones with one bird, as the Americans like to say. He filled out the form with all the fictitious information he had been using and waited. This time it took two weeks to get a response. It was a note on Acme Exterminating and Patio Deck letterhead that said: TOMORROW, 6:45 A.M., TAHQUITZ CREEK LEGEND GOLF COURSE, PAY GREENS FEE FOR THREE, MEET AT FIRST TEE BOX.

Didier had never picked up a golf club in his life. He hadn't even seen a golf course until he'd moved to Nice, where he occasionally met clients at a restaurant overlooking the *Club de Golf Côte d'Azur*. It always seemed to him a sport for people with too much time on their hands. And from what he had observed, playing the game never made anyone happy.

What was he going to do about golf clubs? The only person he knew who played the game was the Italian. Wouldn't it be lovely if Didier went to the meeting with clubs belonging to the man he was arranging to kill? It would make Sammy Dee an accessory to his own murder.

"Samee, comment allez-vous?"

"What is it, Didier?" Sammy growled into the phone.

"Would you be good enough to lend me your golf clubs?"

There was a long pause, during which Didier could almost hear the man's thinking.

"I didn't know you played."

"I am taking the game up. Good for business, no?"

"You ever play before?"

"Here and there. I am, how do you say, a duf*fer.*"

Didier laughed at his own joke and waited for a response.

"These are pretty good clubs—Cleveland driver, Titleist irons."

"I shall take exemplary care of them."

"You know, you can rent golf clubs. . ."

"It makes a bad impression on potential clients, *n'est-ce pas?*"

"All right," Sammy said, after another long pause. "When do you need them?"

"I shall collect them this afternoon. I have an early time to tee up."

"Where you playing?"

"Tahquitz Creek. You know it?"

"Yeah. Fast greens."

"I am indebted to you, *mon ami.*"

The Italian didn't know just how indebted. When he was safely out of the way, Didier would have the leisure to take up golf while he was courting Marcy Gray. They would spend leisurely afternoons swatting the ball around the manicured grass and then. . .a bottle of chilled Pouilly-Fumé and a little siesta. . . .

Appropriate golf attire presented another problem. Didier did not possess anything remotely suitable for a golf course. In addition to not having a T-shirt with a collar, he had nothing for his feet besides sandals and a couple of pairs of Aubercy shoes, which he had bought in Paris during the fat years.

He went to the Big Five Sporting Goods store and spent a couple hundred more dollars on the eradication of Sammy Dee, walking out with a beige Nike Banlon golf T-shirt, a pair of Footjoy brown and white shoes with adjustable cleats, and, per the Italian's suggestion, a Slazenger large left-handed glove, a dozen Titleist golf balls, and a bag of multicolored tees. At the register he took a free copy of OFFICIAL GOLF RULES AND REGULATIONS.

That night he fell asleep trying to decipher the abstruse peculiarities of the game. The Catholic catechism was easier to understand than the rules of golf. He set the alarm for five thirty, ordered a cab for six fifteen, and slept soundly.

Nevertheless, in the cab on the way to the golf course at dawn, he began to experience the first pangs of remorse since he had decided to rid himself of his rival. But they didn't last long. Just as he had learned to quash any guilt he had felt in enriching the junta that plundered Upper Volta, he was able to compartmentalize his feelings about having Sammy Dee removed. The man was not only an obstacle to Didier's own survival, but he was the instrument of misery for the woman he, Didier, loved. The thought of Marcy Gray throwing her life away with this man was unthinkable. *À la limite*, he was performing an act of altruism. *Someone* had to sacrifice himself to save her. It was the very least he could do. *Le moindre des choses.*

He checked in at the pro shop, where he spent another $375 on greens fees and a cart. Didier hadn't been behind the wheel of a moving vehicle since his days tooling around Ouagadougou in his Mercedes. Fortunately, the thing didn't go very fast, and he was able to proceed jerkily to the first tee box, where he found two men waiting for him. They were well dressed, with short hair and clean-shaven faces. To Didier, they looked like narcotics agents, causing an involuntary tremor of nostalgic anxiety until he realized that he wasn't dealing drugs any more. Just phony African art.

They introduced themselves as Walt and Biff—or Bill, he didn't quite catch the younger one's name—and everyone shook hands.

"Go ahead. You got the honors, *Deedeeyay*," the older one said.

"I am a little, how do you say, rus*tee*," Didier said, as he took a club, at random, out of Sammy Dee's golf bag, and approached the tee.

"I wouldn't use a wedge on this hole," the younger one said. "It's four-seventy to the pin, with a head wind."

"But of course." Didier returned to the bag and selected the biggest club he could find. He stuck a tee in the ground, put the ball on it, making several attempts before it stayed there, then looked down the fairway to a tiny flag waving in the distance, took a deep breath and a whack, missing the ball entirely.

"Warm-up swing," one of them said.

On the next swing, Didier managed to hit the ball, or at least a fraction of the surface, and it rolled off the tee and twenty yards to the left.

"Mulligan," said the other one, cheerfully.

At their suggestion, Didier picked up his ball when after twelve strokes he still wasn't on the green. Two holes later, it was decided he would just putt the ball. Meanwhile the two of them continued to play the game with proficiency, and no mention was made of either patio decks or the elimination of Sammy Dee.

They finally got down to business at the tenth hole, where Didier was invited into the W.C. and told to take his clothes off.

"Certainly, you are joking," he protested.

"Not in the least."

"And why, may I ask, do you require this?"

"Do the math," Walt said.

"I see," said Didier, "You are concerned that I am a policeman?"

"Duh," the younger one replied.

"I assure you I am not."

"We'll be the judge of that."

"Must I really?"

"Only if you want your patio deck redone."

Sighing, Didier removed his beige Nike golf shirt and then was told to take everything else off. He suffered the indignity of having his private parts probed, as if he had been arrested in Upper Volta.

"Surely, you don't think. . .?"

"We think of everything, *Deedeeyay*. You can't be too careful in the patio deck business these days."

After they were assured that he wasn't wearing a recording device, Didier was invited to ride in the cart with the older man. They conducted business between holes. The man told him exactly what would have to happen, how and when, if he wanted Sammy Dee taken care of. There was no negotiation; this is the deal, take it or leave it.

Didier was relieved of the necessity of putting for the remainder of the round. He sat in his own cart again and watched the two of them hit the ball great distances with astounding accuracy. He hoped that they were as good at extermination as they were at playing golf.

When they were finished, they all removed their hats, shook hands, and exchanged pleasantries. Didier returned his cart and called for a taxi. As he sat on a bench outside the pro shop waiting for his cab, he marveled at how painless it was to get rid of another human being. All you needed was $25,000, and you got a new patio deck in the deal. *Pas mal.*

At a little after eleven that morning, he knocked on Sammy Dee's door to return the golf clubs. When the door opened, he saw, over the Italian's shoulder, Marcy Gray sitting on a kitchen stool with a coffee cup in her hand. What was she doing there at this hour? Had she spent the night?

Sammy Dee reached to take the clubs, not inviting him in, but Marcy saw him and smiled. "Didier. *Comment allez-vous?*"

"*Bonjour*, Mar*cee*," he replied with a smile of his own.

"Come join us for a cup of coffee. Sammy makes fabulous cappuccinos."

"Merci, Sa*mee*." And without waiting for an invitation from the Italian, he walked past him and took a stool beside Marcy's.

"I didn't know you played golf," she said.

"I am, how do you say, a crack shot."

"No kidding?" Sammy said. "What'd you shoot?"

"Seventy-two."

"Bullshit."

"Maybe it was a *hundred* and seventy-two," he laughed. "I round off a little."

Marcy laughed along with him, and Didier's heart jiggled. He would love to hear that laugh on a daily basis.

"Who'd you play with?" Sammy asked.

"Some customers. They are purchasing art."

"You really selling that stuff?"

"Sammy, Didier's gallery has beautiful things in it."

"Four-hundred-year-old African dildos?"

"They are not, as you say, dildos, but rather authentic fertility rite artifacts, used among the Yoruba to test for virginity as part of the marriage contract."

"Oh, of course. Everybody ought to own a hymen tester. You never know when it'll come in handy."

Didier accepted a grudgingly provided cappuccino, which, he had to grudgingly admit, was excellent. Though he was tired from having gotten up at the crack of dawn and wanted a nap, he was not going to relinquish his stool and allow Sammy Dee exclusive access to Marcy. The thought that he may be, as they said in Africa, milking the goats after the hyenas had already visited, troubled him, but he decided to let it pass. She did not have that flushed *après amour* look that he believed he could recognize in women recently emerging from a sexual encounter. Not a satisfactory one, at least.

As she talked about some movie that she had been in years ago, she skillfully divided her attention between her two suitors, turning first to one, then the other, like a politician making a speech.

Marcy was clearly enjoying their little *ménage à trois*. Why shouldn't she? What woman doesn't like to be pursued? Is it not the ultimate homage to have several men competing for your favors?

They ought to fight a duel. Pistols at dawn. With Marcy sitting in a carriage across the lake, waiting to see which one of them would survive to worship her. Didier liked his chances with firearms. The colonels in Ouagadougou used to take him hunting with them. They would go out on the savannah, drink beer, and fire Kalashnikovs at anything that moved.

". . .and we were five days behind schedule and the studio was freaking out. They flew some suit out to the set—we were shooting in Mexico, or in Costa Rica, I don't remember—to give us a hard time. All the women decided to draw straws to see who was going to fuck this guy's brains out. The wardrobe mistress—a cute little Czech girl—drew the short straw, and she visited the man in his hotel room. He never made it to the set. Talk about taking one for the team. . ."

Both men laughed, each one trying to out-laugh the other. Didier had no problem winning that contest. He had always been a good laugher. The Italian laughed like an old man moving his bowels.

As usual, they waited each other out, until Marcy herself rose to leave. They both got up, as if she were royalty.

"Sorry, guys, I've got to go make some phone calls."

They nodded, almost simultaneously, and watched as she sauntered out the door, all four eyes riveted on the undulating spandex. Then they were side by side, awkwardly staring at the closed door. Didier could smell the Italian's cologne—strong and cheap. Maybe he didn't have to have the man killed after all; the cologne alone should keep him out of Marcy Gray's bed.

Didier quickly followed her out the door, not even bothering to mutter a pretext. The last thing he wanted now was one-on-one time with the man he had just contracted to kill. He would say a few kind words at the man's funeral. *He was generous with his golf clubs and made decent cappuccino.*

Three days later, Didier got another note in the mail, containing detailed instructions on how to proceed with his patio deck. He was told to show up with the money in a FedEx envelope at a car wash in town. This demand presented a problem. He needed to have a car to wash.

He thought about borrowing Marcy's, but immediately thought better of it. He didn't want her involved in any way with the Acme people. Renting was impossible without a driver's license, so his only recourse was to ask his neighbor, the film producer, if he could borrow his old Mercedes.

Didier rang Charlie Berns's bell and asked him if he wanted his car washed.

"Why start now?" the producer asked.

"Why not? I have a friend who has just opened a car wash in town, and he wants to create the impression that there are lots of cars going in there, so others will come, so he asks all his friends to go there today with a car. As you know, I do not have one."

"Thanks, Didier, but I'm a little under the weather today. Allergies kicking up."

"That is no problem, Char*lee*. I will take your car there for you and bring it back. Span and spic."

"I just hope that it runs when it's clean. It's been a couple of years since I washed it."

It took some effort to get the car out of the garage. Backing up in a narrow space was challenging for a man who had never had to parallel park in his life. In Ouagadougou, he would just leave the car in front of a restaurant or a nightclub and not bother with fitting it into a space. There was a lot of space in Upper Volta.

Charlie Berns's Mercedes was an old diesel model that sounded like a coffee can full of nails. Its wood paneling and leather seats were smooth with age. In the glove compartment he found a veritable drugstore of over-the-counter medication, everything from Contac to Rolaids.

He had been instructed to put his car through the car wash and meet Biff in the area where the customers waited to retrieve their cars. He wasn't there. Didier sat with his FedEx envelope and watched the illegals dry the cars and polish the hubcaps until the younger of the two golfers showed up.

Without even saying hello, Biff told Didier to meet him in the men's room in exactly three minutes. Didier nodded, and three minutes later, he got up, ignoring the Mexican who was waving his rag above the Mercedes, and went to the door marked MEN.

The man locked the door from the inside. This time Didier just got patted down and not strip-searched. After the man took the envelope and counted out the cash, he said, "Okay, here's the deal. We'll do our best to take care of this before the holidays, but we don't guarantee it. It's a busy time of the year for us. Holiday shopping."

Didier tried to laugh, but nothing came out.

"When it's done, you'll deliver the rest of the money, in the same manner and probably in the same place. We'll let you know. And I would suggest you don't hold back the final payment, just in case you're thinking of it. We would have no compunction about doing to you what we've done to your guy."

Didier nodded, anxious to get out of the small room.

"We're done."

He unlocked the door, turned back to Didier, and said, "By the way, nice Benz. What year is it?"

"I don't know. I borrowed it."

"Very considerate. You're returning it clean."

And Biff walked out of the men's room with the FedEx envelope stuffed with cash. Didier waited a minute before leaving to retrieve his car. He stiffed the Mexican who had waved a rag at him.

Now that the die was cast, Didier felt liberated. There was no going back. He had invested almost all of his remaining assets on the job. Marcy Gray was now his life raft. He was running out of continents to flee to.

To celebrate, he stopped off at a local wine store for an overpriced bottle of Châteauneuf-du-Pape to stand up to the pizza he intended to have for dinner. And he stopped next door, at the cigar shop, and bought a couple of Montecristos for twenty bucks apiece. Why not? From this point on, it was feast or famine.

That afternoon he took a long, delicious nap, filled with dreams of his days and nights with Marcy Gray. The sun was almost down when he woke. He got into the shower to wash away the cobwebs, and then picked up the phone and ordered a large anchovy pizza with mushrooms and onions from Pizza Hut.

When it arrived, he opened the bottle of wine, sniffed the bouquet, took a sip, and, for a moment, remembered the fragrance of the French countryside. Just as he was sitting down to enjoy his pizza, the phone rang.

Picking up, he heard the voice of his beloved.

"Didier, *bonsoir.*"

"Mar*cee, comment ça va?*"

"*Bon, très bon. . .*"

"*Non, ma petite*, you must say *très bien*, not *très bon*, because it is an adverb, not an adjective."

"Of course, yes. Listen, Didier, I know it's last minute, but I made some boeuf bourguignon for dinner, and I must have doubled the recipe because there's just oodles of it. I thought I'd invite you and Sammy to share it, but he's not home. So how'd you like to help me out?"

It took Didier a nanosecond to say *yes*. Fuck the pizza.

"*Volontiers*, Mar*cee*. I have the perfect bottle of Châteauneuf-du-Pape to complement your boeuf bourguignon. I just opened it."

Didier hung up, changed into one of his exotic dashikis, daubed a little deodorant under his arms, started to put the pizza in the refrigerator and then, remembering that American pizza was bad enough warm and fresh, he tossed it in the black trash bin for non-recyclables outside his unit and walked over to his neighbor's with his bottle of wine.

The boeuf bourguignon turned out to be only slightly overcooked, and Didier resolved that when she was his exclusively, he would improve her culinary skills, along with her French. She looked marvelous in a cashmere sweater, unbuttoned just enough to be alluring without being sluttish, a pair of jeans one size too small, and laced-up calfskin boots. He detected a *soupcon* of Hermès 24 Faubourg emanating from her.

She seemed to be pulling out all the stops, but was it uniquely for him? She'd called the Italian first, or so she said. Was he merely the stand-in? He wished he knew the answer to that question.

In any event, the boeuf bourguignon accompanied the Châteauneuf a lot better than the anchovy pizza would have. And she was a better companion than the six o'clock news. So he relaxed and enjoyed the dinner and her anecdotes, sprinkling a little French lesson in between courses and slipping a chunk or two of beef to Klaus under the table.

When they were finished eating and the bottle of wine was down to the dregs, she pushed back a little from the table, sighing contentedly, emitting a charming little belch. She giggled. He loved it.

She was exhibiting the signs that he had learned to recognize of a woman who wanted to have her dessert in bed. It was the right moment, he concluded, but the wrong time. Sammy Dee was still around, casting his ominous shadow, polluting the air around her. He would wait until the man was safely out of the picture—and she was his prize, to savor exclusively, at a moment of his choosing.

So instead of taking her in his arms, he thanked her for the *repas délicieux*, and returned alone to his condo. He went outside to his soon-to-be-remodeled patio, sat down on the rusty recliner, lit up his Montecristo, and looked up at the stars.

It was a beautiful night, perfectly quiet except for the sound of the Finnish lesbians' cat prying loose the cover of the trash can. Must be the anchovies on the pizza. Good. *Qu'il mange des anchois!*

It wasn't until Didier was face to face with Detective Sergeant Jorge Melendez the next morning that he learned that the anchovy pizza he had tossed in favor of Marcy Gray's boeuf bourguignon had been laced with strychnine. He had apparently slept through the wailing Finns, who had woken almost everyone else in the complex.

Fortunately, Didier was still half-asleep and sluggish enough not to overreact to the news. He stood in the doorway, absently scratching his ass, until the policeman said they wanted to ask him some questions.

Several minutes later, when the cops told him what had happened, Didier understood that someone was trying to kill him, that there was no good reason to share this revelation with the police, and that he would need to think about what this meant before he had the cops thinking about it as well. For the moment, he relied on a reflex developed in Africa and in France to avoid volunteering any information to the authorities that he didn't have to.

"Mr. Onyochinko. . ."

"Onyekachukwu."

"Mr. . . ." he abandoned the attempt to pronounce the name and continued, "Sir, did you order a pizza from Pizza Hut last night?"

"Pizza Hut? You are talking about the take-out pizza establishment?" Didier asked rhetorically, stalling for time to figure out why the cops were talking to him.

"Yes. The place on Desert Canyon Drive."

"Oh, *that* establishment. . ."

"Yes. That establishment. It's the only Pizza Hut in Palm Springs."

"Would you gentlemen care for some coffee?"

"No, thank you."

"No drinking on duty, right?"

Didier laughed his laugh, which crumbled around the edges. "Last night. . .I had dinner with my charming neighbor, Marcy Gray. The actress. You, no doubt, have seen her films?"

"Afraid not. So you didn't order a pizza?"

"Not that I recall."

"Not that you recall?"

"Yes. I do not have a recollection of the event."

Melendez screwed up his features, consulted his pad, and said, "Well, according to them, someone called up at 6:19 p.m. last night, ordered an anchovy pizza, and gave them your address."

"Hmmn. . ."

"It wasn't you?"

"I believe I would recall that."

The two cops shared a look, as if trying to silently convey some sort of strategy for the interrogation. Maybe it was *Bon flic, Sale flic*—a number that he had seen *Starsky et Hutch* use countless times in all the episodes he had watched in Nice.

"And, apparently, someone then called back and canceled the order," Melendez said finally.

"Uh-huh. . ."

"And that wasn't you either?"

"Tell me, why would I cancel an order I had not made?"

At last the other cop joined in. "That's what we want to know."

"An excellent question, no doubt, but I am afraid I cannot help you answer it. Would you mind if I made myself some coffee? I am, how do you say, a trifle hung out. Too much Châteauneuf-du-Pape last night. It did honor to Miss Gray's splendid cuisine."

"Can you think of anybody, sir, who might use your name to order a pizza?"

Didier shook his head and walked over to the kitchenette, his back to them, so as to minimize eye contact. As he poured water into his coffee-maker and scooped several spoonfuls of extra bold French roast into the basket, he tried to slow down his mind. A great deal was going through it at the same time. Who canceled the order? Why were the cops so interested in pizza?

The last question was answered as Didier switched on the machine and stood waiting for it to deliver the coffee he desperately needed.

"Sir, someone poisoned that pizza."

"Oh my dear. Did someone eat it?"

"Yes. Unfortunately."

"Who?"

Another pause for dramatic effect. This was more Hutch than Starsky. Starsky was the fast talker, the friendly guy. Hutch played it close to the vest.

"Tuuli Rennholm's cat."

"How dreadful," he intoned, avidly breathing in the coffee fumes, like a drowning man gulping air.

"Do you happen to know anyone in this complex who didn't like the cats?"

"Well, I believe that Mr. Dee, the Italian who lives across the hall from the cats, had complained several times about them."

Starsky wrote something down in his pad. "Anyone else?"

"No. I am fond of cats. They are beautiful, are they not?"

The cop didn't bother answering the question. "Are you an American citizen, Mr. Oyochinko?"

Didier did not like where this particular line of questioning was going. He considered saying that he was as American as Sergeant Melendez—whose relatives were polishing hubcaps at the car wash—but thought better of it.

"I have a green card."

"Can we see it?" Hutch popped up.

As Didier went to his bedroom for his wallet, he tried to stop thinking about what had happened and concentrate on getting the cops out of there so he could think of what had happened in peace.

After looking at his green card meticulously, they handed it back, along with their cards, and told him to get in touch if he remembered anything about last night.

"Especially about the pizza," Hutch added, with what Didier thought was a sarcastic grin.

As soon as the door was closed, Didier poured a large mug of coffee, didn't even bother with the sugar, and waited for the caffeine to hit his brain. It didn't take long.

Someone had known that he'd ordered a pizza, called the Pizza Hut and canceled it, and then delivered a poisoned one. And had it not been for Marcy Gray's timely invitation, he would have been dead instead of the cat.

Was the pizza meant for Sammy Dee? Did the Acme people somehow cross the two names in their minds and mistake the client for the victim? How could they possibly be so stupid? Or was it someone else? Did someone else want him dead? Did someone have his phone tapped, just waiting for this opportunity to substitute a poisoned pizza?

Didier spent the next few hours reviewing his catalogue of enemies. There were numbers of people, from Ouagadougou to Nice, who, for one reason or another, conceivably might want him dead. But how would they have found him here, in Paradise Gardens? How would they have tapped his phone and substituted the poisoned pizza?

No, there was only one person he could think of who knew where he lived, had his phone number, and had a motive for having him eliminated. The same person whom Didier had just finalized a contract to kill the previous day. And, come to think of it, the same person who recently had *his* patio redone. Was it possible that they were each trying to kill the other? *Nom de dieu. . .*

A few days later, he saw Sammy Dee at the Thanksgiving dinner that Marcy Gray had prepared. The Italian was, as usual, overdressed, trying to impress Marcy with his expensive off-the-rack clothes. In Nice, he would have been regarded as a tasteless American tourist.

As Charlie and Marcy reminisced about making movies, Didier studied the Italian, who sat impassively listening. If he had arranged the pizza murder attempt, he showed no signs of guilt or nervousness. On the contrary, he appeared to be on the verge of falling asleep.

No one mentioned the poisoned cat, though they had all been present at the homeowners' association meeting the evening after the cat had been discovered dead in the garbage bin. To stay on Marcy's good side, Didier had had to volunteer for the community watch. But instead of being assigned to her shift, he got the eight-to-midnight shift with Bert Velum— the eighty-seven-year-old health nut, who claimed he was an insomniac and never slept anyway.

"I've slept enough," he'd told Didier.

Didier didn't show up for his shift the following night.

But he wasn't about to miss Thanksgiving dinner, even though Charlie Berns was there to chaperone Marcy and Sammy Dee. After the meal, Charlie and Sammy repaired to the couch to watch a football game while Didier helped Marcy with the dishes.

"You don't celebrate Thanksgiving in Africa, huh?" she asked.

"No, we don't. But there are many other holidays. When I was a boy, in the village, we would celebrate the full moon. Drink palm wine and dance all night."

"That sounds like fun."

"*A la recherche du temps perdu. . .*" And for a moment he felt a pang of far-off nostalgia for the days before the Jesuits got to him.

"Do you miss Africa?"

"Sometimes."

"You ever want to go back? Just to visit?"

"Africa, Mar*cee*, is a sad place now. There are diseases, civil wars, violence. It is no longer a place of innocence."

"What happened?"

"The Europeans came. And they brought AK-47s, venereal disease, and Jesus with them."

His words had come across more bitter and cynical than he had wanted them to be, and he immediately tried to soften them. "I am exaggerating, of course. There are still lovely places there. Perhaps you will visit someday. . ."

The implication was, of course, *with him*, but he left it at that. More points. Where could Sammy Dee take her? Hoboken, New Jersey? Sicily?

"I'd love to take a safari," she said.

The biggest game that Didier had ever seen were water buffalos, placidly drinking water in the Niger River, but he decided not to disabuse her of the notion that he was a great—if not white, at least virile—hunter. The truth was that he had never been south or east of Lagos, in Nigeria, where the principal hunting prey these days were innocent old people.

"We read *The Snows of Kilimanjaro* in high school," Marcy said, as she scrubbed turkey fat off the plates.

Didier, whose reading at the Lycée was confined to Pascal, Montaigne, and Thomas Aquinas, nodded noncommittally, hopefully giving the impression that he, too, had read it. It was at times like this that he realized how narrowly focused his education had been and vowed to do something about it. But he never did. And, he had to admit, probably never would. Some time ago, he had decided he was as good as he was ever going to be, and he would leave it at that. Except, of course, in pursuit of Marcy Gray.

In that endeavor, he would do whatever it took. If he had to read Ernest Hemingway, he would manage that.

Didier waited out Sammy Dee, as usual, after Charlie Berns had left. The two of them didn't budge until they were dismissed by their hostess, and they slunk off, with heavy stomachs, alone to their condos.

He lay down on his couch, digesting the turkey with the thick gravy and the abominable mix of tasteless starch they called stuffing, and thought about what he had been thinking about compulsively for the last few days. Who the hell had ordered that pizza with his name on it?

Were his Indians, who had become increasingly aggressive in their demands for a larger cut of the African antiquity racket, sending him a message? But what kind of message kills the recipient? Who was going to sell their handicrafts if he wasn't around?

Had one of the colonels from Ouagadougou survived his term in the Saharan prison and gone out to find him and seek revenge? Some sort of freelance African commando with a long memory? He remembered an African proverb: *Do not anger a hyena. You cannot outrun him.*

The more Didier turned it over in his mind, however, the more he came back to the same place. There was only one person with motive and opportunity, and it was someone he had just shared Thanksgiving dinner with.

What he didn't know was whether the Italian had arranged the whole thing himself, or did he, like Didier, contract the job to a specialist? Were there several contract killers doing business in the Palm Springs area, besides Acme Exterminating and Patio Decks? Or had Sammy Dee decided to check out the guys that Charlie Berns told him about? Was Sammy's getting *his* patio deck redone a few weeks ago more than a coincidence?

Were Walt and Biff planning to get rid of Sammy *and* him? Pocket both fees, as well as the completion money from the one they hit last?

No unhappy customers. No witnesses. No traces. *Pas mal. . .*

Didier let this theory stew in his mind for a while, believing it and discounting it at the same time. It seemed both preposterous and plausible.

And then Sammy Dee's car was blown up in the Vons parking lot. Unfortunately, the Italian wasn't in it.

VII
SAMMY

By the time the screaming died down and the sound of police sirens could be heard in the distance, Sammy Dee was standing outside the supermarket looking at the carcass of his Lexus. All that was left were the chassis, with the steering wheel sticking up like a submarine periscope, and one axle. Everything else was scattered—some pieces, the police would later tell him, a quarter mile away. A man sitting outside Der Wienerschnitzel eating a chili dog was injured by a piece of shrapnel that turned out to be a part of the side view mirror.

When his heartbeat slowed down, Sammy considered whether he should disown his car. Just walk away and hope that the job was thorough enough that there would be no way to identify the owner. Within minutes they would throw up a crime scene tape, and no one would be permitted to leave.

But Sammy had watched enough episodes of *CSI* to know that these guys could make you from an eyelash. And if he were seen leaving the scene of the crime, it would make matters worse.

After the uniforms herded everyone back into the supermarket and the paramedics went through checking for injuries, Detectives Melendez and Guthrie arrived, like a couple of gauchos late for the rodeo. They walked with exaggerated slowness, slower even than Marshal Dillon, if that were possible, and conferred with the uniforms. Then they addressed the small group of shoppers and store personnel.

"I'm Detective Melendez, and this is Detective Guthrie, from the PSPD. We'll do our best to get you out of here and home as soon as possible, but first we need everyone's names, contact, and any information you can give us."

People started talking all at once, claiming that they had to leave, that they had groceries melting, that their children had to go to the bathroom. Melendez quieted them with a loud whistle.

"The more cooperative you are, the faster it will go. Now, before we start taking names, we need to know two things. One, did anyone observe any suspicious activity in the parking lot, before entering or leaving the supermarket?"

An old man with a walker said, "There were a couple of gang-bangers hanging around, casing the cars."

"Okay, sir, Detective Guthrie will take your statement." Then he said, "Does the blown-up car belong to anyone here?"

Sammy sheepishly raised his hand, feeling like a school kid volunteering the correct answer. Melendez looked at him and slowly made the connection. He could see the cop's eyes register recognition. *You again?*

The detectives interviewed him in the store manager's office. Melendez sat behind a cluttered desk, Guthrie beside him, and went through his routine, as if he were taking an oral examination at the Police Academy.

"What type of vehicle was it?"

"Lexus, 450."

"Year?"

It took ten minutes to get through the car shit, during which Guthrie sat with his iPad, running numbers through some computer program, no doubt verifying the information that Sammy was providing, down to the date of the last oil change.

Finally, Melendez got down to business. "Do you have any enemies who might want to do this to you, Mr. Dee?"

"Not that I know of."

"Are you sure about that?"

"I mean, I had a couple of teachers who didn't like me in high school."

The detective flashed him one of his cut-the-shit looks and plowed on. "Where were you immediately before entering the parking lot?"

"Playing golf."

"Where?"

"At Tahquitz Creek."

"Who'd you play with?"

Sammy decided to tell his first lie, or, more aptly, half-truth. They would get the information from the golf starter, if they bothered to check, but he didn't want his connection with Walt and Biff undergoing unnecessary police scrutiny, so he fudged. "A guy I'd played with before. Walt Something. Don't know his last name. Big hitter. Seven handicap. And. . .yeah, there was another guy they put us with, some doctor named Ken, or Kyle, I don't remember."

Leaning back in the chair, Melendez tapped his pen a few times, then cut closer to the chase.

"Mr. Dee, do you think it's entirely a coincidence that you have been in-volved in two attempted murder cases within a few weeks of each other?"

"Jesus, I hope it is," Sammy said, and meant it.

"The poisoned pizza could conceivably have been an accident, though we're still looking into it, but this was clearly attempted murder. Cars don't get blown from here to Cucamonga by accident."

"So you don't think it was a bad spark plug?"

"You know something? You need a better attitude."

Sammy reined in the sarcasm for the remainder of the interrogation, which went on much longer than Sammy thought necessary, even for a couple of cops barking up the right tree.

In the cab on the way back to Paradise Gardens, Sammy allowed him-self to ask the question that had been flooding his thoughts since the car went up. Who was trying to kill him? And why? And, more importantly, what the fuck was he going to do about it?

The local six o'clock news led with the story. The teaser was: *Terrorist Attack in Palm Springs?* The same Asian American anorexic who'd cov-ered the dead cat story did a standup live beside the charred remains of Sammy's car.

"A little after ten o'clock this morning, a powerful explosion rocked the 1700 block of Palm Canyon Drive, apparently coming from a bomb set under a car that had been parked in the lot of our local Vons. Stunned shoppers dove under counters, fearful that the supermarket was under attack. Alexandra Flembar of Cathedral City was at the deli counter when the bomb went off."

They cut to a close-up of a woman in a charcoal suntan wearing shorts and sunglasses. "It's very scary. Terrorists right here, in Palm Springs. . . setting bombs off. Where are you safe these days?"

Next, Tracy Tohito interviewed an old man in a yarmulke. "I'm telling you, this is the work of Al-Qaeda. There're a lot of Jews in Palm Springs. It's the Holocaust all over again. I survived the camps for this?"

Then she spoke to an Iraq war veteran, a tattooed guy standing next to his Harley Road King. "Reminds me of Fallujah. The 'ban were setting off IEDs all over the place. . . blew our APCs into the Persian Gulf."

Once again, Detective Sergeant Jorge Melendez had little to say. When Tracy Tohito tried to pin him down about the possibility of the explosion being a terrorist attack, he said, "We're not ruling anything out at this point."

"The police are being particularly tight-lipped about the events surrounding the explosion, but *Eyewitness News* has learned that the investigation is centering on the owner of the car that the bomb was apparently placed under—a retired cement company executive named Samuel Dee, who, as it turns out, was a person of interest in last month's still-unsolved cat poisoning. . ."

It didn't take long for the shit to hit the fan. The news vans started showing up outside the condo complex. Before the reporters began calling, his special WITSEC phone rang.

"Are you all right?" Marshal Dylan asked him, without apparent interest or sympathy.

"For a guy whose car was just blown up, I'm not too bad."

"First of all, do not—I repeat, do *not*—talk to anyone."

"What about the police?"

"We will fix that. But do not say anything to reporters, or even to friends and family."

"As you know, I don't have any friends or family."

"This is no time for self-pity."

"Frankly, I can't think of a better time."

"You need to avoid being photographed."

"How do I do that?"

"You don't leave your house. And keep your blinds shut."

"Anything else?"

"I'll come by tomorrow."

"How will I know it's you?"

"I'll call you thirty seconds before I ring the doorbell. Keep this phone on."

And the marshal switched off. No good-bye, sleep tight, don't let the bedbugs bite.

Before Sammy could close his blinds or take his regular phone off the hook, an Associated Press reporter called. Sammy told him to go fuck himself.

First, he poured himself a stiff Dewars, something he rarely did in the middle of the day, and then he closed the blinds. The sun was already dipping in its short winter arc. Plopping down on his lumpy couch, he took a couple of healthy hits of the scotch before coming up for air.

His first thought, even while he had still been in the supermarket, had been of his old friends from The Island. Nick the Tip had dropped the dime, and they'd sent someone out to do him. The guy had followed him to the golf course and then to the Vons lot, where he put the bomb under the car while Sammy was inside buying Drano. The bomb was on a timer that exploded prematurely.

He doubted it was The Tip himself. They would have contracted with a pro. Phil Finoccio would have set the whole thing up from prison. There were legendary stories inside the family of revenge hits that had taken years to play out. They would say, in Sicilian, *We'll get you in Hell if we have to.*

What if he hadn't stopped off at Vons? What if he hadn't struggled with the choice of frozen pizza after he'd grabbed the Drano? What if there had been no line at the checkout counter, and he had already been in the car when it blew up? What if he hadn't run into Nick the Tip in the CVS parking lot? What if he hadn't decided to buy rubbers *that* day, or had gone to get them ten minutes earlier or later? What if he hadn't met Marcy Gray and decided to revive his sex life?

What if he had chosen to relocate to Ypsilanti, Tempe, or Jacksonville instead of Palm Springs? What if he hadn't sung on Phil Finoccio? What if he had decided to make an honest living instead of shaking people down for the Nassau County mob? And on and on. . .

It was staggering to consider all the crossroads in his life that had led to someone putting a bomb under his car in a Palm Springs supermarket lot. One different turn, at any point, and he wouldn't be sitting in his condo with the blinds drawn and the phone off the hook.

Lost in this maze of what-ifs, he almost didn't hear the knocking on his door. He got up, walked over, and peeked through the tiny hole. Marcy Gray was standing there. With a casserole.

Opening the door narrowly, he moved her inside quickly and closed the door behind her.

"Sorry," he said. "Reporters."

"I know. They're all over the place."

"Tell me about it." Sammy indicated his telephone off the hook.

"I thought you might be hungry."

He wasn't. But he said he was. "Would you join me?"

"I can't. I have dinner plans."

Sammy used all his willpower to refrain from asking whom she was dining with.

"Look, Marcy, the reporters may try to talk to you."

"They already have. I told them to get lost. I know what you're going through, Sammy. Believe me. I went out to dinner once with Jimmy Caan. For a week afterward, they kept calling me and asking about our relationship. I wouldn't even tell them what Jimmy had for dinner."

"I appreciate that."

"Is there anything I can do?"

"Hopefully, it's going to blow over in a day or two."

"Do you really think it's Al-Qaeda?"

Probably better that she thought he was an innocent victim of a terrorist bombing than the object of gangland revenge. "You never know these days," he said.

"You should get some protection."

"I can handle it, don't worry."

He wound up eating the casserole alone in front of the TV, watching the Lakers get their asses handed to them by Portland. He didn't dare go near the local news.

Sammy was deep in an early-morning stupor, after a largely sleepless night, when his WITSEC phone rang. He had set the ringtone to "The William Tell Overture." The Lone Ranger kept riding over the ridge until Sammy dragged himself out of bed to answer the cell phone.

No one was on the other end. Forgetting about his phone call with Marshal Dillon last night, he returned to bed and was nearly back under when there was a rapping at his door. Again, he struggled to get vertical and went out to the living room, scratching his ass and trying to figure out just what he was going to say to the fucking reporter who had the fucking nerve to fucking knock at his door at, what, seven in the morning?

Through the peephole, Sammy saw the clean-shaven face of Ernest Dylan, United States Marshal. In mufti. With sunglasses. And, unconvincingly, a souvenir Disneyland baseball cap. He let him in and closed the door behind him, stealing a quick glance beyond to see the news vans gone.

"Where are the vultures?"

"We had the police clear them. At least for the moment. They'll be back."

The marshal looked around the place with a Bette Davis what-a-dump! look and helped himself to a barstool.

"It's seven in the morning?" Sammy complained.

"This is time-sensitive."

As if in contradiction, Sammy delivered a monster yawn and went to put together some coffee.

"Washington's not happy about this."

"Not half as unhappy as I am."

"They think you should consider relocation."

"No way."

"Sammy, it's only a matter of time before you're recognized. Sooner or later, there's going to be a picture of you in the papers or on the Internet, if there isn't already."

"No one has taken a picture of me."

"That you know of. Someone could have shot you with a camera phone at the supermarket."

"What the fuck do you guys care? They do me, it's one less guy you've got to take care of."

"As I've explained to you several times, we don't like to lose people."

Sammy turned away from the coffeemaker and faced the marshal. As usual, he felt like he was talking to a wall, but nonetheless he said, "Listen, Marshal, I'm not going through this again. If they get me, they get me. You want, I'll sign a statement saying it wasn't your fault, that I was suicidal, that I had terminal cancer and three months to live. . .whatever. But I'm staying here, in Palm Springs, under the name of Sammy Dee. Okay?"

Dylan nodded slowly and took a deep breath. "I think you need to talk to one of our mental health professionals."

"I'm not talking to anybody! This is what I want to do. I'm a fucking consenting adult who is choosing to live the way he wants to live, posing no danger to anybody but himself."

"That's not entirely true. What if they bomb the condo complex?"

"Who?"

"The people who put the bomb under your car."

"That's not the way they work."

"How do you know?"

"I worked for them for forty years, that's how."

"Maybe it's not them."

"What're you talking about? You know anybody else who wants to kill me?"

"The FBI is looking into the possibility that it may be the work of terrorists of some kind."

"What? You buying that bullshit that the reporters are flinging? They're just beefing up their ratings. C'mon, what does Al-Qaeda have against me?"

"You're Jewish."

"I'm Italian," Sammy protested, momentarily forgetting that he was no longer Salvatore Didziocomo.

"According to your cover backstory, you're an Eastern European Jew whose father changed his name on Ellis Island."

"Who the fuck knows that but you and me?"

"It could be racial profiling."

"You mean, Al-Qaeda decided that I looked like a Jew and decided to off me in the Vons parking lot."

"It's conceivable."

"So is the fact that Elvis is still alive."

"The FBI has launched an investigation. At some point, they'll want to talk to you."

"Tell them to take a number."

"All right, Sammy. I can see you're upset. I'm going to give you some time to calm down and rethink your decision. In the meantime, you need to avoid going out."

"What am I going to do for food?"

"Order takeout."

"We know how safe that is around here."

Dylan suppressed a smile, or perhaps it was just stomach gas. "Keep your phone on," he said, getting up and walking slowly to the door. He was gone as unobtrusively as he had arrived. *Who was that masked man*?

In the back of Sammy's mind lurked the possibility that the hit attempt wasn't the work of Phil Finoccio. But the only other explanation, besides the bullshit about Al-Qaeda and the Taliban, was that it was some random error on the part of someone trying to kill someone else.

If Diddly Shit's car had been parked at Vons, if Diddly Shit *had* a car, or if he had taken a cab to the supermarket, then he could have possibly explained it as the work of Acme, mistaking Sammy's car for the African's car. But how incompetent could they have been in their line of work?

Still, the coincidence of someone trying to kill him while he was trying to kill someone else bothered Sammy. Walt was at the golf course earlier with him and could have had Biff put a bomb under his car that was timed to go off someplace else. But if it was Acme that tried to off Sammy, how were they counting on collecting their money after they offed Diddly Shit?

Whatever the case, Sammy wasn't going to spend the rest of his life behind drawn blinds, eating takeout. He needed help.

Salvatore Didziocomo knew a lot of people who could get a lot of things done, but Sammy Dee didn't have a long list of people to call on for help. He knew a United States marshal, a couple of neighbors, and two scratch golfers who moonlighted as hit men.

The only person he could think of whom he could call on was the same guy who had turned him on to Acme—the film producer down the hall. He had the impression that the guy was still wired, or at least knew people who knew people who were wired. It was worth a shot.

Sammy waited until eleven and then picked up the phone and invited Charlie Berns for a cup of coffee. The man wandered over an hour or so later and accepted a cup of Sammy's espresso.

"So, tell me, Sammy, you getting calls about the film rights?"

"The film rights? To what?"

"Your story. You're a famous guy—a national hero. The TV guys are going to be all over you."

"I'm not answering my phone."

"That won't stop them."

"I don't get it. Somebody blows up my car—for all we know, if could be a complete accident—wrong guy, wrong car, random violence, and suddenly I'm a fucking hero."

"It makes no difference—it's a good story. And a good story doesn't have to be true. Listen, if you want, I'll put you in touch with someone to cut a deal for you."

"What kind of deal?"

"I'd go for worldwide media—film, TV, dramatic theater, Internet, apps, the whole ball of wax. You get what you can up front and walk away smelling green."

"Charlie, I got a different problem."

"What's that?"

"I need this to go away."

The film producer looked at him oddly, nodded slowly, took a sip of his espresso.

"Let me get this straight—you don't want to cash in on this?"

"What I want is to be able to go outside without cameras pointing at me."

Charlie Berns nodded, as if digesting this information with some difficulty, then said, "Why don't you just take a vacation to . . . I don't know,
New Zealand? These things usually have a short shelf life."

"I want to stay here."

"Here? Like in Palm Springs?"

"Here. Like at Paradise Gardens."

"You like it here?"

This time Sammy nodded.

"What I need is someone to make this disappear. I need someone to fix
this for me."

"Uh-huh. . .You need a fixer."

"What's a fixer?"

"You ever see *Pulp Fiction*?"

Sammy shook his head.

"Harvey Keitel shows up to clean up the mess that Travolta and Samuel
L make. He scrubs down the car, gets rid of the blood, makes everything
just the way it was before the shit happened."

"You know someone who can do that?"

"Yeah," Charlie Berns said, as if someone had asked if he could recommend a good dry cleaner. "Kermit Fenster."

"Who?"

"He's a guy who once got me out of jail in Turkmenistan."

"You were in jail in Turkmenistan?"

"Long story. Anyway, this guy's a little strange. He claims to be an ex-
CIA agent who still has a pipeline into the agency. I have no idea whether
it's true or not, but I never met anyone who can get things done like him. I
needed to find a telegenic warlord in Uzbekistan—he got me one. I needed
to get out of Azerbaijan without a passport, he got me on a cargo plane to
Brussels. You want an Estonian hooker? He'll get you three."

"And you think this guy can get this story to go away?"

"If anyone can, he can."

"Where is he?"

"I don't know."

"So how do you contact him?"

"There's a phone number in Montevideo. With an answering machine. You leave a message. He calls back. Or not. You never know with him."

"He lives in Uruguay?"

"I don't think he actually lives there. But that's how you have to contact him."

"The thing is, I don't have a lot of money."

"Oddly enough, that doesn't seem to be his motivation. He tells you he'll arrange what you want arranged and then one day he's going to ask *you* for something. You're in his debt. Like the opening scene in *The Godfather*. Remember? The undertaker comes to Brando and asks him to avenge his daughter's dishonor, and Don Corleone agrees to do it, but tells him that someday he'll ask him for repayment? And then when his father's in the hospital, Pacino finds the guy to help protect him. Debt settled. That's the deal with Kermit Fenster."

"Has he ever asked you to pay him back?"

"About three years ago, he calls me. Out of the clear blue sky. No hello, how are you?—he just asks me to get him tickets to the Golden Globes. I had to pull every string I had to get it done. And then, he doesn't show up."

"Jesus. . ."

"Somebody should make a movie about *him*. I've thought about it, but no one would believe it. Anyway, if you want, I'll call him, let him know you have a problem. If he says yes, you can call him directly."

"I appreciate that, Charlie."

"Just being a good neighbor."

Charlie Berns got up, unfolding his rumpled figure from the couch, thanked Sammy for the coffee and left. Sammy crossed to the blinds, cracked them an inch, and looked out. Chris and Edie were sitting on chaise lounges by the pool talking to Tracy Tohito. A cameraman was filming the interview.

Taliban Target Swings! Details at Eleven!

After the police and the United States Marshals Service had interviewed him, Sammy was treated to a visit from the FBI. Two guys drove up from the San Diego field office to ask him a lot of questions he had no answers to. Mostly, they wanted to know about his travels, and when he told them he had never been outside the United States—except for a trip to a whorehouse in Montreal when he was twenty—they didn't want to believe him.

"Never even been to the Caribbean? Or Mexico?"

"Nope."

They had apparently been briefed by the DOJ about his real identity, though they continued to address him as Mr. Dee. It was refreshing to be able to reassume the persona of Salvatore Didziocomo, if only to talk to the FBI. It was as if he were referring to someone else, speaking in the third person about this man he used to be.

"No family abroad? Internet contacts?"

"Afraid not."

The next question made him aware that they had already done some digging on him. "You spend a fair amount of time on porn sites, Mr. Dee, don't you?"

Sammy wanted to ask him what the fuck business it was of his, but knew that the only way to get them out of his house was to be cooperative.

"No more than most men."

"Some of these sites originate from Eastern Europe and Russia."

"So?"

No response. They'd moved on to his Internet purchases, his cleaning lady's name and nationality, the dealership where he bought the Lexus, before finally realizing that they were flailing around fruitlessly. They, too, handed him their cards and cautioned him to get in touch immediately if anyone contacted him or demonstrated unusual interest in him or the car bombing.

And they were gone, leaving nothing behind them but the fading smell of shoe polish.

The next time Marcy Gray came by with a casserole, she brought Diddly Shit with her. With a bottle of Château something or other. They sat around Sammy's kitchen table, drinking the wine and eating Marcy's overspiced coq au vin.

"Why do you not just give them one interview, and then they will go away?" Diddly Shit asked.

"These people don't take yes for an answer."

"In my business," Marcy said, "there is no such thing as bad publicity. The phone starts ringing when you get into the papers. Doesn't matter how. Eddie Murphy got caught getting blown by a tranny on Sunset Boulevard, and the offers didn't stop piling up on his agent's desk."

"I don't understand, Sa*mee*, why are you being so coy?"

Coy? Scared was more like it. Sammy was convinced that Diddly Shit was actually disappointed that he hadn't been in the car when it blew. The African wouldn't even wait till the body was cold. He'd be all over her the night of the funeral. If not before.

Would there even be a funeral? He was struck by the numbing realization of the possibility that there would be no one around to bury him. There was no reason to expect the United States Marshals Service to send him off in style. Would they even bother notifying his daughter? Or if they did, would Sharon show up? And would Howard allow her to pay for his burial? The government wouldn't spend a dime on the cost of disposing of his remains. They'd cremate him in a nuclear waste facility in the Nevada desert.

When Sammy had changed identities, he had signed some sort of DOJ boilerplate will that left his assets, net of government expenses, to his designated heir(s). There was language about the government reimbursing itself for the cost of relocating him. At the time, he had figured that there would be nothing left when he croaked and hadn't bothered to name anyone.

Now he wasn't so sure that he wanted to make it that easy for them. He would make them go through Sharon and account for the fact that there was no money for her. That, at least, would leave some trace of his existence. The thought that he could vanish from the earth without anyone knowing or giving a shit was beyond depressing.

"I'm not being coy," Sammy replied to Diddly Shit's question. "I just don't like my privacy invaded."

"If you tell them what they want, they will go away."

"Not necessarily. You don't know American tabloid reporters."

"Believe me, Sa*mee*, they are better than the French. Have you forgotten Princess Diana, driven into the wall of the tunnel by that pack of *chiens*?"

"That was so awful," Marcy said. "I was in this TV movie about her, back in the nineties. I played a tabloid reporter hounding her. . ."

"Look," Sammy said, eager to get off the subject. "I was the victim of some random act of terrorism or whatever. I just happened to be in the wrong place at the wrong time. I don't deserve this attention, and I'm not going to encourage it by telling them anything. Period. By the way, this is very nice wine, *Deedeeyay.*"

"2009. A very good year in Médoc."

"You know so much about wine, Didier. . ." Marcy purred.

The fucker was showing off again. And she was lapping it up. He hoped they'd poison his wine instead of his pizza next time. He could go out in style.

Then Marcy started with this cockamamie idea that he should let them make a movie about him. She came over, dressed to kill, and pitched him about all the money he could make if he let a writer come and talk to him.

"The story doesn't even have to be true," she said. "Just take the money and run."

It would be serious money. Maybe seven figures. Seven figures could solve a lot of problems in his life. It would, at the very least, move him up over Diddly Shit in the Marcy Gray sweepstakes. And even after Acme removed the African from contention—if they ever fucking actually got the job done—it would be helpful to have enough money to wine and dine her properly. They could forget about early bird specials at the Olive Garden. They could gobble caviar and take Mediterranean cruises. They could move out of this dump and leave the odor of cat piss behind them.

Marshall Dillon would shit a brick, of course. He'd threaten to cut off Sammy's lifeline, but by then Sammy wouldn't need it. God, he would love to tell that asshole goodbye. *Arrivederci,* Fuckface.

He could give an interview in a ski mask to some screenwriter and make things up. He could hire another writer to write an imaginary biography to give to the screenwriter. It would all be bullshit and provide no insight into his real past or present. A cement executive who doubled as a CIA counter-terrorist expert, who was high on Al-Qaeda's hit list.

Sammy played with this pipedream for a few days, while he and Marcy went over various casting possibilities to play him. Jimmy Caan? Harrison Ford? Clint? Pacino? Why the hell not? It was all pie in the sky anyway.

But even the pleasure of pleasing the woman he was in love with or telling a United States marshal to go fuck himself didn't compensate for his blowing his cover. One way or another, those vultures would unpeel the onion and Salvatore Didziocomo would emerge. With a big bull's-eye on his head. They would bury him with his seven figures.

No, it was back to Plan A. Get Diddly Shit out of the way and move in on the prize. Let Charlie Berns's fixer clean things up for him. When the time came, he'd break the news gently to Marcy that there would be no Sammy Dee story at the local Cineplex.

Marcy Gray happened to be there when Kermit Fenster showed up at Paradise Gardens to fix Sammy Dee's problem. Sammy had left a message on the answering machine in Uruguay, as instructed by Charlie Berns, leaving his WITSEC cell phone number—in direct violation of his agreement with them. It couldn't be helped. Sammy wasn't answering his land line, which rang a dozen times a day with interview requests.

How the man found out just where Sammy lived without calling was obviously not beyond the talents of a man who could get you out of Azerbaijan without a passport. Sammy and Marcy were sitting out on his patio talking about the upcoming Christmas holiday, which neither of them was looking forward to.

Sammy wasn't happy about being besieged in his own home, reduced to eating casseroles and watching TV. Though the tabloid coverage had died down, he was convinced that all it would take would be one sighting of him—at Vons, on the golf course, at a restaurant—and the jackals would be all over him.

For her part, Marcy claimed to be suffering from her annual seasonal depression. The Holiday Blues, her shrink called it.

"I don't have any family, except my actor friends," she bemoaned.

"That's more than I have."

"Sammy, everybody at Paradise Gardens likes you."

"Your friend Didier isn't a big fan."

"You know, it would be nice if the two of you got along better. I mean, why not? You're about the same age, you're both smart, well-informed men."

If only he could tell her she was sitting on ceramic tile that constituted the down payment for Sammy's contract on the African. Is there anything more flattering to a woman than a man passionate enough to have his rival killed?

These thoughts were interrupted by his doorbell. He chose to ignore it.

"You're not going to answer it?"

"It's probably some reporter. Eventually, they go away."

The ringing, however, did not go away.

"Let me answer it," Marcy volunteered. "In case they have a camera."

She'd never met a camera she didn't like, Sammy thought, as Marcy walked inside, crossed the living room, looking delectable to him, as usual, in a pair of well-cut toreador slacks and platform shoes.

She opened the door to a short, slender man in a Dacron summer suit and Panama hat. The man had no visible camera or recording device. He took his hat off, revealing a seriously receding hairline, and said, "Kermit Fenster. Nice to meet you."

At the sound of the name, Sammy walked into the living room, surprised to see Charlie Berns's fixer standing in his doorway.

"Come in."

Fenster entered, closing the door behind him. He took a long, admiring look at Marcy and then smiled. "Marcy Gray, am I right?"

Marcy nodded eagerly.

"You're even better-looking in person," Fenster said.

She blushed a beautiful pale burgundy that Sammy wanted to sip slowly.

"Marcy was just going," Sammy said.

"Nice meeting you," she smiled thinly, clearly a little miffed at his not-so-subtle dismissal of her.

"Likewise," Fenster said, his eyes following her out the door. "Good-looking broad," he said to Sammy as Marcy disappeared.

"How'd you find me?"

Fenster looked at him as if Sammy had asked how he had managed to walk in the door. "This place secure?" he asked, ignoring the question and looking around the condo.

"Secure?"

"Can anyone hear our conversation?"

"Doubt it. Mrs. Epstein next door can't even hear when you're shouting at her."

"Bugs?"

"Who would bug me?"

"Let's see. . .how about the United States Marshals Service? Or the Finoccio family out of New York? For starters."

Sammy looked at the man incredulously. What the fuck?

"How'd you know that?"

"Mind if I sit down? I got a bunion on my foot that's killing me. And I could use a cup of coffee. Two sugars, low-fat milk."

Kermit Fenster helped himself to one of the kitchenette stools while Sammy scooped some coffee into the coffeemaker.

"You know everything?" he asked.

"I know what I need to know."

"What did Charlie tell you?"

"That you needed something fixed. I told him I'd take care of it, as long as it wasn't a hit. I don't do hits."

Sammy closed the sliding glass door to the patio and then lowered his voice, as if someone could actually overhear them. "I need to get this story of me and the bombing out of the news, at least enough so I can go outside without being photographed."

"That's all?"

"You can do that?"

"I can do that."

"How?"

"That's need-to-know, Sammy, and you don't need to know."

"How long will it take you?"

"A week, maybe ten days. Depends on what else happens over that period. Of course, if the North Koreans lob a warhead at Hawaii, or Angela and Brad break up, it'll be a lot faster. You'll be buried in the ashes."

Fenster elaborated: "You need to be overshadowed by something bigger. And that shouldn't be very hard. You see, celebrity is a zero sum game. There's only so much of it to go around. One person gets famous, someone else fades into the woodwork. Never fails. July 18, 1969—Mary Jo

Kopechne gets drowned by Teddy Kennedy. Two days later, Neil Armstrong walks on the moon, and it's Mary Jo *who*?"

"Charlie told you that I didn't have any money?"

"Sammy, I am not a whore. I'm a fixer. I fix things for people I like or friends of people I like. Charlie and I go back a long time. He's a standup guy."

"That's great," Sammy said, pouring the coffee. "If there's anything I can do for you, now or later, just let me know."

"I will. You can count on it."

Ten minutes later, having drunk his coffee, Kermit Fenster left. Sammy sat wondering how this strange man was going to manipulate the media and get him out of the spotlight, and decided he didn't want to know. There were a number of things in life he didn't want to know—his cholesterol count, whether the Iranians really had nuclear weapons, just what had transpired between Marcy Gray and Diddly Shit when he wasn't there. . . and he didn't want to know how Kermit Fenster was going to make it possible for him to go into Vons without people aiming camera phones at him and posting his picture on the Internet, where Phil Finoccio and his band of underemployed, vengeful goons would see it and send a guy out to Palm Springs with a high-powered assault weapon.

Or why.

In the week following the bombing at Vons, replacing his car was the last thing on Sammy's mind. He hadn't even bothered to report the loss to the insurance company, assuming—erroneously, as it turned out—that everyone, including his friends at State Farm, knew what had happened to him.

The day after Kermit Fenster paid his visit and eight days after the incident, he finally made the call and, after surfing through endless automated options on the 800 number, got some woman who was apparently operating out of a bunker in Kansas.

"May I have your policy number, please?" she asked.

"I don't have it handy." He didn't. To the best of his knowledge, it was somewhere with his papers in one of several places in the condo, or, just as possibly, he may have thrown it out along with other superfluous pieces of paper.

"Name, last name first, and social security number?"

He gave them to her and waited for what seemed a very long time. Then, she said, "Dee, Samuel. Date of birth and mother's maiden name, please?"

The DOJ had given him a fictitious mother's maiden name, but he couldn't for the life of him remember it. "I just have my date of birth, okay?"

"You don't know your mother's maiden name?" She uttered these words, as if to say, *What kind of son are you?*

"She got remarried a bunch of times. I keep getting them mixed up."

"*Maiden* name, not married name."

"Gimme a break. . ."

"Is this for a claim, Mr. Dee?"

"Yes."

"Involving the 2012 Lexus?"

"Yes."

"Date and time?"

"It was a week ago Wednesday—no, a week ago Tuesday, eight days ago. . ."

"You're first reporting it now?"

"I've been kind of busy."

"Is there a police report?"

He was about to ask her if she had been watching television over the last week, but then he realized that the story may have died quickly in Kansas.

"You bet," he said.

"Any injuries?"

"None. I mean, people were shaken up, but. . .somebody put a bomb under my car in the parking lot at Vons. . ."

This time the pause lasted a full ten seconds. "Excuse me," she said finally. "Did you say a bomb?"

"Yes. A bomb. It completely destroyed the car."

"We're going to have to get back to you, Mr. Dee."

"What do you mean, *get back to me*? This is the claims line, right?"

"Accidents brought about by acts of terrorism are handled by a different department."

"Act of terrorism? Somebody was trying to kill somebody and they just hit the wrong car."

It was to no avail. The woman told him that he would be contacted by someone in the policy coverage department within seven working days and disconnected him. But not before saying, "In the meantime, I suggest you try to remember your mother's maiden name."

The only person who had that information was someone he didn't want to talk to. He got the Lone Ranger out and dialed the number.

"What's the problem, Sammy?" the marshal answered, without bothering to say hello.

"I forgot my mother's maiden name."

"That's not good."

"I realize that."

"We've stressed the fact that you need to indelibly memorize the data of your new identity."

"Yes, you have. Now can you just give it to me?"

"Why do you need it?"

"Why do you need to know why I need it?"

More silence. This was a lose/lose strategy. Sammy told him about his problem with State Farm.

"You know, you should have reported the accident immediately."

"I was in shock."

"For over a week?"

This time Sammy resorted to silence until he heard the keys of the marshal's computer. "Lebow," he pronounced, finally. "We chose it because it's a swing name. Could be any ethnicity."

"Thank you."

His real mother's name was Angela. Angela "Angie" Didziocomo, née Grazziani. When his father was pissed at her, he would grumble: "She thinks she's Angie Dickinson, your mother." And his mother would glare back at him with a look that said, *If I didn't marry you, I could've been.*

Their mutual hostility was no doubt some sort of mutated form of love, but you could've fooled young Salvatore, who felt as if he were growing up in a combat zone. The family apartment in Corona often resembled a rowdy music hall in Palermo, the audience tossing rotten tomatoes onto the stage accompanied by a volley of guttural slurs.

Now he had the opportunity to change all that. His fictional past was his to re-create. Mrs. Lebow could be a warm, nurturing woman, instead of the bitter, frustrated Angie Didziocomo. Why not? It was one of the few things he liked about witness protection: he could reinvent his past. If he did it convincingly enough, maybe he could learn to believe it.

They didn't give her a first name, so he made one up. Sophie. Sophie Lebow. A nice name. She was a big woman, warm and tender, spent hours in the kitchen preparing dishes for him, a pampered only child whose father sent generous support checks from his home in Oyster Bay.

Jesus. He shut down the fantasy before it got completely out of hand. Maybe he really did need to see one of the Marshals Service's mental health professionals, revisit the apartment in Corona and his toilet training. And when they got through with that stuff, they could move on to why he had spent a good chunk of his life sitting around in cars and restaurants with a bunch of dumb fucks waiting to do something he never enjoyed doing.

Sammy wasn't sure he wanted the answer to that question either.

Being without a car was not a major inconvenience for Sammy, at least not until the publicity fatwa was lifted. The fact was he had no place to go. They were still out there, lying in wait with cameras. Marcy did his shopping and brought cooked dishes over. Unfortunately, she often brought Diddly Shit, too.

They became a peculiar ménage à trois, hunkered down dining and drinking wine while the Indians surrounded the stockade. Marcy, for her part, seemed to be enjoying the situation, especially when the odd camera caught her going in or out of Sammy's place. It was as if she were on the red carpet at Cannes, being snapped up by the paparazzi.

Whatever it was that Kermit Fenster did to get him out of the news, it worked. Like gangbusters. A week to the day after the man had paid him a visit, Sammy was watching the Lakers when a news bulletin flashed across the screen: BREAKTHROUGH IN VONS PARKING LOT BOMBING: DETAILS AT 11.

They led with the story. Jason Echeverra, the Latino anchor with the sculpted hair, announced that the police had uncovered new evidence in the bombing. They cut to Tracy Tohito standing at the now-vacant spot in the Vons parking lot—a small crater, set off by construction sawhorses, replacing the police tape—microphone in hand.

"I'm standing here at the site of the terrorist bombing ten days ago. *Eyewitness News* has learned that Samuel Dee, the retired cement mogul, was not, as previously believed, the target of the assassination attempt. A car belonging to Esfandyar Fahran, an undercover Afghan informant, was parked next to Samuel Dee's 2012 Lexus, and was the real target of the bombing, the terrorist apparently mistaking his car for one belonging to Fahran. The Afghan national had been on the Taliban's hit list ever since he furnished allied intelligence with drone targets in Kandahar in the Pashtun region of Afghanistan. He was apparently traced to Palm Springs, where he had been laying low. His whereabouts at the moment are not known, but FBI sources believe he is no longer in the area. Sources at the PSPD are saying little about this new development in the case. . ."

They cut to Tracy Tohito ambushing Detective Sergeant Jorge Melendez exiting Palm Springs Police Department headquarters in a Hawaiian shirt and a plaid bowling ball carrier.

"We have no comment on that, Tracy," he said, getting into his late-model SUV and driving off—to the Desert Oasis Lanes for his bowling league night.

Then there was some banter between Tracy Tohito and Jason Echeverra: "Don't know about you, Tracy, but I'm going to look around me a little more carefully before I park my car at the supermarket," the anchorman said with a little smirk on his face.

"Talk about being in the wrong place at the wrong time," she replied, shaking her head ruefully.

"In other news," Jason Echeverra plowed on, "all two-hundred seventeen passengers and the crew of a Chilean jumbo jet were killed when their plane skidded off the runway at Santiago airport this morning . . ."

Sammy hit the remote, turning off pictures of the smoldering carcass of the Chilean airplane and breathing a sigh of relief. Along with relief came a sense of incredulity. How the hell did the funny little man in the wrinkled suit pull it off?

Sammy went to bed that night relieved that he was no longer tabloid bait, but still aware of the fact that someone—and it wasn't the Taliban—

wanted him dead. Whatever bullshit Kermit Fenster managed to get the public to accept, Sammy Dee still had to deal with the fact that Phil Finoccio had tried to whack him, and that there was no reason to believe that he would stop after one failure. *We'll get you in Hell if we have to. . .*

He'd been living with this fear ever since the car went up. But he was learning that fear had its own law of diminishing returns. Every day it receded a little farther from his consciousness, overtaken by the events of the day. It had induced in him a sense of fatalism that was actually liberating. If his number was up, it was up. If it wasn't a hit man, it would be cancer or a Chilean jetliner. No one was getting out of here alive.

The next morning, after making sure that the reporters were, in fact, gone, he walked out of his condo, squinting into the flat desert sunlight like a prisoner who had been locked in a cellar. He knocked on Charlie Berns's door to thank him and was greeted by the film producer in his bathrobe and slippers.

"Sorry, Charlie, hope I didn't wake you?"

"I always get up twelve hours before I go to work, gives me time to shower and grab a cup of coffee. . .Old Lenny Bruce routine he used to use when people called him in the morning. Come on in."

"Thanks, but I got a bunch of things I got to do in town."

"The reporters gone?"

"You didn't see the news last night?"

"No. What happened?"

"They found out that the target of the Vons bombing wasn't me."

"Really? Who was it?"

"An Afghan double agent. The Taliban are after him."

Charlie chuckled, shook his head in admiration, and murmured, "Fenster."

"Yeah. Just wanted to thank you for him."

"The Taliban. He's good."

Sammy decided to check out the lease prices on a new Porsche. Why the fuck not? *Carpe diem. Carpe* everything, for that matter. Now that he was no longer a prisoner in his home, he would escalate his campaign. When he got back from car shopping, he'd call Marcy. Invite her for a weekend at La Costa. They'd drive down in the Carrera, which, fortunately, sat only two.

State Farm finally got back to him. Now that the Taliban was involved, the destruction of his car was officially deemed the result of "an act of terrorism," and, as stipulated by Article 16, Paragraph 6, Subsection F, not covered by his policy. He was, as his Good Neighbor put it, shit out of luck.

With no Lexus to trade in, he would have to lease the Porsche. And that would require a financial background check, which he may or may not survive. He still owed money on his home improvement loan and had already tapped into the equity on the condo. The computer might very well spit him out. He was going to have to convince them to hand over the keys to a sixty-thousand-dollar vehicle with only his mortgaged condo as collateral. Worse, if the car dealer made him as the guy whose car was blown up, mistakenly or not, in the Vons parking lot, he would no doubt consider him a poor risk.

Did he dare ask Marcy Gray to co-sign his car lease? She had co-signed his patio deck contract. If he kept coming to her for money, she would start to see him as the deadbeat he was. It was bad enough that he was living in Paradise Gardens with a limited wardrobe and the ashes of a Lexus in an urn above his fireplace. But a Porsche was still a Porsche. Wasn't it? What woman could resist a man behind the wheel of a new Carrera?

So once again, he knocked on her door and told her that the worst thing that could happen would be that she would have to take possession of a brand-new automobile. She could sell it, pay off the lease. Or she could drive around the Springs stopping traffic.

So he got the Carrera—silver gray, in her honor—with black leather interior, walnut dash, and racing tires. $4,999 down and $890 a month for thirty-nine months. By then he would either be at the bottom of the Salton Sea wearing a cement boot, or, preferably, living off the fat of the land with Marcy Gray.

He drove it home from the dealership and pulled into the parking space beside her car. As he emerged from the parking garage, car keys jangling from his fingers, ready to knock on the door to announce the good news, he heard the loud piercing sound of a pneumatic drill. And it was coming from the African's patio, where two men in Acme Exterminating and Patio Deck jumpsuits were chewing up the old deck in preparation for installing a new one.

He put the Porsche keys in his pocket and walked to his condo. Inside, he double-locked the door. Then he poured himself a very large glass of single malt and allowed the realization to sink in that it was not Phil Finoccio who'd blown up his car. While he had been playing golf with Walt and his periodontist, Biff was booby-trapping his car. If Sammy hadn't gone into Vons to get the Drano. . .

Holy shit.

VIII
MARCY

Sammy Dee's car getting blown up in the Vons parking lot had a definite effect on Marcy Gray's program of due diligence in determining which of the two men would be her lover, if not her next husband. It gave her pause, to put it mildly. What kind of man gets his car blown up at a supermarket?

Best-case scenario: Sammy was a victim of random violence; his car just happened to be parked in the wrong place at the wrong time. But there was the cat poisoning—for which he very well may have been the target—and Evelyn Duboff's opinion that Sammy was trying to hide his past. It seemed increasingly improbable that he was merely a nice half-Jewish retiree who had made a little money selling cement.

Reporters were camped outside Paradise Gardens, waylaying residents and pumping them for stories about their neighbor. Though Marcy had never been publicity-shy, she refused to answer any questions about Sammy Dee. It was bad enough that he had narrowly escaped getting killed, but did the poor man have to be harassed by the tabloid press?

These feelings, however, did not prevent Marcy from taking extra care with her appearance. She no longer went out in running shoes and tracksuits, and she chose a lipstick shade that complemented her outfits. After all, there was no reason to look like a poorly dressed Palm Springs matron with nothing better to wear than shmatas she picked up in the bargain bin at Penney's.

Au contraire. She was the companion, potentially the girlfriend, of a man whom the media were pursuing. She was a mature, fascinating, enticingly *damaged* woman, whose life was lived on the edge of intrigue. And she had to act and dress the part. Sharon Stone in *Basic Instinct*. Okay, that was a bit of a stretch. More like Glenn Close in *Reversal of Fortune*.

With the reporters camped out in front of the building, she brought hot dinners over for Sammy, who was trapped in his condo with the shades drawn. As the flashbulbs popped, she was careful to turn her face profile right, her good side, but resisted smiling or waving. That would have been really tacky.

Sammy was visibly shaken. Yet she resisted asking questions about why there had been a bomb under his car. If he wanted to talk about it, that was fine, but she wasn't going to pry. She had hired Evelyn Duboff to do that.

As if he had some sort of sixth sense that told him when Sammy was alone with her, Didier showed up, with a bottle of wine, and the three of them had dinner together. Sammy didn't say or eat very much, and Didier dominated the conversation, such as it was, talking about the art business. Things were apparently a little slow in the African antiquity market.

"It is the recession. No one seems to have the money. And yet they still throw it into the stock market. *Incroyable*. They might as well toss it into the ocean, to be washed out by the tide. They must know that art, like gold, increases in value during difficult times. It is tangible, not to mention beautiful. . ."

Sammy didn't bother commenting. Usually he would offer some deflating remark about Didier's life and business, but he was too preoccupied to indulge in running down his rival. Instead, he stared blankly at the camera lights leaking through the blinds.

Occasionally, he shook his head and murmured, "Vultures." There was nothing more forthcoming from him about why his condo was besieged by reporters. And, as usual, Didier didn't leave until she did, waiting her out as they got sleepy from the wine. Sammy refused to turn the TV on. "I don't want to encourage them," he said with endearing, if faulty, logic.

The next morning, the reporters were gone. Ethel Esmitz said that the police had dispersed them late last night, claiming that they were disturbing the peace. They were replaced by ACLU picketers defending the right of journalists to harass people. It didn't take long for the Arab Anti-Defamation League to show up to protest racial profiling in the assumption that the people who tried to kill Sammy Dee were Middle Eastern, and they, naturally, brought out the Jewish Defense League. Which, of course, brought the police back to keep these two groups from each other's throats. And, eventually, the reporters returned to cover the confrontation with the police.

"My God," the PGHOA president declared. "You'd think we were in Iraq, or Paris, or someplace like that." She was holding court in the multipurpose room, where a meeting had been called to discuss the latest development.

"We are going from cat murderers to senior citizen bombings," Tuuli complained. Majda agreed, nodding demonstrably. They looked like a couple of crones in an Ingmar Bergman movie, *The Witches of Skövde*. They sat there in matching cardigans, knitting contrapuntally, the surviving cat on one of their laps.

Mrs. Epstein—Sammy's neighbor, wearing a seersucker dress that was probably out of fashion when she'd bought it during the Second World War—kept clicking her tongue, shaking her head, and repeating, "It's awful, it's terrible," and other lamentations that Marcy thought were in Yiddish.

The one positive result of the deluge of press attention coming from the car bombing was that they no longer needed a community watch program. No one was getting in or out of Paradise Gardens unobserved.

Sammy didn't show up. He wanted, no doubt, to avoid the hostility—spoken or silent—of his neighbors, who considered him the cause of their sudden notoriety. It was bad enough that he was a suspected cat assassin, but now he was also a possible terrorist, or counter-terrorist, or just a run-of-the-mill criminal who had crossed powerful underworld elements. His empty parking space stood gaping at them like a gravesite waiting for an occupant.

Sammy Dee's brush with death had a peculiar effect on Marcy. The incident should have moved him down the short list, well below Didier. Did she really want to spend the rest of her life worrying every time she got into a car with him? At this point in her life, she was looking more for security than adventure.

And yet—go figure—she found herself more attracted to Sammy Dee after the bombing than before. Her pulse quickened in his presence. Her body felt unfamiliar stirrings. It was as if the danger around him emitted some sort of pheromone.

She was perplexed enough about this reaction that she decided to have a phone session with Janet.

"It's like I'm back in high school, turned on by the bad boy. James Dean in *Rebel Without a Cause*. After I saw that movie, I went home and masturbated. Can you believe that?"

"Yes."

"You can?"

"It's a post-adolescent reaction against your parents."

"My parents have been dead for twenty years."

"That's what *you* think."

"Huh?"

"On some level, our parents never die. Erikson says we don't really become adults while our parents are still alive."

If Marcy was looking for solace, she had dialed the wrong number.

"So I just ignore these feelings? Pretend they don't exist?"

"You don't have to ignore them. You just don't act on them. Unless, of course, you want to."

"Get involved with a guy whose car gets blown up?"

"It would seem that you already are involved with him. Emotionally, at least. The rest of the deal is up to you."

"I just wish I knew what his story is."

"Ask him."

"Right. Hello, are you in witness protection, and is somebody trying to kill you?"

"Why not? If it's important for you to know?"

"What if he lies to me?"

"Then you'll either be falsely comforted or falsely alarmed. That is, if you discover that he didn't tell you the truth. Which might not be the case. Some people are very accomplished liars."

Marcy let out a long, aspirated sigh to express her frustration with this psycho-talmudic wisdom.

"Listen," Janet said in her let's-wind-up-I-have-another-patient tone of voice. "If I were you, I'd just go with the pitch."

"That's some fella you got there, darling."

Evelyn Duboff's flat New York diphthongs came over the phone the morning after Sammy Dee's car was blown up. Marcy was on her second cup of coffee, hung over from Didier's bottle of first-growth Bordeaux, as well as groggy from a sleepless night trying to figure out why she wanted to have anything to do with a man that people were clearly trying to kill.

"You heard?"

"Heard? It's all the over the TV. Apparently your condo complex is surrounded by reporters."

"Yeah, it's terrible. We're like trapped inside."

"So it looks like someone wants your guy dead."

"You don't think it was some random thing?" Marcy asked, but without conviction. She had been over and over it in her mind, groping for some reason to believe that Sammy had merely parked his car over a bomb meant for someone else.

"The short answer is *no*. Anyway, it looks like our WITSEC scenario is right on the money. It's got to be somebody he testified against."

"Who do you think it is?"

"I got a couple of ideas, but nothing specific yet. I'm working the data on recent canaries on the East Coast. If I can get you a physical description, maybe we can do a match and get you his real name."

Marcy wasn't sure she wanted Sammy's real name. At this point, what difference did it make whether his name was Sammy Dee or Dean Martin?

"They're going to try to relocate him."

"Shit. Really?" Marcy blurted before she could stop herself.

"The DOJ doesn't like their stoolies to get made. It puts a damper on their attempts to get other people to talk."

"Can they do that to him if he doesn't want to?"

"Technically, no, but they can put pressure on him. They can cut off his living allowance. They can stop his mail drop. They can even take away his social security and medicare if they really want to get nasty."

"There still hasn't been any picture of him on the news, or in the paper."

"Well, it looks like *somebody* knows who he really is. Somebody with a bug up their tush. Listen, darling, if I were you, I'd keep a little distance. I wouldn't want you to be collateral damage."

Marcy couldn't see herself walking away totally from Sammy Dee, especially now, when he really needed her. Who was going to bring him hot meals and go shopping for his beer and pretzels?

And even if she wanted to walk away, how would she do it? Relocate herself? Move back to LA, to that apartment in Studio City with the postage-stamp pool and the cottage-cheese ceiling? Get her agent to put her up for laxative commercials?

No, for better or worse, she had to stick by Sammy, his own damaged woman—even if she ended up like Faye Dunaway, getting shredded by machine bullets alongside Warren Beatty.

"You want to hear about the African?"

"Is this good news or bad news?"

"I don't know yet. It could be either. Or nothing. But your guy applied for a home improvement loan."

"Didier took out a loan?"

"Twenty-five grand. From Wells Fargo."

"What for?"

"A new patio deck."

"That's exactly what Sammy did."

"I know. Strange coincidence, huh?"

"Yeah. Wow. What does it mean?"

"Beats me, but does it seem kosher to you that both a WITSEC stoolie and a former drug dealer would be that concerned about their patio decks?"

Marcy silently shook her head. After a moment, Evelyn Duboff said, "Stay tuned, darling. I'll be back to you when I have more."

That was the first interesting phone call of the day. The second was from her agent, Artie Reman. She hadn't spoken to him since she had moved to Palm Springs.

"How you doin', doll?"

"Okay, I guess. *You're* calling *me*?"

As she asked the rhetorical question, she remembered the sick joke about the actor who comes home to find his wife beaten and raped. When she tells him it was his agent who did this to her, he beams and says, "My agent *came by*?"

"I saw you on television."

"Really? Oh, you mean on the news?"

"Yeah. You were going in to see your famous neighbor, Sammy Dee."

"Oh *that*. . .he's just a friend."

Marcy waited for the pitch. There was no way that Artie Reman had called her just to say hello.

"So, listen, at the staff meeting this morning, guess whose name came up?"

"Mine?" she replied, playing along with what she hoped wasn't just a cruel game.

"You bet."

"Meryl die?"

He laughed. It was a bad joke, but it cleared the air. They had been in business for twenty years, and the least he could do was not bullshit her.

"Give me the emmis, Artie? Okay?"

"Okay. After the meeting, my office was full of lit agents. They all want to get the rights to this guy's story, for their clients. It's a clean seven-figure option deal for whoever walks in with his rights. But nobody can get to him. He's not answering his phone."

"So?"

"So I'm figuring you can get to him."

"So?"

"So if you can get to him, maybe we can put something together."

"Like what?"

"A movie deal."

"I'm not a writer, Artie."

"What I'm talking about, Marcy, is putting you up as the girl in a movie about this guy."

"The girl?"

"Yeah. There's got to be a girl, no?"

"I'm sixty. . .three." She was still lying but not by as much as usual.

"This guy's like in his sixties, right?"

"Come on, Artie, you ever see Tommy Lee Jones or Harrison Ford, or even Clint with a woman his age? And he's nearly eighty."

"Okay, so you could be his mother."

She almost hung up, but years of playing this game kept her on the line. Where there was light, there was hope. Artie Reman picked up on the thickness of the silence and quickly corrected his suggestion.

"I meant his sister—his *younger* sister. You can play early sixties, right?"

"Of course." She was right back in.

"So you talk to him and see if he's willing to let us put him with a writer. And then we'll go from there, okay?"

"I'll get back to you, Artie."

"ASAP, doll. CAA's going to be all over this. Like flies on shit. Call me any time, night or day."

The agent gave her his cell phone number, a privilege she hadn't enjoyed even when she was earning money for him. He had just reeled her right back in. And it hadn't been very difficult. Just when she was getting to the point of accepting the reality that she no longer had a career, he had dangled a little bait in front of her and she was biting. Big time. Marcy could just hear Janet's reaction. *What planet are you living on?*

Clint Eastwood's younger sister? Why not? If they got the DP to light her well, she could play sixty, sixty-one. Maybe even late fifties. Clint's first wife? Better—a woman he was having an affair with. A damaged woman. But on the way back to rebuilding her life. Thanks to the love of a good man.

Before she went over to see Sammy, she dressed the part of the fifty-five-year-old—she could get there with a *really* good cinematographer, a serious diet, and a wardrobe magician—the fascinating woman who would conquer the heart of whoever they got to play the ex-mobster in witness protection. Marcy Gray was already in makeup.

This time, she waved at the reporters. That's how good she looked. What harm could it do? They apparently already knew who the mystery lady in Sammy Dee's life was. Or, at least, the woman who was showing up with casseroles.

She brought pastries. Truffles and champagne were a little much at 11:00 a.m. So were the Manolo Blahniks that she had splurged on when a large residual check had fallen out of the sky last summer, but she looked incredible in them, and there was nothing wrong with the reporters getting an eyeful.

Sammy answered her knock by opening the door a crack and letting her slip in. He was unshaven and wearing a bathrobe. She liked the look—Tony Soprano after a night of burying bodies.

"Hey," he muttered, and then added, "You look great."

"Thanks. I got an audition later," she lied.

"No kidding? What for?"

For Clint Eastwood's love interest. "Just some TV thing."

He took the plate of pastries from her, put them down on his kitchen counter, and started to pour water into his espresso machine. She sat herself on one of the kitchenette stools. Uninvited. Lately, they had unconsciously assumed the intimacy of a married couple.

"So. . .this is all pretty exciting, huh?" she led with, trying to recast the incident in a more positive light.

"It's a pain in the ass, is what it is."

"Of course. But still, you know, there could be some good things happening for you."

"Like what?"

"I'm sure people want to talk to you about your story."

"They're coming out of the woodwork."

She took a moment, dangling her Manolos in an alluring fashion. "What's so bad about their writing a book or even making a movie about you?"

"I don't need the publicity."

"There could be a lot of money, serious money."

"C'mon. Who wants to make a movie about a retired cement guy whose car happened to be parked in the wrong place?"

"The writers will change all that stuff around. They do it all the time."

"Charlie Berns offered to set me up with something, and I turned it down. I don't like the idea of being a celebrity."

Sammy took a couple of espresso cups from his dish rack, put saucers underneath, and extracted two tiny spoons from a drawer. There was something charming about his fastidiousness. He was going about his daily rituals in the face of threats against his life.

"Money's always nice. You can get yourself a nicer condo, travel. You don't even have to see the movie. They'll probably change the story so much that no one will even know it's you. Just take the money and run."

He nodded, wavering, but still wasn't biting. It was time for one final gambit. She'd go right for the ego.

"What if they got like. . .Tommy Lee Jones or Harrison Ford?" The façade cracked just a bit, enough for some light to sneak through, and she went for the kill. "You'd have casting approval, of course."

"No shit?"

"You'd be calling the shots. You could get, I don't know. . .maybe Jimmy Caan, or even Clint Eastwood."

He let his gut out a little and shrugged. "I'm thinking more Al Pacino."

Bingo.

While the literary agents in Artie Reman's agency did a triage of their A-list writers, Marcy kept the pressure on Sammy not to back out. He seemed torn between the idea of cashing a big check and allowing his life to become public. Thanks to Evelyn Duboff, Marcy knew why. She was walking a very fine line.

She came by at dinnertime with a lasagna and her Jimmy Choos—right behind the Manolos in her closet hierarchy—hoping to shore up the deal. She had called Didier and told him that she was under the weather, so he wouldn't pop in for dinner.

As soon as she saw him, she could tell that he was wavering. "Pacino's gained weight," he said.

"Really? How do you know?"

"I saw him on *Letterman*. And he's got this beard that looks awful."

"It's just probably for some role he's playing."

"I don't know. Besides, the guy's not Jewish."

"So what? Paul Newman played an Israeli in *Exodus*."

"Newman was half-Jewish."

And you're Italian. "Sammy, they're talking to Sorkin."

"Who's he?"

"The man has an Academy Award."

"They give them to *writers*?"

Jesus. This man was a serious civilian. She knew more about cement than he knew about the movie business.

"You're damn right, they do. Writers are big players in Hollywood."

"Well, I never heard of him."

They ate for a while in silence, Sammy playing with his pasta, as if he weren't hungry. Then he said, "So, instead of Pacino, what do you think about Kirk Douglas? He's Jewish, at least."

"He's also ninety-seven, and he's had a stroke."

"What about his kid?"

"Why not?"

Later that night, she lay in bed and indulged in the luxury of evaluating the men she wanted to play opposite. Clint really *was* too old. They'd let him direct, and there'd be endless script rewrites, and the movie wouldn't be made for years. She'd already worked with Jimmy Caan, who, at 73, was still doing Sonny Corleone. Pacino was in his seventies, too, and they'd never cast her as his love interest. She'd wind up as his older sister, or, worse, his therapist.

Maybe she should give Sly a call. *Hey, Sly, how're you doing? Remember me—the complex, damaged USO worker in Bangkok you had a one-night stand with in* Rambo—*or was it in Kabul in* Rambo III?

She drifted off to sleep with the fantasy of walking the red carpet at Cannes, where her powerfully understated performance in "The Sammy Dee Story" had gotten her a lot of buzz. When she gave her acceptance speech, she would make sure to mention all the people who'd never hired her.

The next day, Artie Reman called with news that they were in negotiations with a Triple-A writer.

"Who?"

"Can't tell you until it's closed."

"Who are you negotiating *with*?"

"Can't tell you that, either. Let's just say it's with a major studio."

"What about me?"

There was a pause on the line—a pause she knew well. Whenever Artie Reman had bad news to communicate, he sucked in air like a vacuum cleaner on a dusty carpet.

"We're getting a little pushback there."

"What do you mean, pushback?"

"The studios don't like to be locked in on casting."

"Did you explain that there's no deal without me?"

"You can't put a gun to their heads, Marcy."

"If it wasn't for me, you wouldn't have access to Sammy."

"I'll get you an associate producer's credit and some money."

The old back and fill. Three steps forward, four steps back. Deals fell apart every hour, if not every minute. They just swept you under the rug and moved forward. Okay, they wanted to play hardball? She was ready.

"Listen, you just better hope that Kirk Douglas dies before the first day of shooting," she said with edge in her voice and hung up on him. Five seconds later, her phone rang again, and she let it go to voice mail.

"Marcy, I'll make it work. Somehow. Maybe a smaller role—a supporting role. You could get a nomination. . ."

She went over to Sammy's in platform shoes and a pair of toreador pants that she knew did marvels for her bottom. She had worn them on their first date, at the Olive Garden, and if she wasn't mistaken, he had been very happy to see her.

They sat outside on his resurfaced patio and talked, in a desultory manner, about the upcoming holidays. She had hated this time of year ever since her divorce from Neil Breslau, forty-odd years ago. Especially in Palm Springs, where there were no sleigh bells or snowmen to cheer you up. There was nothing but the canned carols in the malls and plastic poinsettias. Her mantelpiece was bereft of Christmas cards. Her fridge was sans fruitcake.

The doorbell rang. Thinking it was a reporter, she went to answer it and found a thin, balding man in a wrinkled linen suit and a Panama hat standing there.

"Kermit Fenster. Nice to meet you."

At the sound of the name, Sammy came in from the patio, as if he were expecting the visitor. The two men shook hands, and Sammy said, "Marcy was just going."

The little man smiled through his gold inlays. "Marcy Gray, am I right?"

She nodded. It had been a long time since anyone had recognized her in public.

"Loved you in *The Last Hard Man*. You blew Jimmy Coburn off the screen."

"Thank you, but that was Barbara Hershey," she pointed out, flattered nonetheless.

"They should've given you the role. You're better-looking."

Blushing, she walked out the door, into the firing range of Leicas with telephoto lenses. The police had made the photographers move a hundred yards away, across the street, which was fine with Marcy. These days, she looked better in long shots.

Back in her own condo, she wondered who this strange man was and why Sammy didn't want her around. Kermit Fenster didn't look like a mobster, or some federal marshal from witness protection. He looked like Harry Dean Stanton in *Cool Hand Luke*. Harry was too old now to play him in the movie. They could go out to Richard Jenkins or, better, Greg Kinnear. A little young for the role, but better box office sales.

They could make him the cop who tries to protect Sly from the mobsters who want him dead. And she could play a scene, maybe two, with him, working to keep the man she loved alive. In the end she would go into witness protection along with Sammy, running off with him to a life in the south of France, where they could walk the beach hand-in-hand as the surf crashed against the shore and the credits rolled.

Just as it was all coming to fruition, as the elements were coming into place, as the writer's deal was closing, as Sammy was almost leaning toward Sylvester Stallone, the deal fell apart. Abruptly, fatally.

"The deal's going south," Artie Reman said on the phone, in the same tone of voice he used for good news.

"Why? What happened?"

"You didn't watch TV last night?"

"No. I went to bed early."

"Turns out your guy's car was just in the wrong place at the wrong time. Some Taliban crazy put the bomb under the wrong car."

"Huh?"

"Sammy Dee was parked next to an Afghan informant who was working for the CIA."

"Really?"

"Really, I'm afraid your guy couldn't get arrested now if he walked down Hollywood Boulevard with his dick hanging out."

The familiar wave of disappointment washed over her—the feeling of a role slipping away to another actress, or of the evaporation of funding, or of any of the hundred other reasons that a movie job fell apart. It had been years since she had allowed herself to indulge in the exquisite surge of self-pity that these moments brought on. She would wallow in them, assuaging her pain in an orgy of self-destruction—taking to her bed with a half-gallon of mint chocolate chip ice cream and a bottle of Portuguese rosé.

"No movie?"

"Nope. Even Lifetime's walking away. Maybe there's a web series in it. I don't know. . .some guy whose life is changed by his accidentally being mistaken for someone famous, but I think it's a serious long shot."

"Jesus, Artie. I was going to call Sly."

"Stallone only sells movies in Bulgaria these days. Sorry about this, doll."

And he hung up before she could humiliate herself further. Typical. No consoling remarks, no reason to hold out hope, not even false hope that the situation would improve. The man had no bedside manner. Never had.

Marcy walked over to the window, opened the blinds, and looked out. The reporters were gone. There was no one there at all. Not even the homeless and the curious.

Sammy Dee was now officially chopped liver. And with it, her. For a long moment, she stood at the window and gazed out into the void, trying to look at these events in a positive light. This was good news, wasn't it? Sammy's life was no longer in danger. He could start his car once more without worrying, that is, of course, when he had a car. He still hadn't replaced the Lexus.

She forced herself to let some light into her thoughts. They could go back to their life before the explosion. Reporters were no longer besieging Purgatory Gardens. She could stop with the fucking casseroles.

Try as she may, however, she was fighting a losing battle with the delicious pain of her rejection. It had been so long since she had even been in the position to lose out on a role that, in some sick way, the defeat actually felt reaffirming. She was in the game enough to strike out.

Exhaling deeply, Marcy went to get her car keys to drive to Vons. She had an irresistible yearning for mint chocolate chip ice cream and Portuguese rosé.

Two days later, a liberated Sammy—now just another senior citizen, free to come and go as he pleased—came over to ask her to co-sign the lease for a new car. A Porsche. Marcy agreed to do it with the same lack of concern that she'd had when she'd co-signed the contract for his new patio deck. He showed her the brochure—silver gray, with racing stripes.

She thought he was a little old for a midlife crisis. It was one thing to dye his hair, but quite another to tool around in a car with racing stripes. But who was she to criticize his vanity? She had spent almost as much redesigning her face.

"So I guess it's good that no one was trying to kill you after all, huh?" she said.

"Oh yeah. A load off my mind."

"I bet. And thank God those reporters are gone."

"Tell me about it."

"You got to be careful where you park your car these days," she said with a smile. And he smiled back. It was the smile she liked, the Lino Ventura smile that she hadn't seen in a while.

Oddly enough, however, as the danger around Sammy Dee dissipated, so, to some extent, did his allure. He was no longer a man people wanted dead, but a poor schlub who had parked his car in the wrong place. Accordingly, he inched back down the short list to his previous position, more or less parallel to Didier's.

Then Didier got *his* patio deck redone. And things really got crazy.

The botched attempt on Sammy Dee's life in the Vons parking lot pissed Didier Onyekachukwu off. He thought he had been dealing with professionals, but now it looked like Acme Exterminating and Patio Decks didn't know what they were doing. If you're going to put a bomb under someone's car, at least make sure that he's in it when it goes off. In Ouagadougou, for one-tenth the price, he could have hired an out-of-work colonel to gun the Italian down in his doorway. It wouldn't have been pretty, but it would have been done.

Now he would have to wait for another shot, and the shot would be more difficult because Sammy was aware that someone was trying to kill him. To complicate matters, the man was now some sort of celebrity, the place surrounded by reporters. He was barricaded in his condo with the shades drawn, not answering his phone.

Worst of all, the whole business wasn't helpful to Didier's pursuit of Marcy Gray. Being the target of a foiled assassination attempt had given Sammy Dee cachet. The press was making him into some sort of national hero, a target of Al-Qaeda, the Taliban, North Korea, you name it. And Marcy was rushing over there with cooked dishes.

Didier had half a mind to make the truth public: that Sammy Dee was the target of a neighbor who wanted him out of the way for romantic purposes. That he'd escaped his fate only because he walked into a super-market at just the right time. A minute or two earlier, and he would no longer be around. Instead, Didier would be standing beside Marcy Gray at the Italian's funeral, consoling her with great tenderness.

As soon as he saw Marcy heading to Sammy Dee's condo with dinner, Didier selected a bottle from his wine rack and followed her over. It was a shame wasting good wine on them, but it was the price he had to pay to neutralize the Italian's growing allure.

They sat around and ate Marcy's under-spiced casserole, sipping first-growth Bordeaux, until Sammy fell asleep at the table. Then Didier was out the door after her. He walked her to her place, squeezed her hand with empathy, but refrained from greater familiarities.

He knew enough about women to understand that it was not the appro-priate moment to make a move. She was preoccupied with the attention surrounding Sammy Dee. In fact, Didier had the impression that she was actually enjoying it all. Since the photographers were outside the building, Marcy had been dressing as if she were on the runway in Paris, and not mere-ly bringing a covered dish to a neighbor in a condo complex in Palm Springs.

Didier debated whether or not to contact Acme and find out what the timetable was for the next attempt. It would be nice to know that they at least had a plan to try again. There was nothing in the patio deck contract that provided for a refund if they didn't do the job. And taking them to court for non-performance was obviously out of the question. Though in this country you could find a lawyer to take any case—even failure to as-sassinate. And they could probably even get a judge to order that Acme fulfill its contractual obligation as stipulated.

In France, if Didier got caught, they'd give him five years, or even less, because it was a *crime passionelle*. They'd put him on the late-night talk shows, direct from prison. Women would flood him with propositions to wait for him until he got out. Imagine—a man who killed for love. What more fitting tribute to a woman you adored? *Quel sentiment exquis!* Didier sent Acme a note asking if there was an adjusted date for his patio instal-lation. Three days later, he got a pre-printed Christmas card.

SEASONS' GREETINGS FROM YOUR FRIENDS AT ACME EXTERMINATING AND PATIO DECKS.

And then in ink at the bottom: BEST WISHES, WALT AND BIFF.

Meanwhile, things at Afrique Ouest continued to deteriorate. His client list dwindled to a trickle. Authentic pre-colonial African art was not a hot item in Palm Springs, where tastes ran toward Leroy Neiman prints. Clive wanted more money and fewer hours. And the Indians were shaking him down for a bigger cut.

George Kajika had taken to stopping by the gallery regularly to see how the pieces were moving, his narrow dark eyes scanning the shelves in a silent inventory. The 92 percent Choctaw—a great-grandmother had had a fling with a Chinese railroad worker, he explained—wanted to see his books.

What books? Didier's concept of accounting was limited to moving money from one pocket to another. Even when he was stealing money for the colonels in Upper Volta, he had not written things down. Writing things down just got you in trouble. It left footprints, and Didier Onyeka-chukwu had gone to great lengths in his life to leave as few as possible.

They sat in his office, or what passed for an office—a redecorated supply room with a gunmetal-gray desk and an empty file cabinet. George Kajika chain-smoked unfiltered Camels and uttered a series of not-so-subtle threats to cut off Didier's product supply.

"My people are not so happy."

"I'm sorry to hear that."

"They are suffering from illness."

"That's regrettable."

"Medicaid sends them to far-off places."

"How unfortunate."

"Many travel a hundred miles in their pickups to get medicine."

Didier nodded, with as much sympathy as he could muster.

"Many miles in pickup creates hemorrhoids."

This would go on for a while—George Kajika smoking, coughing, and uttering his pointedly oblique threats—until Didier put some cash in an envelope and the Indian would leave. He would rise, like Sitting Bull at a war council, gathering his threadbare California Angels windbreaker around him like a ceremonial robe, and walk out the door.

Didier considered replacing the Indians with illegal Mexicans, but he would have to retrain the labor force to produce items that looked something like African art objects and not souvenirs from a Tijuana tourist stand. He thought of replacing Clive as well, but it would mean that Didier himself would have to spend his days at the gallery watching nobody come in.

What he needed was a game plan. That charming American sports metaphor had no translation in French. Not to mention an end game. Once Sammy Dee was out of the way, things would fall into place. But in the meantime, he was scrambling just to keep his head above water—like a football team with a one-goal lead in injury time.

He even considered taking the job over from Acme. He could put poison in Sammy Dee's pizza himself. Or just buy a gun and shoot him. Self-defense, Your Honor. It was either him or me.

But violence was never something that Didier Onyekachukwu was comfortable with. He had spent his life accommodating the people who actually committed the violence, insulating himself from both danger and distaste. He believed that he was, at heart, a decent human being. Maybe not Nobel Peace Prize material, but not Idi Amin either.

When Marcy was exclusively his, he could devote himself to good works. He could teach French to migrant workers, produce Moliere plays in the lettuce fields. He could make an attempt to track down his numerous children and send them money to get out of Burkina Faso. He could stop selling bogus African antiquities to unsuspecting suckers who needed to feel better about the forlorn continent of Africa by displaying a Yoruba fertility fetish on their coffee table.

And he could live happily off Marcy Gray's retirement income, cooking for her and making her happy at night. Maybe he'd even take up golf. In memory of Sammy Dee. It would be the least he could do.

At four o'clock in the morning, as Didier lay awake trying to figure out if there was a way he could unload his entire supply of pre-fab African art on some wealthy ignoramus with empty wall space, he had another idea. What if he capitalized on all the publicity surrounding Sammy Dee and Paradise Gardens to promote the business? Since the Italian's car had been blown up, they had all been pestered by reporters looking for next-door-neighbor stories. Didier's voice mail was cluttered with the names and numbers of people wanting to talk to him.

Why not do an interview at the gallery? Get a TV crew over to Afrique Ouest and make sure they shot him in front of the artwork? He could make up some *merde* about the Italian and slip in a few plugs for the business. *My good friend Sammy is a serious collector of Benin bronzes...*

Who would know? Sammy refused to watch the news on TV. Marcy, well, she'd get a kick out of it. He hoped. And it was reasonable to surmise that the French narcotics police would not be watching the Palm Springs ABC station, nor would any of his former wives and children.

Among the messages on his voice mail were three from Tracy Tohito. Didier remembered seeing the *Eyewitness News* reporter, pert in a beige knit suit with too much eye makeup, standing with a microphone near the crime scene tape around the empty space where Sammy Dee's car had been parked and talking about Al-Qaeda plots. The message said to call her anytime and left her cell phone number.

As soon as he'd had his morning coffee, Didier dialed the reporter. She picked up on the first ring.

"This is Tracy."

"Miss Tohito, I am Didier Onyekachukwu."

"Who?"

"A neighbor of Samuel Dee, at the Paradise Gardens community. You have been leaving me messages."

It took only a microsecond for her reporter's reflexes to kick in. She sucked in air and said, "Thank you for calling back, Mister..." Like most people, she didn't bother trying to pronounce his name.

"I would be willing to speak with you about my good friend and neighbor, Samuel."

"Great. Wonderful. So you know him well?"

"Intimately."

"Fabulous. Would you do it on camera?"

"I would be pleased to, but I do not want to do it here. There is too much publicity already, and I do not want to displease my neighbors."

"Of course. I understand. Where would you want to do it?"

"At my place of business, which is a gallery of art, a stone's toss from Paradise Gardens."

Didier could hear her reporter's brain taking this in, no doubt already figuring how to frame the story. *Intimate friend of Al-Qaeda target's art collection.* "Okay, so I need to run this by my producer and round up a crew. I don't think there'll be any problem. Are you talking to anybody else?"

"Not at the moment."

"I need to sell this as an exclusive, you understand?"

"That should not be a problem, provided that you allot sufficient amount of time to the interview."

"Of course. We'll lead with it at six and eleven. Okay?"

"All right. I am available this afternoon, at three o'clock."

"You got it."

He gave her the gallery address and hung up. Then he took a long shower and composed a fictional version of his intimacy with Samuel Dee. He went to his closet and foraged around for his most African wardrobe, settling on a colorful *pagne* that he had gotten by mail order from a place in Dakar while he was selling art in Nice. He'd put a little makeup on his cheek, below his eyes, to accentuate the tribal scars, which had long since started to fade.

". . .Samuel and I have both been interested in African art since the days when we first met, in New York. We had invested in a restaurant downtown and had done quite well with it, using the profits to purchase authentic art from the Benin basin on the West Coast of Africa, hence the name of this gallery, 'Afrique Ouest,' which is spelled the French way, O. . .u. . .e. . .s. . .t."

Tracy Tohito stood beside him in front of a wall of Yoruba masks, holding the microphone as a camera followed them through the gallery.

"Can you explain, Mr. Onyekachukwu"—she had spent five minutes practicing it before they began—"why Al-Qaeda is so interested in eliminating your good friend and former business partner?"

"I am not confident that I can tell you that, Tracy. A good deal of the information is classified."

"Are you. . .a CIA operative, as well?"

"I can neither confirm nor deny that."

"Perhaps you could speculate."

"Well, for a while now, Al-Qaeda and the Taliban have shown a vibrant interest in West Africa. As you know, there is an appreciable Muslim population in those countries, which they would like, *naturellement*, to radicalize. So they are looking for operatives who have some connection in the region."

"And you being African. . ."

"Oh, not me. I am too obvious. They are using less transparent people."

"Like Sammy Dee?"

"As I say, I cannot comment on that. But I can tell you that Samuel is particularly fond of Benin bronzes, from the Niger River delta, encompassing Nigeria, Benin, Togo, Ghana, and Ivory Coast. We have quite a few here in the gallery, a stone's toss from downtown Palm Springs, open ten to six every day. . ."

Tracy Tohito's editors edited the story severely, but enough of it remained to give Afrique Ouest the kind of free advertising that he couldn't afford to buy.

For a few days, traffic at the gallery picked up. Mostly lookie-loos interested in visiting the venue where Sammy Dee, undercover CIA operative, bought his art. Didier showed pieces similar to those that his dear friend *Samee* Dee owned, and people took pictures with their camera phones and posted them on their Facebook pages.

But with the exception of the two middle-aged sexual perverts from Paradise Gardens—who bought an Ashanti fertility fetish that could be used as a dildo—no one wrote checks. George Kajika came by to assess the action, and pointed out with satisfaction several little red dots next to pieces that supposedly meant they were sold, but which Didier had put up to give the impression that the exhibition was a success.

He had to pay Clive for overtime and put out a spread of wine and cheese, to which people helped themselves liberally. Word quickly spread among the town drunks that there was free chardonnay in the gallery, and they showed up in numbers, staggering around the gallery with plastic cups of wine.

All in all, Didier's scheme to capitalize on Sammy Dee's notoriety to sell art was a crashing failure. The only bright spot may have been the reaction of Marcy, who seemed to be amused by the stunt. She showed up in a big straw hat and lovely cotton dress, looking like a Renoir painting, and circulated with him, admiring the art.

Didier vowed that when she was his, he would give her an education in art appreciation so that she would no longer be impressed by the shit he was selling. He would take her to the Louvre and teach her about chiaroscuro and brush stroke techniques. And when they went on their tour of Africa, he would show her genuine art pieces that he couldn't afford even on consignment.

The two Palm Springs police detectives who had questioned him after the poisoned pizza canard showed up fishing for leads. They stood around in their atrocious sports jackets, the outline of their holsters making a visible impression in the polyester, their eyes darting back and forth, as if the people who placed the bomb under the Italian's car would be dumb enough to attend.

Didier approached the cops and said, "Detectives, how nice to see you."

They nodded quickly, not happy to have been recognized.

"Are you gentlemen off duty?"

One of them looked at the other for guidance and then said, in an attempt at ambiguity, "We're not here. . .*officially*."

"Well, in that case, could you *unofficially* remove the drunk who is throwing up in the toilet?"

The whole deal fell apart completely when it was discovered that Sammy Dee was not a target for the Taliban, but an innocent victim who had inadvertently parked his car beside an Afghan double agent that they had trailed to Palm Springs. It was all over the TV—a CIA spokesman in a dark suit reporting from Washington that they had managed, without resorting to a drone, to take out one of the Taliban's most notorious agents. And that America was safer for it.

Not to be outdone, the two local cops who had shown up at Didier's gallery got some camera time to announce that the collaboration between federal, state, and local law enforcement had functioned the way it was meant to function, and that Palm Springs was safer for it.

Didier watched it all with mixed feelings. Certainly, he was happy to be rid of the pack of reporters who had been parked outside Paradise Gardens since the incident, and not to have to waste decent wine on Sammy Dee for dinner every night, but at the same time, this new development freed his rival to go out and pursue his advances on Marcy Gray. He could take her out to dinner or to a movie, invite her to his place without worrying that the reporters were watching his door, or take her away for the weekend, God forbid.

It was clear to Didier that he would have to escalate his attack, now that his rival was no longer *hors de combat*. This was no time to relax his guard. He would go back on the offensive, pursuing Marcy with renewed fervor until Acme Pest Control got rid of his problem for him once and for all. He would keep up the attack by inviting Marcy for afternoon Scrabble games by the pool, something that the Italian could not compete with—English clearly being at least his second language, after Sicilian and God knew what else.

Didier would buy a state-of-the-art grill, on credit at Sears, and cook exotic dishes for Marcy. At night, the two of them would dine, *à deux*, on his patio, enjoying châteaubriand *au point* with a bottle of Château Margaux. He would play Juliette Greco on the CD player and take her in his arms to seal the deal. *Parlez moi d'amour*. He would speak to her of love, under the desert moon, and she would be his. Finally.

X
SAMMY

That the African was trying to kill him was weird enough, but that he had contracted with the same outfit that Sammy was using to do *him* was seriously weird. Okay, there was a chance that Acme occasionally redid a patio without killing anyone, in order to keep up appearances, and that Didier Onyewhatever just happened to decide to redo *his* patio after Sammy did his. But the coincidence was hard to swallow, even for someone as desperate as Sammy Dee.

Biff must have put the bomb under his car while Sammy was playing golf with Walt and the periodontist. And his unscheduled stop at Vons to pick up the Drano had saved his life. Incredible. Those fuckers had taken the contract without batting an eye and were trying to cash in on both of them. The one who was fortunate enough to be dead would not have to remit the final ten grand, but he wouldn't put it above them to go after the estate.

Did Charlie Berns put the African on to Acme? Or did Diddly Shit stumble on Walt and Biff's Facebook page? Unfuckingbelievable.

What to do about it was another matter. Contacting Acme involved the inevitable invitation to golf. And then what? On the third green, matter-of-factly drop: *Nice shot. By the way, you guys trying to whack me too?* He wouldn't put it above them to assure him that it was not personal. *Just business, Sammy. You're on the tee. . .*

He could put Marshal Dillon on to them. Agreeing to hit someone in a WITSEC program had to be some sort of federal crime. But, then again, so was taking a contract out on someone. He and Acme would do time together. Conspiracy to commit murder. Ten to twenty. Marcy would visit him in San Quentin with a file baked into a lasagna casserole.

Or he could break down and accept Dillon's offer to relocate again. Let them send him to Kalamazoo with a new name. He'd go to Marcy and convince her to come to Kalamazoo with him. He'd get snow tires for the Porsche. There was Jacksonville or Tucson, but the program didn't give you your choice of locales. This time of year, warm weather relocations were undoubtedly very much in demand. He could be dead by the time one opened up.

Nevertheless, he decided to see what was available from WITSEC. Then he would evaluate his options. Unfortunately, there was no way to get into this with Marshal Dillon over the phone. Even though Sammy had been given a special, untraceable cell phone, the marshal told him it could still be hacked. *The only communications that are secure are face-to-face in an unbuggable location.*

The unbuggable location turned out to be one of Dylan's favorites, the deli next to the Movie Colony Hotel with *the best pastrami in the Coachella Valley.* For breakfast, no less. The marshal ordered it, while Sammy stayed with a bagel and coffee. They sat in a booth in the rear, next to the kitchen, Dylan facing the door. In case Al Capone walked in.

He was wearing pressed Dockers, a Lacoste T-shirt, and Hush Puppies. As far as Sammy was concerned, you could make him as an undercover cop from a hundred yards. Taped to his calf there was undoubtedly a 45-caliber Glock with six rounds.

"You're not looking very good, Sammy."

"I've been through a lot of shit."

"Well, you're out the other side now."

"What do you mean?"

"They made the guy whose spot you parked in."

The man actually believed that shit.

"I'm thinking, Marshal, of maybe taking you up on the relocation deal."

Dylan chewed his pastrami with his usual thoroughness, then put the sandwich down for a sip of root beer. "Why is that?"

"Like you said, I'm in the news. Someone could make me."

"You *were* in the news. Not anymore. Now you're just another retiree walking around the Springs in polyester."

"Yeah, but still, someone could've made me *while* I was famous."

"You assured me that no one did."

"Well, I assumed so. . .but I'm not a hundred percent sure."

"I don't get it. Last week you told me you refused to go anywhere, and now you're not so sure. What's going on?"

There's a contract out on my life with two ruthless scratch golfers who just missed offing me in Vons parking lot, that's what's going on.

"I just want to know my options. Is there anything open in Jacksonville or Tucson?"

"This time of year? You kidding?"

"What about like. . .Kalamazoo or Duluth?"

"Sammy, you know what it costs to relocate someone?"

"A lot, you told me. But still, if I get killed. . ."

"Why should you get killed? You're off the hook. They were going after someone else. Unless, of course, you want to tell me that the bomb at Vons really *was* meant for you."

It was a no-win situation. He was fucked if he did, and fucked if he didn't. The odor of the pastrami was turning his stomach. There was no way he was going to get what he wanted from this man. Now, or ever.

"Well, if I get hit, it's going to be on your conscience," he said, limply.

"I'll live with it."

"I gotta go," Sammy said, getting up abruptly and sliding out of the booth.

"Sammy?"

"What?"

The marshal handed him the check and went back to his breakfast.

Sammy took the Porsche from the valet, under-tipping the guy with two singles. One of the problems with driving a sixty-thousand-dollar car was that you were expected to tip big. He put it in first, let out the clutch, and burned rubber, enveloping the valet in a cloud of noise and exhaust. In the rearview he saw the guy give him the finger. Fuck him! He was parking cars for a living.

The way Sammy saw it, he was down to two options. They both involved hitting someone. The question was who. If he did Diddly Shit, then presumably Acme wouldn't bother going after him, since they couldn't collect the final money for the African's contract on him. But he'd still be on the hook to them for his own money, whether or not they actually did the job. There had to be something in the boilerplate of the patio contract that stipulated that they got paid if the job got done, one way or another. And if he were alive, they'd go after him.

Or he could whack Walt and Biff. Use the money to hire another contract killer to do them. This option had the advantage of getting rid of the people trying to kill him, but it left the African alive. Which would defeat the purpose of his having taken out the contract in the first place.

Anyway, there was no point thinking about who to hit if he didn't know who was going to hit the one he'd decided to hit. Back in the day, there were button men Finoccio used when he needed someone done. Salvatore Didziocomo had never been high enough in the family to know the names of these guys, but there were men who did. Nick the Tip ought to be one of them. Tuccieri had been one of Finoccio's inner circle. He had been invited on the Vegas trips and down to Miami Beach in the winter for deep-sea fishing and hookers. If anyone knew if there was a West Coast guy, it would be The Tip.

It was the week before Thanksgiving when he'd run into his old colleague in the CVS parking lot and dropped the condoms. Sammy would have to tell him that the marlin weren't biting in Jacksonville and that he was back in the Springs. On business.

He'd make up a story. Some guy had stiffed him out of serious money. He could give Nick a grand off the top as a referral fee. *Whad'ya say, Nick? For old times?*

Sammy managed to dig up the card that his old colleague had given him. VICKY AND NICKY, with a Palm Desert address and a phone number.

A woman answered the phone.

"Hi. Wonder if I could speak to Nick?" Sammy used his cheerful voice, one he rarely used.

"Who's calling?"

"Tell him it's his old friend, Sal."

"Sal?"

"Yeah. From the Island. He'll remember."

After a moment, The Tip got on. "Sal? How're the marlin biting?"

"They're not, Nick. Couldn't catch a fucking minnow. I'm back in the Springs."

"No kidding? What are you up to?"

"A couple of things. Listen, I thought I'd take you up on your invitation. You know, drive over, say hello. . ."

"Great. Why don't you come by for dinner? We'll throw a couple of steaks on the barbecue, mix up some Mai Tais. Like old times."

"Okay. Sure. How about. . .tonight?"

"Tonight? Let me check with the boss."

Tuccieri shouted to his wife, who apparently okayed the deal. "You're on. Six o'clock for drinks. Bring one of your girlfriends. We'll play a little pinochle after dinner."

"Well, I'm kind of between women at the moment, Nick."

"Too bad. You don't want to let those condoms go to waste, Sal," he chuckled, then gave him directions and hung up.

When he got to Vicky and Nicky's split-level on the edge of the desert, there was a woman waiting for him. Of course. He should have seen it coming. As a straight single male who drove at night and presumably made a living, he was low-hanging fruit. She was a refugee from Jersey named Connie wearing skin-tight toreador pants and a gold lamé top that accentuated a recent tit job.

The woman put down three Mai Tais and got flirty over the steaks. She was the widow of some made guy on the Island who had left her with enough krugerrands to relocate to Palm Springs and fish for her next husband. Sammy was clearly a candidate for the job.

When Sammy said after dinner that he had some business to discuss with Nick, the women repaired to the kitchen. The good thing about family wives was that you didn't have to explain this kind of shit to them.

"I thought you were retired, Sal," Nick said, lighting one of his Tiparillos.

"I wish I was. Unfortunately, I can't afford it."

"I'm sorry to hear that. You got nailed on that fucking audit, huh?"

"Big time. Lennie The Kike told me I was going up for three to five, on the inside. Which is why I. . .you know?" Sammy couldn't bring himself to actually say that he blew the whistle, even though Nick knew he had.

"Of course," Tuccieri said sympathetically. "It's water under the bridge, Sal. I would've done the same thing in your shoes."

"Well, I don't feel good about it, but it's done. Time to move on."

"You bet."

"Anyway, Nick, I got some action going on out here. Nothing big. A little laundry business. I'm making a living. Or at least I was until a couple of weeks ago. I got a problem I need taken care of."

"Uh-huh," Nick said, taking a long inhale from the cigar. "Serious problem?"

"Yeah. Maybe I can get away with just scaring the guy, but I may have to set an example. You understand?"

Nick nodded gravely. There was no need to define the problem any more clearly. They had spoken the same language all those years and were still fluent in the subtext.

"Preferably someone on this coast."

"Right. You can't get on a fucking plane with a piece anymore."

"Wasn't there a guy that Phil used when he had a job to do out here? Someone in LA?"

"Tino from Tarzana."

"Right. Tino. The guy was pretty good, if I remember correctly."

"The best. The guy wired ignitions like a fucking brain surgeon. But we're talking like ten, twelve years ago. Who knows if he's still in business?"

"You know how to find him?"

Nick shook his head. "I don't even know where the fuck Tarzana is. Can you believe they name a place after some fucking guy who swings from trees?"

"You know anybody who might know?"

"The only guy who could tell you is Phil himself. He kept the number in his head. He never even met the guy. He called, gave him the info, wired him the money, half up front, half when he did the job. When we had a West Coast job, Phil would say, 'I'm calling Tino in Tarzana.' And that was it. A done deal."

Sammy escaped after two rounds of pinochle with Connie's phone number. On the back of her card she wrote, *I'm always home.* He drove through the clear, cold desert night, taking the Porsche up to eighty-five on the straight-aways. There was one person who might be able to track down Tino from Tarzana. Though he wasn't happy about owing this guy two favors, he didn't see any other way.

The message was specific. Sammy didn't have time to fuck around. On the answering machine in Uruguay, he said, "I'm trying to locate a button man named Tino who lives in Tarzana, California. Call me any time."

The response came back a few hours later. Sammy had no idea what time it was in South America, but in Palm Springs, California, it was around 3:00 a.m. and Sammy was fast asleep with the phone ringer on silent mode.

Typical of Kermit Fenster, the message consisted simply of a phone number. Nothing more. Sammy stood in his pajamas, drinking a mug of espresso and waiting for the caffeine to kick in. Then he made the call.

The voice was thin and spidery, with a thick Mexican accent. "*Sí?*"

"Tino, this is Gus Malvolio, a friend of Phil's."

"Phil who?"

"Phil Finoccio."

"He's in the joint."

"Right. But he's still doing business."

"I don't do New York."

"This is local, Tino. Palm Springs."

"I don't do the desert."

"It's an hour and a half away."

"I don't drive at night."

"You can handle it during the day. Leave LA at six, you'll be home by noon, three the latest."

Sammy heard the sound of a nose being blown, then: "How much you got to spend?"

"Ten."

"I'd have to pack a bag."

"Why? You're not staying overnight."

"Colostomy bag."

Jesus. What was he thinking? Anybody who blew cars for Phil Finoccio was probably pushing eighty.

"I'll get back to you, Tino," Sammy said and hung up.

Sammy started back toward the bedroom, meaning to go back to sleep. But the caffeine was tap dancing through his brain. He glanced at his watch. Nine thirty. His eye caught the date. December 24. It was Christmas Eve. Holy shit. The night before Christmas, and all through the house, Sammy Dee was trying to arrange a hit. That wasn't going to look good if there was a Guy up there, and if The Guy was paying attention.

When you thought of it, getting rid of the African was actually the Christian thing to do. The man was clearly some sort of criminal. If he wasn't smuggling drugs, he was smuggling guns. God knows what he had been up to in Africa. Some sort of genocide, no doubt.

But, more importantly, if Diddly Shit wound up with Marcy, then Sammy would wind up in the homeless shelter and become a drain on society's resources, consuming vital public funds that were needed for truly destitute people. Limbless veterans and fallen nuns would be turned away in favor of an able-bodied man who had failed to support himself in his old age.

This equation made sense to Sammy. He would go with it. Or at least make his case when his day in court arrived. He would explain to The Guy that he had done what he did for the greater good.

A half-hour later, his phone rang. It was Marcy Gray, inviting him to midnight mass. He said yes, in the desperate hope that it would cancel out his earlier activities. He'd eat a wafer and explain things to The Guy.

XI
MARCY

When work began on Didier's patio, Marcy didn't give it much thought at first. Yes, it was a coincidence, but not that big of a co-incidence. A number of residents of Purgatory Gardens had gotten their patios redone. If she had the money, she would have her own redone. Every time she looked out at her forlorn flower boxes on the bare con-crete, she thought of Stanley. *Your patio should be condemned as a public eyesore.*

With the reporters gone, she was once more officially chopped liver. Artie Reman wasn't calling with updates on the movie deal; photogra-phers weren't shooting pictures of her going in and out of Sammy Dee's condo; the possibility of the phone ringing at any given moment was no longer there. For so many years, she had lived with that possibility—to the extent that even now, she still felt a quickening of the pulse whenever her phone rang. This could be *the* call, the one that turned it all around, the role that put her on the map for good.

After a series of plaintive emails, Janet had relented and called in a pre-scription for Zoloft, but the effects of the anti-depressant hadn't kicked in yet. All it had done was blunt her sex drive—not that it had been very acute to begin with. She couldn't even dish up a nostalgic memory of what it had been like to be in bed with a man, let alone take steps to make it happen.

Which wouldn't have been very difficult. She still had two men humping her leg and was convinced that either of them would be happy to accommodate her if she so much as dropped a hint. She had actually resolved to do it after her last face-to-face session with Janet, when the therapist had told her she was in the Catbird Seat. But then Sammy's car was blown up, and everyone was a little too jumpy to think about sex.

They were back to their strange, three-way slow dance, while Marcy waited for the Zoloft to start working and Christmas to be out of the way. She spent her afternoons playing Scrabble with Didier at the pool and her evenings in front of the TV tearing up at the Christmas specials and feeling sorry for herself. It all looked to be dissolving into one big blah.

Until Evelyn Duboff called with an update.

It was late in the afternoon, and Marcy was sitting in the dwindling light of her living room, trying to decide whether to have cottage cheese and frozen pizza or cottage cheese and frozen enchiladas, when her phone rang. She almost didn't answer it, that's how depressed she was.

But Marcy Gray was congenitally incapable of not answering a ringing phone. She picked up and heard Evelyn Duboff's voice.

"You got a moment, darling?"

"I guess so." She had lots of moments, but she wasn't up to hearing more bad news about her suitors.

"You might want to sit down."

"I'm sitting."

"Okay, so listen. I've done some more digging on your two Lotharios, and came up with some really interesting information. . ."

"Evelyn, I'm not sure I want to hear this right now. . ."

"I think you'd better."

"What?"

"I have reason to believe that these two clowns are trying to kill each other."

"Pardon me?"

"They both may have taken contracts out on the other one."

"What!"

"Wait, it gets better. With the same hit man."

"Sammy and Didier have hired hit men?"

"Looks that way."

"Why would they do that?"

"Duh. . ."

"What're you talking about?"

"Sweetheart, they're fighting over *you*."

"Oh, please. . ."

"It appears to be the only explanation for what's been going on. There were attempts on both of them, right? First the African with the bad pizza, and then Sammy and the blown car."

"That was the Taliban."

"The Taliban could easily have been the cover story. WITSEC does that kind of thing to protect their people, so that they don't have to relocate them again. And then, we got the patios."

"What does that have to do with it?"

"There're a couple of contract guys who operate out here in the desert. They charge twenty-five grand for a hit, and their cover is that they're exterminators and patio deck refinishers. They have a company—Acme Exterminating and Patio Decks—and they make you sign a contract to get your patio redone. That's in case you stiff them, so they can go after you. And, this is the capper, they actually put the facacta patio deck in to cover their asses."

"So?"

"So, didn't you tell me that both of them have had their patios redone recently? Two schnorrers like them are going to spend twenty-five grand just to fix up their property? I don't think so."

"How do you know this?"

"I have a pipeline into the Riverside County prosecutor's office. Apparently, both federal and state have been trying to nail Acme for a while, but so far they've been able to cover their tracks. These guys are good. They're top of the line, your Chivas Regal of hit men."

Marcy let the phone slip from her ear as she tried to assimilate the astounding information that Evelyn Duboff had just imparted to her. It was both absurd and made complete sense. It explained a number of things that needed to be explained. But still. . . *killers*? Sammy and Didier? Men she'd had in her home for Thanksgiving dinner and played Scrabble and almost slept with?

"Darling, you there?"

Marcy put the phone back to her ear. "Yeah. . ."

"Look, I known this is upsetting, but you needed to know it."

"What should I do?"

"You could talk to someone in the DA's office, tell them what you know."

"Why would I do that?"

"Build a case against Acme."

"Yeah, and in the meantime Sammy and Didier go to jail."

"Maybe they can cut a plea deal."

Marcy took a deep, cleansing breath, then another.

"Don't hyperventilate on me, darling."

"Evelyn, it's the holidays. I can't deal with this shit now."

"You want my advice? I'd cut them both loose."

"Thank you."

And she hung up. In a trance, she walked over to her freezer, took out the frozen enchiladas, unwrapped them, and stuck them in the microwave. Then she took out the cottage cheese and poured herself a large glass of recorked chardonnay. Sitting at her kitchen counter, she ate the cottage cheese right out of the container, washing it down with the souring wine. She stared at the phone and did everything in her power not to call Janet's emergency number. *This is only for when you're on the ledge.*

As far as Marcy was concerned, if she wasn't already on the ledge, she was eyeing it through the window.

She left a message on Janet's non-ledge number to call her as soon as possible. *I'm not on the ledge, but I'm pretty fucked up.* Then she polished off the rest of the wine, washing down the curdling cottage cheese and the overdone enchiladas, slopped herself on the couch in front of a *Law and Order* rerun, and turned the sound low. She used TV as white noise. Better to have something in the room with her, even if it was stale cop dialogue, than to be completely alone with her thoughts. Which, at the moment, were all over the place.

Oh. My. God. Could this really be happening? Sammy and Didier actually trying to *kill* each other? Over *her*? How awful! And then, like Rex Harrison in *My Fair Lady*, she did a one-eighty. How *delightful*!

Two men felt passionate enough about her to try to kill each other. She had to admit that it was pretty titillating. It was like some gothic romance novel, with rivals fighting a duel at dawn over the attentions of a beautiful woman. A *damaged* beautiful woman.

Okay, calm down. Maybe Evelyn Duboff was wrong; maybe they both decided they needed a new patio deck at more or less the same time. They had both come into some money and were going to spend it upgrading their property. *Right.* So why did Sammy ask her to co-sign the contract if he had come into money? And why would Didier put money into his patio when his gallery was having trouble keeping the doors open?

Okay, they *were* trying to kill each other. But not over her. There was some sort of feud between them, some business deal that went wrong, or some back story that she didn't know about. She just happened to be in the middle; the innocent bystander who became collateral damage. She wasn't a femme fatale so much as a damsel in distress.

Well, Marcy Gray didn't do damsels in distress. And she wasn't about to start now. Damaged women were her meal ticket, and she would go with that. It made sense. They were trying to kill each other. Over her. Why not?

Tuuli and Majda's cat ate a piece of poisoned pizza that had been ordered by Didier, and a bomb had gone up under Sammy's car at Vons. As far as she was concerned, there had never been a satisfactory explanation for either of those two incidents. And now there appeared to be one, far-fetched as it might be.

The whole thing felt like a cop show plot. Reflexively, she looked up at the screen, and there was Jerry Orbach, questioning some perp in the pea-green interrogation room at the stationhouse. She imagined Sammy and Didier sitting side by side, in handcuffs, as Jerry worked them over.

You expect me to buy this poisoned pizza and Taliban bullshit?

And then, before they could answer, they cut to an extreme close-up of a woman in smeared eye makeup, lighting a cigarette. Her hair was disheveled, her eyes milky and distant from drugs and alcohol. And then the voice, dripping with pain and regret, said, "You think you have it all figured out, don't you?"

God, she looked awful. They at least could have done something with her hair. Okay, she was playing a pill freak, but she could have gotten it together enough to make it to the beauty parlor.

It was a show she had done over twenty years ago, in the early days of *Law and Order*. A couple of days' work at scale plus ten, and then a nice flow of residuals for years after. Now it was coming back to haunt her. For a moment, she thought she had hallucinated the whole thing, but as they widened to a full shot of her with Sam Waterston in a three-walled set in Long Island City, she remembered the job. They had flown her first-class and put her up at the Hilton. Those were the days.

Her performance, as usual, transcended the cheesy dialogue. There was depth and subtext in her line readings. You could hear the whole history of drugs, cigarettes, and bad men in her voice. She watched the show, transfixed in nostalgia, until her character, high on Vicodin, walked in front of a taxi on Sixth Avenue and that was that. Another damaged woman meeting her fate.

It seemed, if anything, prophetic. Was she glimpsing the future, reflected in the past? Was she to become a victim of the men herself, caught in the line of fire between Sammy and Didier?

She wondered if there would be a taxi with her name on it roaring down 111 as she crossed from the Movie Colony Hotel to her car, baking in the sun across the street, the glove compartment full of melting Zoloft. At the very least, she deserved a better death scene.

She clicked off the TV. Sometime in the next six months, she'd be getting a residual check for a dollar-twenty. If she was lucky. She ought to make a collage of all the miniscule checks she was getting and hang it in the bathroom. This was Hollywood's parting gift to her—bupkis.

In the meantime, she had to figure out what to do. She hadn't a clue.

Janet called her back the next day, just before noon. Marcy was still in bed, unable to muster the fortitude to get up. This was clearly the onset of a monstro depression; if the Zoloft didn't kick in soon, it would be two weeks in bed.

"What's up?" Janet greeted her, with her usual lack of bedside manner.

"It would have been nice if you'd called last night," Marcy said, in her mawkish teenage-girl voice.

"You said *as soon as possible*. This is *as soon as possible*."

"You must be very busy."

"It's the high season for mental health. What's going on?"

Marcy took a beat, for dramatic effect. When you had a key line to deliver, you never wanted to rush it. That way they couldn't cut away from you in the editing room and put the line over someone else.

"The two guys I'm involved with? They're trying to kill each other."

There was a long moment of silence. If they were face-to-face, Janet would simply have nodded. On the phone, the silence was disconcerting.

"Did you hear what I said?"

"Uh-huh. The two men are trying to kill each other."

"Isn't that crazy?"

"If they go through with it."

"They've hired a hit man."

"I see. . ."

"You *see*?" Marcy said, trying unsuccessfully to contain the sarcasm in her voice. "And don't say I'm in the fucking Catbird Seat."

"Marcy, let's not act out, okay?"

It was moments like this that Marcy contemplated putting a contract out on Janet. Was it still considered transference if you didn't want to sleep with your therapist, but wanted to kill her instead?

"It's the weirdest thing," she went on. "I should be freaked, and I'm not. I mean, I'm freaked, but I'm also kind of, you know, turned on."

"How? Like sexually?"

"No, I'm too depressed to think about sex. It's more like this romantic thing about men fighting over you. I mean, that's kind of a turn-on, isn't it?"

"If you're twenty-one."

Typical of Janet—raining on her parade. Even if she was right, she could be a little more understanding.

"Okay, I get it," Marcy sighed. "It's not a good thing that these guys are doing this. But still. . ."

Still *what*? There was no *still*. She'd been over and over it in her mind ever since Evelyn Duboff had told her. They weren't living in the Middle

Ages with knights jousting to win the hearts of fair maidens. This was a couple of retired suitors trying to poison each other's pizzas and blow up cars. This was Purgatory Gardens, not *The Romance of the Rose*. And yet. . .

Janet didn't do *and yet*. One of her mantras was, "Fantasy is a nice place to visit, but you don't want to live there."

"I'm just wondering if. . .if I did anything to encourage them. Am I to blame here?"

There was an audible sigh. Marcy recognized the language. It was Janet's way of telling her that she was building a bullshit castle. If they had been in her office, the therapist might have even looked at her watch to let Marcy know that they weren't going down that road.

"Listen, Marcy, you have enough guilt going in your life without taking it on over something like this. Even if you wiggled your ass in front of them and led them on, it doesn't justify going to the extremes that you tell me these guys are going to. This is not just aberrant behavior. This is criminal behavior. In fact, this is moving into the area that could obligate me to notify the authorities."

"Are you serious?"

"You bet. Impending behavior that could imperil lives is not protected by patient-client privilege. I could lose my license if one of these guys pulls the trigger and they find out that I knew it was possible."

"Who would tell them?"

"You could."

"Why would I do that?"

"Marcy, I don't know why you would do that, but you could. In some sort of post-transference anger, you could do that and rationalize it some way. And I don't want to expose myself to that liability. So we're not going to be able to continue this conversation."

"What? You're cutting me loose?"

"I have to. Unless you call the police and tell them. Then we can proceed, but I spent too much time and money getting this license, and I'm not about to put that in jeopardy."

"That's it?"

"We can talk about other things—your career, your parents, your marriages. . ."

"Let's not forget my weight!"

"Okay, Marcy, I'm going to have to wrap this up."

"Just like that?"

"I've got a number of other calls to return. Merry Christmas."

It was a soft click, at least. Unlike Artie Reman's hard clicks. It always felt to her like her agent was already on the next call before he'd finished with hers.

So there it was: She had just been fired by her shrink. *Fuck you, and Merry Christmas.*

Could it get any worse?

It did. But not right away. The situation was making her both anxious and claustrophobic. A double whammy. She recognized the symptoms. Zoloft wouldn't touch them.

In the past, she would go for a long drive in an effort to combat the claustrophobia. Once, in the midst of a serious depression caused by her missing out on a series role that would have given her five years of well-paying work, she drove all the way to San Luis Obispo without stopping until she got pulled over by a highway patrol officer for doing eighty. She broke down in tears, trying to explain to the impassive face behind the Ray Bans that she had lost five years of work because of menstrual cramps that had fucked up her network callback. Her performance was so moving that the cop didn't write her a ticket.

Driving fast crystallized her thoughts. It helped her breathe. So Marcy gassed up the car and headed north. Whenever she did this, she let herself believe that she wasn't going to stop, that she would continue going north, all the way to Canada, if she had to, to outrun her problems.

This time she kept the car below eighty, not trusting her ability to cry her way out of a speeding ticket. Or flirt her way out of it, for that matter. Twenty years ago, all she had to do was look at a man the right way, purse her lips, and let her eyes go soft focus. But Marcy had enough self-awareness to appreciate that those days were gone—certainly with California Highway Patrol officers.

Back in the seventies, she had done an episode of *ChiPs*, in which she'd played a damaged motorcycle babe who had a fling with Erik Estrada. The last residual check she'd received for it was three cents. Literally. She had put it in the birdcage and let her parakeet shit on it.

Marcy was past LAX before she was able to focus. Okay. She was not going to go to the police. That much she was sure of. She was temperamentally unsuited for the role of witness for the prosecution. She couldn't play it, not even with a great director. And even if she could, what would it accomplish? After they were both shipped off to Victorville, she'd be all alone again—bereft, penniless, unprotected. Months away from being a bag lady.

By the time she was approaching Santa Barbara, she was convinced that she ought to do nothing and just let the whole thing play out. Whichever one of them got the other one would be her guy. She'd surrender to him, living with the knowledge of what he had done to get her, never confronting him. And she would secretly revel in her realization that a duel had been fought over her.

She continued north to Pismo Beach. She parked and got out of the car. Kicking off her shoes, she walked across the sand and sat on a dune looking out at the Pacific. The beach was deserted in the chilly, damp December air.

Staring at the limp waves, falling over one another in a slow cascade of foam, she realized that, flattering as it may have been, she wouldn't be able to live with a killer. Part of her would always be aware of what the man had done to another man she'd had feelings for. No, she wasn't going to be able to let a man touch her whose finger—directly or indirectly—had pulled a trigger. There were limits to her self-delusion.

No. She would get Sammy and Didier to call it off. She would conduct an intervention. Just the three of them. She would confront them with their behavior and demand that they stop the madness. *This has gone far enough. Look at yourselves. Seven-year-olds fighting in the schoolyard. Grow up!*

For dramatic effect, she would do it on Christmas Eve. She would invite both of them to midnight mass, and then afterward, when their hearts were full of love, she'd conduct the intervention. Peace on Earth, goodwill to men.

XII
DIDIER

The communal sauna was an amenity at Paradise Gardens that Didier tended to avoid, not being fond of perspiring in public or having to listen to one of the geriatric occupants with leathery skin chatter about their health problems. But he thought that the dry heat might soothe his nerves and allow him to think clearly.

Wearing only a pair of bathing trunks that highlighted his burgeoning middle, he sat, waiting for the sweat to begin dripping, hoping for an inspiration. He needed one. He was running out of both money and time. If the Italian wasn't out of the way soon, Didier might have to take matters into his own hands.

After the Italian's car went up at the supermarket, Didier had assumed it had been a foiled attempt on the part of the contract killers he had hired. Then the story about the Taliban double agent emerged, and he wondered if that wasn't some cover story to explain that Sammy Dee was not an assassination target, but an innocent bystander, a canard put out by Acme to cover their tracks.

Didier's attempts to contact Acme had resulted in nothing but a printed Christmas card and a couple of Mexicans to redo his patio. Up until then, he had forgotten that Sammy Dee had had *his* patio redone in November. And that realization started him along a new train of thought. Was this just a coincidence? Or. . .?

It was equally plausible, *n'est-ce pas*, that Sammy wanted him out of the way for the same reason that Didier wanted the Italian gone, to give him *carte blanche* with Marcy Gray.

What did *she* know? He couldn't believe that she knew that either or both of them were trying to kill the other one over her. If she did, she would certainly try to stop it. Of course. *Bien sûr. . .*

And then, as the sweat began to flow, another thought occurred to him: Maybe Marcy *did* know. Maybe she was secretly thrilled that two men would go to such extremes to win her. Maybe she would look at the victor as the man who had fought a duel to capture her affections.

Well, if that were the case, then Didier would just have to make sure he won. There was no second place. *Qui ose gagne!* He would take care of business and claim his prize, then carry her away with him on his white horse, leaving Sammy Dee spinning his Porsche wheels in the dust.

He closed his eyes and envisaged Marcy and him at a café on the Promenade des Anglais in Nice, sipping chilled rosé and eating perfectly sautéed prawns as the sirocco drifted in off the Mediterranean. After a barefoot walk on the beach, they would go up to their suite at The Negresco and make love until the sky lightened and they woke in each other's arms, inhaling the sweet perfume of their bodies. . .

"Have a drink, *Deedeeyay.*"

Didier looked up and saw Chris and Edie sitting just below him, proffering an open bottle of tequila. So lost had he been in his reverie that he hadn't heard the two swingers enter the sauna.

They were both naked. Unfortunately. Edie, her artificial breasts fighting gravity in the wet heat, gave him one of her lecherous smiles and said, "Why don't you slip out of that bathing suit, big boy?"

"I was just leaving," he murmured as he climbed over her spread-eagled body and, closing his eyes, beat a hasty retreat.

Christmas had never been much of a holiday for Didier Onyekachukwu. He barely knew it existed before the Jesuits got to him, and then, as far as he was concerned, it amounted only to extra choir practice to learn the Christmas carols instead of afternoon recreation on the soccer field. And the endless retelling of the story of the birth of Jesus with the manger and the wise men and the frankincense and myrrh. The fathers didn't feel it necessary to explain how, if Mary was a virgin, she was able to produce Jesus.

Since leaving Africa, his feelings about Christmas hadn't changed much. In France, it wasn't a particularly good time of the year for the drug business. His clients made resolutions to stop using—resolutions that would be broken by the middle of January, but for a couple of weeks around the holiday, things were dead.

And, with the exception of the weather, December in Palm Springs wasn't much better. There was an artificial gaiety in the air, the hanging of plastic wreaths on the doors, the fake tree with tinsel in the multi-purpose room, the endless carols in the stores. And the need to put cash in envelopes and give them to the mailman, the *femme de ménage*, and to anyone else whose goodwill you depended upon.

This year, however, he was in the middle of a deadly ménage à trois that was playing out, one way or the other, as Christmas approached. It was very possible that either he or the Italian would be dead by New Year's. So when Marcy Gray called on the 24th and invited him to attend midnight mass with her and Sammy Dee, Didier almost said no. And then he quickly thought better of it. Having to get through the evening with a man who might be trying to kill him was preferable to leaving him alone with her.

The evening was to start out with a drink at Marcy's. Which meant that there would probably be an exchange of presents. He couldn't give her another "authentic" African artifact. He'd already given her a Yoruba tribal mask and a Benin bronze, both manufactured in the Coachella Valley.

He'd gift-wrap a bottle of 1991 Pauillac and tell her it was the best vintage that Bordeaux had produced since 1961. She wouldn't know the difference. There was no way he was getting the Italian a present. But then, he thought, what if the man got *him* something? What would Marcy think?

Perhaps he could sprinkle a little strychnine on a slice of pizza and present it. *Merry Christmas, Sammy. Requiescat in Pace.* There was a pair of fake gold-plated cufflinks that he'd had since his days running the art gallery in Nice. He'd put them in a box and tell the Italian that they were from the Gold Coast. He wouldn't know the difference, either—unless he went to pawn them.

A little after ten o'clock Didier showed up at Marcy's in his best African outfit, a multi-colored Senegalese *pagne,* carrying his two presents, both elaborately wrapped.

"Didier, how sweet!" Marcy cooed. "Sammy got a present for you, too!"

Sure enough, the Italian, no doubt having used the same reasoning, had brought something for him. Pewter salt-and-pepper shakers, marked *Sel* and *Poivre.* They couldn't have cost more than ten dollars.

Marcy unwrapped her wine and threatened to open it right then and there, but Didier objected.

"Mar*cee,* '91 is a great vintage. You must put it in your cellar for at least another ten years." *When it would be completely vinegar.*

"What cellar?"

"You must have one." When they lived together, he would put one in and use the '91 Pauillac for spaghetti sauce.

Sammy grunted some words of gratitude for the cheap cufflinks. Which, if Didier remembered correctly, he had spent less than ten dollars for at a flea market in Nice. It was a close call which gift was worth less—the cufflinks, or the salt-and-pepper shakers.

Marcy opened a bottle of California champagne and poured out three glasses. Then she proposed a toast.

"To peace on Earth, goodwill to men."

Didier and Sammy mumbled some sort of assent as they eyed each other over the raised glasses, murder in their eyes.

They drove to the Apostolic Church of the Desert, on Dinah Shore Drive, in Marcy's car. Sammy grabbed the front seat beside her, relegating Didier to the back. *Tant mieux.* He had more leg room.

The congregation was made up chiefly of Mexicans and gay men. Father Luis Espinoza performed the mass and gave an interminable sermon. Something about how it was never too late to turn to Jesus.

Au contraire. It was indeed too late. Here they were—two Jews, one alleged, the other non-practicing, and an animist (or, more accurately, a devout atheist)—in a church on Christmas Eve in Palm Springs, California. There wasn't a wise man in sight. Two of them wanted to kill each other in order to fuck the third one.

Still, when it came time for the wafer and the wine, all three of them kneeled before Father Espinoza and accepted the Eucharist. *Pourquoi pas?* A little grape juice wouldn't hurt anybody. Didier would have preferred palm wine. He could remember the taste of *nsafufuo*, the potent palm wine that was drunk in West African villages. It was the worst hangover on the face of the earth.

Afterward, they walked quietly to the car, one of them on either side of her. How long could this go on? At this point, he was ready for the two of them to settle it by hand-to-hand combat. Just go out into the desert and finish it off. One way or the other. Didier outweighed the Italian by twenty pounds, but the man had the nasty look of a street fighter. There was a scar on his cheek that was no doubt the result of a knife fight.

They got back in the car, Didier grabbing the front seat this time. Before starting the engine, Marcy said, "I'd like to invite both of you back to my place for a drink."

The two men looked at each other, hoping that the other one would decline. When neither did, they each nodded, more or less simultaneously.

Marcy didn't say anything else during the short drive back to Paradise Gardens. She dispensed with her usual breezy banter and concentrated on driving. He could feel Sammy's eyes on the back of his head, as if to say, *One move and you're dead.*

Back at her condo, she excused herself to go into the bedroom, leaving the two men alone in uncomfortable silence. Klaus wandered in through the doggie door and glared at both of them. Then he delivered a powerful fart and lay down on his cushion with *Hundebett* stitched in purple thread, looking up at both of them as if to say, *That's what I think of you.*

When Marcy finally came out of the bedroom, she had redone her makeup and changed into a pair of expensive and uncomfortable-looking pumps. She looked delicious.

"Would you like me to open a bottle, Mar*cee*?"

She shook her head. "Sit down, both of you. On the couch."

There was a commanding tone in her voice, one that Didier was not familiar with. As if to back her up, Klaus got up off his cushion and started to pace at her side, like a second lieutenant attending the commandant.

"*Plotz*, Klaus," she ordered. The dachshund waddled back to his cushion and plotzed.

The two men sat down side-by-side, facing her. She stayed standing, listing slightly in the three-inch heels. She looked from one to the other, like a mother addressing two naughty boys.

"I want to say something to both of you," she said. "Something very important." She paused for dramatic effect. Then: "I've chosen Christmas Eve to have this conversation with you, because it's a time when our hearts should be full of love and goodwill toward our fellow man."

It sounded to Didier like she was reciting her lines from a script. The two men leaned forward in their seats, in anticipation. Didier was ready for anything. Except, as it turned out, for what she said.

"First of all, I'd like you both to know how happy I am to consider you my friends. You are both very dear to me, extremely dear—possibly the closest friends I have these days. This time of year, especially, we should stop and give thanks to our friends, the people who make our lives more meaningful. . ."

Nom de Dieu. Where was she going with this? She sounded like one of those dreadful greeting cards full of high-sounding *merde* that Americans sent one another.

"It is a time for forgiveness, for reaching out and making amends to those we may have injured, inadvertently or not. As well as to those who we might wish to injure. . .in the future."

Didier felt the first drop of perspiration underneath his *pagne*.

She paused, as if to gauge their reaction. He looked over at Sammy, who seemed as catatonic as Didier felt.

"I debated a long time before I decided to do this," she went on. "It's not an easy thing to do, but I think it's necessary to. . .to *intervene*."

She emphasized this word for dramatic effect. Didier felt his stomach go queasy, usually an indication that he sensed he was going to hear something he didn't want to hear.

"So. . .I want you to consider this as an intervention."

The two men looked blankly at her. She elucidated: "You don't know what an intervention is?"

They shook their heads simultaneously.

"An intervention is a psychological technique in which family and people who love someone involved in destructive behavior communicate their awareness of it to him, and their willingness to help him overcome it. It's usually associated with drug or alcohol addiction, but it can be used for other types of behavior—infidelity, kleptomania, anger management. . .you following me?"

Rhetorical nods. The Italian was no doubt as apprehensive as Didier was, but he wasn't talking. They were both waiting for her to cut to the chase, as Americans so charmingly phrased it.

"Sammy. . .Didier. . ." she looked each one in the eye as she pronounced his name. "Violence is never a solution. *Never.*"

Marcy waited for a response. But both men just continued to sit there and nod compulsively.

Her voice got deeper, more theatrical. "I want you both to renounce your plans to do the other one harm."

Then, in response to their astonished looks, she said, "I know everything."

Didier thought she might be bluffing, fishing for information based only on a hunch, but that idea was quickly squelched when she elaborated: "*Every*thing. Acme, the patio decks, the whole deal."

The chase. *Enfin!* He felt Sammy deflate beside him, as if some burden had been lifted from him. Didier was lightheaded, giddy. It was finally out in the open. She knew. Sammy knew. Sammy knew he knew. He knew Sammy knew he knew. Everyone knew. He had no idea what to do.

Nobody said a word. The only sound in the room was Klaus's light snoring from his cushion.

"So here's what we're going to do. We are going to stay here in this room until both of you make amends, call off your plans, promise me that this will never happen, and embrace."

"Embrace?" The word slipped out, involuntarily, from Didier's mouth.

"Yes. It will signify you're ending this feud and starting to build love for each other."

Then it was Sammy's turn to say something. "Marcy, I'm not sure this is such a good idea."

"Sammy, you're in denial. You're blinded by your problem and can't see it clearly yet. You need to do this."

"Or else?"

"There is no *or else*. This is an intervention. You don't get a vote. We're staying here until it's done. And. . .if you don't like it, tough."

"What if I just left?" Sammy said, beginning to sound like he was really pissed now.

"I wouldn't try it. Klaus, as you know, was trained by a retired agent of the *Bundesnachrichtendienst*. I have various commands for him to subdue you. They're German words which will call him to action. I would hate to use one, but I will if I have to."

Then she turned to the dog and said, "Klaus, *achtung*!"

The dachshund sprung to life, immediately alert, eyeing the two of them with menace.

"Do we get to use the bathroom?" Sammy grumbled.

"Just let me know first, and I'll give Klaus the 'stand down' command."

XIII
THE CHASE

By two in the morning, Sammy Dee and Didier Onyekachukwu had not embraced. But they had said a number of things that they presumably wouldn't have said under normal circumstances. Marcy conducted the intervention like a group leader in a consciousness raising exercise. She had done EST, The Forum, Landmark, a couple of twelve steps, and knew the drill. Keep them on the defensive. Don't let them out of the box. Make them see their denial in undeniable light.

They were both tired, cranky, and combative. They kept eyeing the door, checking the location of Klaus, asking to go to the bathroom.

"You made the first move, Sammy. So you need to look at where that decision came from," Marcy said.

Sammy looked back at her, shrugged, murmured. "I don't know."

"*I don't know* is not an acceptable answer."

"Okay, so I wanted him out of the way."

"Was putting a contract out on him the only way to accomplish this?"

"It was the easiest."

"So that's what you do—take the easy way out?"

"I didn't know what else to do."

"Why didn't you talk to me about it? I could have solved the problem for you. Could have saved you a lot of time and money."

"What was I going to say? 'Marcy, which one of us do you like better?'"

"Why not? A hell of a lot easier than having someone killed."

"But. . .but what if you chose him?"

"Okay, I get that. But, Sammy, why would you want me if I preferred Didier? Would you have wanted to win by default?"

"I don't know. . ."

"Uh-uh."

"I. . .didn't. . .want to know the answer."

"Because. . .?"

"Because I didn't want to know."

"Uh-uh."

She looked directly at him, her eyes boring in. This time he really didn't know the answer. She prompted him. "Maybe, Sammy, you didn't want to know because you were afraid to lose."

"To *him*?" he said disdainfully, indicating Didier, who was sitting smugly beside him and enjoying the spectacle of Marcy raking his rival over the coals.

"Was there anyone else in the picture?"

"*You* tell *me*."

"Uh-uh."

Sammy stole a glance at his watch. Ten after two. He was exhausted, hungry, disgusted.

"Marcy, I'm really tired."

"You want to go to bed?"

"Yes."

"Then make amends. Admit that what you did was terrible. Embrace Didier. Forgive him. Forgive yourself. And promise that you will never hurt him in the future."

At this point, Didier piped up. "Come on, S*amee*, just admit it. You did a terrible thing."

Marcy whirled on him. "Uh-uh, Didier. First of all, you're not supposed to talk yet. This is Sammy's turn to own up to what he did. You're next."

"I'm willing to embrace him. If he's willing."

"You need to admit your guilt first."

"I was just acting in self-defense, Mar*cee*."

"Really? Are you telling me that you knew there was a contract out on you?"

It was Didier's turn to squirm on the couch. "Well, I suspected so. You see, there was the pizza incident. That was clearly his work."

"If it was clearly his work, why didn't you report him to the police?"

"I had no evidence."

"Then why did you assume he was responsible?"

"He was. He just admitted it."

"You only know that now. At the time, you didn't know that. Otherwise you would have done something."

"Well, I was unsure that justice would prevail."

"What do you mean, Didier?"

"You are well aware that in this country, they don't like blacks."

"Whad'ya mean?" Sammy whined. "O. J. Simpson walked."

"But now he is prison, *n'est-ce pas*?"

"Irrelevant," Marcy ruled, like a judge in a courtroom. "We are not talking about O. J. Simpson. We're talking about the two of you."

Klaus started snoring again. Marcy jolted him awake with a forceful, "Klaus, *achtung*!" The dachshund snapped out of his stupor.

Sammy looked at the dog and started, involuntarily, to giggle.

"You don't want to piss Klaus off, Sammy."

"I'm sorry. It's just hard to imagine him as an attack dog."

"Klaus, *bereit zum Angriff*!" She snapped.

The dog raised himself up on all fours and bared his teeth.

"That's the penultimate command. The next one is attack."

Sammy backed down. "Sorry. Just kidding, Klaus."

She ordered the dog to stand down. "*Rührt!*" The dachshund relaxed back into his at-ease posture.

Marcy decided it was time to switch into good-cop mode. She sat down on one of the kitchenette stools and worked up a smile. "Look, guys, I know you're both exhausted. But that's part of the process—fatigue makes your defenses crumble. You see, you've built these fortresses around yourselves to protect you from your own feelings, like. . .like some sort of stockade. But here's the thing—there are no Indians out there. There's nothing but your own fears and insecurities. You need to acknowledge them for what they are—limitations, hang-ups, rationalizations, all the stuff we make ourselves believe rather than looking the truth in the face. You understand what I'm saying?"

Marcy was winging it, tossing around the vocabulary of all the self-help programs she had taken over the years, hoping that some of it would penetrate.

But these guys were hard cases. They had built very sturdy stockades. If she was going to wind up with either of them—and at this point, she wasn't entirely sure she wanted to—they would have to transform themselves from the Neanderthals they were into something a little more evolved.

"So. . .who's ready to take the first step?" She looked from one to the other expectantly.

"What must we do?" Didier asked, without a great deal of enthusiasm.

"First of all, you have to get up, turn to Sammy, and ask for his forgiveness."

"Will he do it, too? At the same time?"

"We can go in order. But you both have to do it."

"What if I do it, and then he backs out on the deal?" Didier asked.

"Then we'll still be here," she sighed.

"Well, I'm not going first," Sammy snapped.

"Why not?"

"Because *he* was the one who moved in on *me*. He knew I was interested in you, that we had gone out on a date, and he just barged right in. With no respect for my. . .rights."

"What do you mean, *your rights*?" Marcy stared at him hard. "Are you saying that I'm property that you can claim to have a right over?"

"He has no respect for women," Didier attacked.

"Who the fuck asked you?"

Didier turned to Marcy for support. "He doesn't, does he, Mar*cee*?" But before she could say anything, Sammy shot back: "Right. Not like you people over there in Africa, making your women walk around with their tits exposed."

"So! You banish your women to the kitchen to make spaghetti!"

Sammy got up and confronted Didier.

"I'm not Italian!"

Didier got up and stood his ground.

"Bull*sheet!*"

"I'm a Jew!"

"If you're a Jew, let's see your circumcision!"

"You want to show me yours?"

"I don't want to embarrass you, *mon cher.*"

They were both about to unzip their flies when Marcy interceded. "Stop it! Both of you! You're acting like a couple of ten-year-olds measuring their penises."

The two men stood there, fists clenched, ready to spring.

"Sit down, both of you," she ordered.

Each one waited for the other to sit first. Finally, they did it—more or less simultaneously—crossed their arms, and waited.

"All right, we don't seem to be moving in the right direction. And I'm getting tired, not to mention disgusted. So here's what we're going to do. I am going to bed. But before I do, I am going to put Klaus in front of the door in lock-down mode. He's been trained by the *Bundesnachrichtendienst* to keep suspects at bay—prevent them from escaping, but not kill them. Just maim them so that they remain available for interrogation."

"Jesus," Sammy exhaled. "You're not serious, are you?"

"Perfectly. Maybe you'll make some progress if I'm not present. So when you are ready to make amends, call me, and I'll get up to witness it. Then we can all have breakfast together to celebrate."

With that, she pulled Klaus's cushion in front of the door. He hopped on it, looked up at her expectantly.

"Klaus, *Vorbereitungsmodus!*" she commanded. Then, she turned to her two captives and said, "Goodnight, gentlemen."

She walked into the bedroom, closed the door behind her, and removed her Jimmy Choos mere minutes before blisters would form. Then she lay down on her bed, closed her eyes, and fell asleep.

Neither of them said anything for a while. They remained side-by-side on the couch like a feuding married couple, their arms folded stiffly. Finally,

Sammy said, "You think if I got up and sat over there, the dog would at-tack?"

"I have no idea."

"Maybe this whole dog thing is a bluff."

"Why don't you try, and we'll find out?"

"That would be convenient, wouldn't it? The dog does me, you'd have a clear shot at her."

More silence. Klaus sat there, keeping his eyes on both of them. Didier yawned. Sammy belched. The air conditioner cycled back on.

"Okay, what I want to know," said Sammy, "is how you got to these guys?"

"The same way you did, apparently."

"The movie producer?"

"Of course."

"You asked him to recommend someone?"

"No. I overheard you talking. As you know, he keeps his windows open."

"So you called them?"

"As you know, you must write to them. And then play golf."

"So that's why you borrowed my golf clubs."

"There is no other way to do with business with them."

"How much they charge you?"

"The same amount that they charged you, I would imagine."

"Five grand?" Sammy lied.

"Yes," Didier lied back.

"So when they did my patio, didn't you figure out that I had made a deal with them, too?"

"When they did your patio, I had not spoken with them yet."

"But after you did. . .?"

"It occurred to me, yes. But it seemed too much of a coincidence."

"Jesus, I'm thirsty," Sammy said. "You think if I just went to the kitchen and not near the door, he would attack?"

"As I have said, I have no idea."

"You're not thirsty?"

"No."

"Right. You're probably used to it out there in the desert, where you're from."

"I am from Côte d'Ivoire, where there is no desert."

Sammy stretched his neck, keeping an eye on the dog.

"So, what are we going to do about this?"

Didier shrugged the classic Gallic shrug that he had acquired from the French—their insincerely polite way of saying, *Whatever gave you the idea that I would possibly know the answer to that question? Or, for that matter, give a shit?*

"You want to sit here for the rest of your life?" Sammy muttered.

"All right. What if we just said we were sorry, had a quick embrace, and got on with things."

"That's not what I'm talking about."

"I see. What *are* you talking about?"

"We need to figure out what to do about Walt and Biff."

"Perhaps we should go to them, together, and tell them that we do not want to kill each other anymore."

"I don't think that's going to fly. The contract is irrevocable. They're going to come after us, one way or the other."

"They are going to come after *one* of us."

"Maybe they'll only bother *killing* one of us, but they're going to come after both of us for the rest of the money. That's why they went to the trouble of redoing the fucking patio decks and getting the contract co-signed. You want them to come after Marcy?"

"Of course not."

"Because they'll do it. These guys are ruthless."

"Perhaps we should go to the authorities."

"No good," Sammy shook his head. "They got a clean cover. And if it doesn't work, they'll really be pissed. They'll do both of us, just out of spite."

"Maybe you can go back to. . .Italy?"

"For the last time, Diddly Shit, I am not Italian."

"*Samee*, come on, let us at least, how do you say, level with each other."

"What about *you*? You really from the *Côte* Whatever?"

"Yes," he lied.

"Who gives a shit? You can be Nelson Mandela, if you want."

"He's dead."

"That won't stop you. Look, whether we like it or not, I think we have to cooperate here. It's the only way."

Didier nodded, as reluctantly as he possibly could.

"If we don't figure out how to deal with this, we're both fucked."

"What do you propose?"

Sammy took a deep breath, stifled a yawn. He was exhausted and bewildered. He really didn't know what to do, but at this hour, he was open to just about anything to get off the couch and go home.

"I think we got to go after *them*," he said finally.

"Go after? You mean, have them killed?"

"Yes."

"How do we do that?"

"I know a guy."

"Another contract killer?"

"Yeah. He's in LA."

"How much do we have to pay him?"

"Ten grand."

"I don't have ten thousand."

"Yeah, but I bet you have five thousand."

"I'm afraid not."

"Didier, what about the final payment on the hit?"

"That is only three thousand."

"Okay. Cards on the table. I know that the hit on me cost ten. And I know that it was five up front, and five on the back end. Right?"

"Perhaps."

"Don't fucking *perhaps* me. We need to get down to business here. If we each have five pending, and we pooled it, we could afford my guy."

"Then we have nothing."

"But we'll be alive. That's something."

"I don't know. . ."

"I'll see if I can get my guy down to seven."

"I need to think about this."

"No, you don't. If you think about it too much, you won't do it. And one of us will be dead soon. It's Russian roulette with only two chambers. You can't like those odds."

"What do we do about Mar*cee*?"

"First, we kiss and make up. Then we figure out how to do this."

"Do we tell her what we are thinking of doing?"

"No. We have to protect her in case things go south."

"Go. . .south?"

"Jesus, how long have you been in this goddamn country? Look, *Deedeeyay*, these guys are very good at what they do. Which is kill people. If they think we're dicking around with them, there's no reason to believe that they won't do both of us. And if they find out Marcy knows what went down, they could go after her, too."

"Mar*cee*, too?"

"You bet. These guys are equal-opportunity killers."

Didier flexed his shoulder muscles, cramped from having sat on the couch for several hours. It was an unconscious gesture he adopted when confronted with two undesirable alternatives.

"Now are you ready to do the kissy-face shit?" Sammy pressed.

"I suppose so."

"I'm not any more thrilled about it than you are. So let's get it over with."

Then Sammy cupped his hands and shouted, "Marcy! We're ready!"

It took almost ten minutes for Marcy to emerge from the bedroom. She had combed her hair and slapped on a little mascara, just enough so that her eyes didn't look as groggy as she felt.

She sat down on a kitchen stool and said, like a director on a movie set, "Action."

They looked at her blankly. "Just kidding," she said. "Movie joke."

"Is Klaus back on the leash?" Sammy asked, glancing at the dog, who had perked up again at his mistress's entrance.

"Oh, he would never hurt a fly." Marcy smiled.

"You made up the whole attack dog shit?"

"Uh-huh. He's a good actor, isn't he? I taught him how to growl. It wasn't easy. He's a sweetheart." She giggled her lovely, non-damaged giggle, and called to the dog, "Klaus, *kommen hier*." The dachshund waddled over and put his snout in her lap.

"Okay guys, let's see a hug."

The embrace was as minimal as it could be and still be called an embrace. Marcy understood that this was about as good as it was going to get. A step in the right direction, at least.

"Okay, so now what, guys?"

"I could use a little sleep."

"It's Christmas Day, Sammy."

"You and I are Jewish, Marcy. And I don't know what he is," Sammy said, indicating Didier, who was slumped on the couch half-asleep.

"I was educated by the Jesuits," Didier murmured, eyes lidded.

"Jew persecutors. . ."

"Come on! No more sniping at each other. You've made amends. You've embraced. We need to move forward with positive energy."

They nodded, still checking to make sure that the other one was nodding, too. It was clearly a fragile peace.

Marcy let her eyes rest on each of them for a few seconds, then said, "Okay, I am going to assume that you will deal with your joint problem together."

"We shall do that," Didier assured her.

"I don't want to know the details."

Sammy put on his best cement-salesman manner and said, "Marcy, consider it taken care of. And you're right—the less you know, the better. It's safer for you."

"That's very considerate of you. Both of you."

"*Le moindre des choses,*" Didier said with a gallant bow.

"You're in America. Speak English," Sammy snapped.

She flashed Sammy a look, and he relented. "Sorry."

"All right. I'll let you guys get some sleep. You look like you need it." Then she turned to the dachshund and said, "Klaus, *Rührt!*" When the two men froze, she broke into the smile that they both loved and said, "Just kidding."

They headed for the door gratefully. As they turned to wave goodbye, she said, "Guys, I think this is the beginning of a beautiful friendship."

When they were gone, Marcy plopped down on the couch, still warm from their bodies, and slowly exhaled. Wow.

What a performance! Barbara Stanwyck in *Double Indemnity*. It was time for a remake. She was a little old for the role, but she could make it work. She'd go on a serious diet and do another little lift—nothing drastic, just tone up the flesh around her neck, and maybe a little tuck in the butt. Right after the New Year, she'd call Artie Reman, put it on the freeway, and see if it got run over.

Both men slept through Christmas, in spite of the boisterous holiday party hosted by Chris and Edie. The tequila flowed. There was carol singing and a spontaneous conga dance around the pool. The two swingers tried to get Marcy to go skinny-dipping with them.

"What do you say, doll?"

"Maybe ten years ago," she demurred.

"You kidding?" Chris said. "You are one foxy lady."

Marcy sought refuge with Charlie Berns, who was on a recliner at the other end of the pool.

"Merry Christmas, Charlie," she said, sitting down beside the movie producer.

"Back at you."

She leaned back on her recliner, sucked in her stomach, took a sip of her watery margarita, and said, "You ever see *Double Indemnity*?"

"1944. Paramount. Barbara Stanwyck, Fred MacMurray, Edward G. Robinson. Billy Wilder directed from a script by Raymond Chandler and James M. Cain."

"Wow. You know all that stuff."

"Occupational hazard."

"Has there ever been a remake?"

"Universal fucked it up in 1973. Richard Crenna, Lee J. Cobb, Samantha Eggar. Crashed and burned on the runway."

She took a moment, in an attempt at some sort of disinterested interest.

"You think it's time for one more?"

"You'd have to make it as a period piece. The insurance companies discontinued double indemnity clauses years ago."

"What if you kind of just. . .I don't know, took the title? And changed the story."

He looked at her, puzzled, but not without interest. "How?"

"I was thinking of a story about a woman. . .caught between two men, both of whom are in love with her. And these two guys are both, like, mysterious characters. She doesn't know whether she can trust either of them. So she hires a private eye, but it's a woman detective, to investigate them, and she finds out that both of them are trying to kill the other one. Over her."

"Not bad," Charlie mused. "So what happens?"

"Here's the twist. They both hire the same hit man. A kind of offbeat killer type—Johnny Depp, or maybe. . .Daniel Craig, or someone."

"And?"

"I haven't figured out the ending."

"Uh-huh."

"That's why writers were invented, right?"

"Great role for a woman."

"Yeah. I was thinking it would be better with a. . .mature woman."

"Fortyish?"

"I'd go even higher. Fifty. You know, older women are an underserved demo. They love to go to the movies, but they're not interested in Jennifer Lawrence foraging for food. No, they want to see women they can identify with, mature, vibrant women, women who run with the wolves. . ." She stole a quick glance at him, then said, "Don't you think?"

"Intriguing," he agreed, nodding.

Marcy decided to leave it there, let it percolate in his brain. Never over-sell, Artie Reman always told her. In the meantime, she could look for a writer who could flesh out the story, solve the ending. Or maybe the ending would magically reveal itself. Art imitating life. Or was it the other way around?

By the time Sammy Dee was up, the party was winding down. He cracked the blinds, peeked outside, and saw Edie and Chris in the pool, naked, and Ethel Esmitz yelling at them that indecency was against the CC&Rs.

Sammy took a long shower to clear out the cobwebs and figure out what the fuck to do about the new mess he was now in. Doing nothing was not an option. Walt and Biff might decide to come after him first and leave

Diddly Shit to make a separate peace. Then the African would wind up with the prize. Insult to injury.

He could try to get the hits called off, offer them another grand or two and see if it flew. Maybe this extreme prejudice bullshit was just some sort of bluff. Like Klaus. Right?

Maybe. Maybe not. He didn't want to find out. No, there was only one way of dealing with Acme. It was clean, surgical, and final. It would solve the problem once and for all.

Sammy shaved, dressed, and made himself some coffee. He would have to bring Diddly Shit in on the deal. He would need his money, and he wanted his complicity. Spread the risk. Eliminate the possibility of Sammy taking the rap, going up to maximum security alone, and leaving the African free to move in with Marcy. Besides, he could use a caddie.

It was dark when Sammy knocked on Didier's door. The African answered it in one of his colored robes.

"We need to talk."

He walked in without waiting to be invited. The place was dark with the weird African shit everywhere. It smelled of strange vegetables and olive oil. There was a large aquarium with nothing in it but murky water, and an empty birdcage.

"This place soundproofed?"

"I do not know. But there is only Charlie Berns on one side and the old man who does not hear on the other. Why?"

"Sit down," Sammy said, as if he were the host.

"You would not care for a glass of papaya juice?"

Sammy shook his head and waited for Didier to sit down on some sort of carved mahogany stool.

"This an Ashanti chief's stool."

"Fantastic. Listen, we need to deal with this. And we need to do it right away."

"Are you proposing. . .?"

"Yes. My guy."

"I don't know, Sa*mee*. . ."

"Yes, you do. We talked about this last night. We don't have a choice. It's self-defense—them or us."

"Still, arranging a murder. . ."

"You didn't have any problem arranging to murder *me*."

"That was for. . .love."

"Well, this is for survival. Look, *Deedeeyay*, these guys are scumbags. They're evil. The world will be a better place without them. We would be doing the moral thing here."

Didier kept looking at the door, as if he could somehow walk away from the whole problem by walking out of his condo.

"Have you spoken with him?" he asked finally.

"Not yet. First, we got to get these guys someplace where my guy can do them. Unless you happen to know where they live."

Didier shook his head.

"Okay, so I contact them. I explain that it is urgent that I speak to them, set up the golf bullshit. Then both of us show up."

"They will be suspicious."

"Of course they will. But this way they'll know the jig's up. And, better, you and I will be in the clear. We'll have an alibi."

Didier pondered this for a moment, then slowly nodded. "I see. We shall be present when they are killed."

"No, my guy does ignitions. But we'll have our names on the tee register as playing in a foursome with them when their car blows."

"But they will not be in it?"

"Yes, they will. My guy will wire the car while we're playing golf. We walk them to their car, shake hands, step away. By the time they turn the key, we'll be out of range. Then we call 911. Help! Someone just killed our golf buddies. How could we have set the ignition bomb if we were playing golf with them when their car was being wired?"

"Can you trust your. . .guy to do the job correctly?"

"He's a professional."

"From the cement business?"

"Didier, don't go there, okay? I'll stay out of your past, you stay out of mine."

"*Entendu*."

Tino from Tarzana picked up on the ninth ring.

"*Hola.*"

"Tino. It's Gus Malvolio."

"Who?"

"I talked to you a couple of days ago about a job. In Palm Springs."

"I don't do the desert."

"We talked about that. It's a seven-thousand-dollar job."

There was a long silence on the other end. Sammy wondered if the man had hung up.

"Seven large?"

"Yeah."

"I'll have to pack a bag."

"Of course. Sure. Listen, it's probably going to be soon."

"I could work you in tomorrow."

"No, not that soon. Hopefully a couple of days. And here's the other thing. It's probably going to be early in the morning."

"I don't like working before noon."

"Tino, this is going to be a two-hour window. Starting around six a.m."

"You want me in the fucking desert at six in the morning?"

"You can come down the night before."

"You paying for a hotel?"

"Sure."

"Get me a room at Bally's."

"That's Vegas, Tino. We'll put you in the Morongo."

"Okay. Make sure there's a minibar in the room. And a wide-screen."

After he hung up with Tino, Sammy struggled to compose a note that would get a quick reply. This deal needed to happen fast, before Diddly Shit backed out. The man was very shaky.

He settled on: Dear Walt and Biff, I'd like to see you a.s.a.p. golf this week? New business. SD. Handwritten, in stenciled letters. In case the cops found the note and tried to trace it.

On the way back from mailing the note, Sammy stopped at a drive-thru McDonald's and threw the pen he had used for the note in the trash bin. Then he went to the driving range and pounded the shit out of a hundred balls.

It took only two days to get a response, but they were very long days. Sammy stayed out of sight, calling Didier to keep him warm. When he told Marcy that he wasn't feeling well, she wanted to come by with chicken soup, but he told her that it was his stomach, and he couldn't eat anything.

"Can't keep anything down," he lied.

"You sure there's nothing I can do?"

"No, thanks. I just need a couple of days of rest."

He spent the days lying around in his bathrobe, watching daytime soaps and dozing on the couch, eating soup and chips. Acme's response came early on the 29th, in a FedEx envelope. A guy in shorts delivered it with a smile and a Merry Christmas. Sammy took a fin out of his pocket to tip him, but he said that it was against company rules to accept it. What was this fucking world coming to?

As usual, Acme didn't waste words: 12/31, 6:45 A.M., TAHQUITZ CREEK.

Sammy shredded the message and the envelope manually, using a serrated kitchen knife. It took him almost an hour.

First he would call the Morongo, book a room, then call Tino, then call Diddly Shit, then go to the bank for cash.

The Morongo was booked solid for New Year's weekend. After another half-dozen calls, he managed to find a room at the Ramada that had a thirty-six-inch flat screen, but no minibar. It would have to do. It was a little after ten when he dialed Tino from Tarzana.

This time it was twelve rings. "*Hola,*" Tino said, sounding like he had been yanked from a sound sleep.

"It's Gus Malvolio."

"Who?"

"From Palm Springs."

Eventually Sammy managed to get Tino to recall their previous conversation and to communicate the narrow window of opportunity he would have to work with. Sammy told him that there was a room booked in the name of Tino Mercado at the Ramada, and that Sammy would meet him there at nine that evening with the money and the location of the job.

"It got a minibar and a fifty-two-inch?"

"Tino, it's a holiday weekend. It was the best I could do on short notice."

"Make sure it's not near the ice machine."

Then he called Didier and told him they were a go for December 31st at 6:45 a.m.

"Ah yes, that is their preferred time, is it not?"

"It's apparently their only time."

"Is your. . .man arranged for?"

"He's coming down tonight. We're putting him in the Ramada. Two hundred and forty-nine bucks. You're in for half of it."

"What about golf clubs for me, Sa*mee*?"

"You won't need them. You're going to caddie for me."

Sammy took the Porsche to the car wash, then stopped by the drive-in window of the bank with a two-thousand-dollar withdrawal slip. He handed it to the teller with his driver's license and waited for what seemed a very long time, watching the woman pecking away at the computer keyboard, then calling over a supervisor to check the screen.

The supervisor said through the microphone, "I would suggest you make a deposit soon."

"And why is that?"

"After this withdrawal, you will have fourteen dollars and seventy-one cents in the account."

"Thank you," Sammy said, with as much dignity as he could muster.

"How would you like the cash, sir?"

Sammy took it in hundreds and pulled out of the drive-thru lane. As he drove home, he began to figure out how much cash he could raise on his credit cards before they ran dry. He would have to do some serious kiting or hit up Marshall Dillon for a raise. But first he had to stay alive. Then he'd worry about how to feed himself.

Diddly Shit came by at four with his money. Sammy counted it in front of him.

"You do not trust me?"

"As far as I can throw you."

"*Vas te faire foutre, espèce de macareau*," Didier said with a smile.

"*Va fongool*," Sammy smiled back.

Marcy was right. It looked like this really was the beginning of a beautiful friendship.

"What are we going to tell them?"

"Leave that to me."

"If I am part of this deal, I would like to know."

"What difference does it make? You barely speak English."

"I am paying for half of this, Sa*mee*."

"I'm planning on kind of playing it by ear."

"Why don't you just have your man set a bomb in their car? And we can avoid the golf."

"I want them to know it was us."

"If they are dead, what difference does it make?"

"As they're blown through the roof of their car, I want them to realize who did this to them. So they can remember us in hell."

"If you tell them it's us, then why will they start their car?"

"Jesus, Didier, leave it alone. Don't worry. This is going to work. If it doesn't, we're dead anyway. So what the fuck difference does it make?"

Sammy tried, unsuccessfully, to take a nap, before having two bags of Doritos and a glass of Chianti for dinner. At nine o'clock sharp, he walked into the lobby of the Ramada on Frank Sinatra Drive. Tino Mercado had not checked in yet.

Sammy sat at the bar, nursing a Dos Equis, wondering if Tino was going to show and thinking about what he was going to do if he didn't. Finally, at a quarter after ten, a short, wiry Latino carrying a metal suitcase and wearing shorts, a tank top, and flip-flops approached the desk.

Sammy waited for him to get his room key, then followed him to the elevator. The doors shut, and Sammy said, "Tino?"

The man blinked at him a couple of times and handed him the suitcase, as if he were a bellhop. It was heavy.

"You're over an hour late."

"Fuckin' traffic on the San Berdo."

That was the extent of the conversation until they were safely inside room 725, with the door closed. Tino looked around unhappily.

"This the best you could do?"

"I told you, it was last-minute."

"Got the money?"

Sammy took the envelope out, but didn't give it to him. "Listen, Tino, this has got to go off right. You can't be late tomorrow morning. You understand?"

"Yeah."

"You need to be ready, downstairs, at six a.m. sharp. It's fifteen minutes to the golf course. You'll follow me in your car. You'll park next to me in the lot and I'll point out their car when it arrives. Then the next time you see me is when I show up in LA with the rest of the money."

"What happens if the cops get you?"

"If you do your job right, they won't."

"I been doin' this for years, man. Phil never had no problem with me."

Sammy held his eyes for a moment, as if cementing some sort of oath, then handed him the envelope full of cash. Tino peeked inside but didn't count it.

He nodded and said, "Okay, now get outta here. I got to change my bag."

Sammy got maybe an hour's sleep, in spite of the ten-milligram Ambien. He had set two alarm clocks and laid out his clothes. His clubs and shoes were already in the trunk of the Porsche, along with six sleeves of Pro V1s. When the second alarm went off, he emerged from a nightmare about being trapped in the sauna with Chris and Edie. He felt as if his brain were wrapped in gauze.

The first thing he did was call Didier. The African growled into the phone, "I am awake, Sa*mee.*"

"Thirty minutes. And don't wear any of that African shit. It's a golf course."

Then he took a ten-minute shower, thinking about the first hole at Tahquitz Creek—a long par four with a couple of gaping bunkers flanking the green. He did his best to visualize a straight shot into the fairway, but all he could see was the thick copses of ice plants on either side.

He made himself a double espresso. Lying on the couch were a pair of beige polyester slacks, with forgiving room in the crotch, a Greg Norman orange pastel shirt, and a down vest. He would look good at least when he hit the ball into the ice plants.

Walking past Marcy's doorway on the way to get Didier, Sammy imagined her curled up in bed with Klaus. She didn't have a clue. Someday, he hoped she would understand the trouble he had gone to on her behalf.

He knocked softly on Didier's door, waited, then knocked again. On the third knock, the African came to the door in a Nike Banlon golf shirt and a pair of brown and white FootJoys.

"You're not going to need the golf shoes for caddying."

"They are the only appropriate shoes I have."

That was the extent of their conversation until they were heading south along 111. There was just a smear of gray light coming over the rim of the mountains. Sammy had the top up and the headlights on.

"This is a very crazy thing we are doing, Sa*mee*."

Sammy just nodded. It was amazing what men did for pussy.

The Porsche pulled up in front of the Ramada, and, miraculously, Tino was waiting for them, sitting in a parked two-tone Chevy with spinners on the hubcaps and a vomiting llama decal. A seventy-five-year-old gangbanger.

"This is your man?" Didier asked, his eyebrows erect.

Instead of answering, Sammy got out of the car and walked over to the Chevy. "You ready?"

Tino tapped the metal suitcase on the passenger seat beside him and said, "Let's roll."

Sammy drove slowly, keeping the Chevy in his rearview mirror. Fortunately, the traffic was light, because Tino drove like a serious senior citizen. Sammy never got the Porsche out of third.

"This man is older than we are," Didier said, after a while.

"So?"

"Does he know what he is doing?"

"Why shouldn't he?"

"Have you employed him before?"

"I didn't need this kind of service in the cement business."

"I thought we were going to be honest with each other, Sa*mee*."

"Why start now?"

"Why not?"

"Look, *Deedeeyay*, this is not the time for a heart-to-heart. We're both full of shit. I know it, and you know it. Let's leave it at that for the moment, okay?"

"You are a very cynical man."

"For chrissakes, I'm trying to keep us alive. If that's cynicism, I plead guilty. Now, listen, here's what's going to happen. We drop Tino in the lot, point out their car to him. We check in at the pro shop, using our real names. That's going to be our alibi. They'll meet us at the first tee. When they see the two of us together, they'll know something's up. I will suggest that you ride with Biff, the younger one. I'll get into the cart with Walt. Hopefully they'll dispense with the strip search in the men's room. I'll tell Walt that we're calling off the hits. And we'll go from there."

"What do I say to *Beef*?"

"Anything. Talk about Africa, art, wine, I don't give a shit. Just don't talk about the hits. If he asks you, just say that I am discussing it with his father."

"If he says yes, do we then just shake hands and go home?"

"No. I want to play at least three holes, give my guy enough time to wire the car. He says he only needs seven minutes, but I want to give him an hour, in case he runs into problems."

"*Merde*. . ." Didier sighed.

"What the fuck does that mean?"

"It's French for *sheet*. You say it when you want good luck."

"Jesus Christ. . ."

He pulled the car into the Tahquitz Creek lot, the Chevy right behind him. The Acme Exterminating and Patio Decks van with the PATSNUFF plates was not there. Sammy's watch said six-twenty-five.

"They are not here?"

Sammy shook his head.

"What are we going to do?"

"I don't know. I'm thinking."

He thought. He didn't want Walt and Biff to see the two of them together in the parked car. They could very easily turn around and leave.

"Okay," he turned to Didier, "Go up to range as if you're going to warm up before teeing off."

"I have no clubs."

"Take mine out of the trunk. It's open."

"But, as you know, I cannot hit the ball very well."

"Nobody's going to give a shit. Go, quick. Before they show. I don't want them to see us together. Yet."

Didier got out of the Porsche, opened the trunk, took out the clubs. Slinging them over his shoulder, he walked with his ambling gait toward the pro shop, looking more like the arms dealer he was than a professional caddie. As soon as he was out of view, Sammy got out of the Porsche and into the Chevy. The car smelled like a bodega.

"What's the story?" Tino asked.

"They're not here yet."

"Maybe they don't show?"

"They'll show."

"I keep the front money if they don't show."

"Yeah, yeah. . .sure. . ."

The next five minutes were among the longest of his life. He tried not to think about the fact that he was sitting in a Chevy with bad springs, reeking of salsa and beer, beside a Mexican hit man with a colostomy bag at a golf course at six thirty-five in the morning on New Year's Eve Day, waiting for a van to show up so he could point out where to put an ignition bomb. He couldn't begin to count the number of things that could go wrong.

"Someone coming," Tino said, moments later, and Sammy opened his eyes and saw the Acme van pull in and park on the other side of the lot.

"That's them. Okay, tell me when they're gone."

With some difficulty, Sammy scrunched down on the seat.

"You want to hit cockroach guys?"

"Long story," Sammy managed.

Two more minutes went by as Tino described how he was going to get in the car, defuse the alarm, and wire the ignition, then reset the alarm so they wouldn't suspect anything.

"A hundred percent professional job, man."

When Tino told him they were gone, Sammy said, "Don't fuck up." Then he got out of the car and walked to the pro shop without looking back. Walt and Biff were waiting for him in their white-and-beige designer clothes and Titleist golf bags with the perfectly aligned club covers. Walt's in blue; Biff's in brown.

"Morning," Walt said, in his breezy tone. "We were getting a little concerned that we weren't going to make our tee time."

"Traffic," Sammy said, unconvincingly.

"Where're your clubs?"

"My caddie's got them, at the range."

"Are you paying for all three rounds, sir?" the pro shop guy asked.

"He sure is," Walt said, with a chuckle. "It's the least he could do with the amount of business we throw his way."

Sammy slapped down his VISA card, praying that the computer wouldn't spit it back up. If he wasn't over his credit limit, he was close. He waited for the reassuring sound of the printer printing out his receipt before he breathed easily.

"Since when are you using a caddie?" Biff piped up.

"Back's acting up."

He glanced at the receipt before signing it. $550. Jesus. Besides the greens fees and the carts, they had added a caddie fee. Fuck it. At this point, it was just numbers in a checkbook.

As they walked out to get their carts, Sammy could just make out Didier on the driving range, about two hundred yards away, flailing away with a driver. Walt and Biff didn't recognize him, apparently, because Walt said, "They're letting *anyone* play on this course these days. Twenty years ago, there were no blacks allowed. Or Jews, for that matter."

"Guy looks like he could use some lessons," Biff said.

"That's my caddie," Sammy said.

"I hope he reads greens better than he hits balls."

"I'll meet you on the tee," Sammy said, and drove the cart down the path toward the range. The moment of truth was about to arrive. He was both dreading it and anticipating it. It would all be out in the open, cards on the table. He would say what he had to say, and while he was saying it, Tino would be wiring their car. God willing. Another hour, and Acme Exterminating and Patio Decks would be out of his life forever.

To their credit, Walt and Biff did not blink when Sammy pulled up to the tee box with Didier beside him in the cart.

"I think you know my caddie," Sammy said.

"Yes, we've met," Walt said crisply. "Why don't you tee off, Sammy? I'd use a three-wood on this hole if I were you. Narrow fairway."

Sammy took his three-wood out, walked over to the box, teed his Titleist Pro V1—a five-dollar extravagance—took three warm-up swings, then addressed the ball, wriggling hips, before topping it and watching it roll about seventy yards to the right of the fairway and into some serious rough.

"Take a mulligan," Biff said.

"No, thank you."

Then father and son both hit long, straight drives, and walked back to their carts.

"I'm going to ride with Walt," Sammy said.

Father and son exchanged a barely perceptible look before Biff got into the cart beside Didier. Sammy took the wheel of the other cart. He was only about twenty yards down the cart path when Walt said, "This better be good."

"It is."

"Okay. It's your dime, Sammy. I'm listening."

"Let me cut to the chase here."

"Go ahead."

"Putting aside the fact that you took a contract *on* me from the guy who you were supposed to take care of *for* me—which, besides being bad business ethics, is fucking slimy—I suggest we reach some sort of accommodation."

"What did you have in mind?"

"You cancel both contracts and we all walk away."

"They're binding contracts."

"Let's cut the shit, Walt."

"With the completion money paid, we might consider it."

"You're not going to get any more money from me. Or from him."

"That so?"

"Yup."

"I've got your signatures on enforceable contracts."

"Good. Take me to court. Five years from now, if we're both still alive, I'll testify to the terms of the deal we made. We'll see what a jury says about your patio deck business."

"I want you to think about this very carefully, Sammy. Because once I get out of this cart and walk away, you and I won't see each other again."

"My pleasure, believe me."

"I know where you and your caddie live."

"So?"

"You want to spend the rest of your life afraid to order a pizza?"

"I'll take that chance."

"Because we're very good at what we do."

"Could have fooled me. You fucked up twice already."

Walt looked hurt by Sammy's attack on his professional competence.

"Okay. We're done here," the man said petulantly.

"Not quite. Listen, you may know where I live, but I know who you are and what you do. All I have to do is go to the DOJ and sing. I happen to have friends there."

"If you're alive to talk to them."

"Don't worry. I've written it all out, chapter and verse, on how you do business—the patio decks, the Pizza Hut, the Vons parking lot, the whole thing—and left a copy with the United States Marshals Service with explicit instructions to open it if and when something happens to me. Or to Mr. Onyekachukwu."

Walt laughed. But it was a flimsy laugh, with cracks around the edges. Sammy read the tell. The guy was holding a pair of deuces.

"You expect me to believe that?"

"I don't give a shit whether you do or not."

The cart was on the path beside Sammy's ball, buried in the rough. He couldn't get it out of there with a blowtorch. As he sat there next to Walt, Sammy could feel the man's ambivalence. He had revealed his ace, and Sammy was still in the pot. Not only calling, but raising. The bluff had worked.

And as he realized this, he had an epiphany. They didn't have to kill Walt and Biff after all. The man had bought the story. Enough, at least, so he wasn't going to risk coming after them. What was the point of killing two men if there was no money in it, and the possibility of a grand jury indictment to boot?

Sammy had gone almost seventy years without actually murdering someone, so why start now? He didn't need a mortal sin on his plate. You never knew. Maybe that shit about heaven and hell was true. Maybe the priests knew what the fuck they were talking about after all.

"Tell you what," Sammy said. "You talk it over with Biff. But before you even do that, call the Palms Springs PD bomb squad and tell them to come out and unwire your ignition."

"You're bluffing."

"Go ahead. Make my day."

Sammy put the cart in reverse and backed up until he was alongside the other cart. "Let's go, Didier. We're out of here."

Didier got out of Biff's cart and into Sammy's. As they drove toward the parking lot, Sammy said, "Don't ask any questions. I'll explain everything to you later."

Sammy put the clubs in the Porsche and pulled out of the lot. Sitting at a light a mile away, they heard the explosion. Five minutes after that, as they approached Paradise Gardens, they passed fire trucks speeding down 111 in the opposite direction, sirens blaring.

At six o'clock that evening, Sammy, Didier, and Marcy were at the Olive Garden taking advantage of the early bird New Year's Eve dinner. For $12.99, they got a glass of champagne, a salad, a pasta dish, dessert (choice of ice cream or tiramisu), and a half-bottle of Chianti. The place was mobbed.

"So, how was golf today, guys?" Marcy asked.

"It was most satisfactory, Marcee."

"I'm so glad you two are getting along."

Neither of them contradicted her.

Marcy recited her New Year's resolutions.

"This year, I am going to eat less red meat, exercise more, learn to dance the salsa, and read *Anna Karenina*. And, of course, be kinder to my fellow man and woman."

"That sounds like fun," Sammy quipped.

"What about you?"

"Stay alive," he responded without hesitation.

"Is that all?"

"That's enough."

When she turned to Didier and asked him about his resolutions, he shrugged his Afro-Gallic shrug and said, "Who knows what the future holds? *La vie est un longue fleuve tranquil.*"

"Speak English, for chrissakes," Sammy barked.

"It would not hurt you, Sa*mee*, to expand your horizons."

"My horizons are expanded far enough, thank you very much."

"Guys. . ." she said. But there was a touch of softness on the edge of her rebuke. They were bickering, she was convinced, like old friends, and not like the enemies they had been before her intervention. They were pals. And they were both still sniffing her bottom.

As far as she was concerned, it remained a difficult choice between them. Her jury was still out. Maybe it would stay out for a while. Why not? What was the hurry? There were advantages to enjoying the attentions of two men at the same time. For centuries, men had been doing it with their wives and mistresses. What was good for the goose. . .

She'd have two lovers. Both ardently devoted to her. What's not to like?

They finished the evening at Marcy's, watching the Times Square ball drop on tape delay. They sang "Auld Lang Syne." Off-key. Everyone kissed one another, more or less. Klaus looked on from his cushion, farting contentedly.

It wasn't until the two men left, together as usual, that Marcy turned on the late local news. There was Tracy Tohito, standing beside the yellow crime scene tape earlier that day. She was wearing a knit suit that accentuated her tight little Asian body. How do you compete with that? They were born that way. They didn't have to exercise. They could eat anything they wanted.

"I am here in the parking lot of the Tahquitz Creek Golf Course, where at approximately seven forty this morning, a bomb went off in the van of a local exterminating and patio deck company. Fortunately, the owners of the van, Walt and Biff Keller, were not inside the vehicle. They had used a remote device to start the engine, which apparently exploded on ignition. This is the second vehicle explosion within the past month, and police are once again being tight-lipped about their investigation. . ."

They cut to Tracy Tohito talking to Detective Sergeant Jorge Melendez, as he sat in his car trying to eat a Subway sandwich, a napkin covering his Kmart trousers.

"Do you think there's any link between this car bombing and the one at Vons?" she asked, sticking the microphone into the car.

"We're very early in the investigation, Tracy."

"Is it possibly the work of the Taliban again?"

"We are not ruling out anything at this point in time."

"Have the Kellers made a comment?"

"No comment."

They cut back to the reporter at the crime scene for the wrap-up. "Very little is clear about what appears to be an attempted murder. The two men who escaped death when their van blew up have remained unavailable for comment. All we know is that they are father and son and own Acme Exterminating and Patio Decks, a local business. The good news this New Year's Eve is that no one was hurt, except a squirrel that had wandered too close to the car when the blast went off. Animal rights activists are looking into the possibility of a negligence suit. This is Tracy Tohito, *Eyewitness News*, at the Tahquitz Creek Golf Course. Have a very Happy New Year."

She flashed her bleached-white smile and dissolved into a commercial. Marcy hit the remote and sat on her couch, letting it all wash over her. Son of a bitch. They weren't in Kansas anymore. This was really getting interesting. This was classic film noir. This was *Double Indemnity* with a modern twist.

And Marcy wasn't Ann-Margaret in *Grumpy Old Men*; she was Jeanne Moreau in *Jules and Jim*. The three of them were in an old car, heading over a bridge that ended midway over the river. Nobody would ever know what happened. Fade Out. Roll credits.

Tomorrow she'd pitch the story again to Charlie Berns. With the new ending. The three of them at the Olive Garden on New Year's Eve. The subdued gaiety. The dialogue, rich with subtext. The old year fading away. The new one on the horizon. *Que sera?*

They'd get Jack Nicholson and Morgan Freeman to play Sammy and Didier. Ed Harris and Sam Rockwell to play the father-and-son hit men, Kathy Bates for Evelyn Duboff—or maybe even Meryl. Why not? She could do the accent. But she'd have to read. The only casting locked in was Marcy Gray as the beautiful woman who had driven two men to explore the darkness within them. She'd kill.

The movie star climbed into bed with Klaus. Nuzzling up to the dachshund, she lifted up his floppy ear and cooed, "*Schlaf, mein lieber Hund.*"

Then she turned her good side to the camera, allowed the light to bathe her eyes—distant, mysterious, *damaged*—and whispered, "I think this is going to be a very good year."